WORLDS END

DAVID RHODES

SEVERED**PRESS**

WORLDS END

ACKNOWLEDGEMENTS

Thanks to Linda and David for giving it a read.

Thanks to Lacey for all of her proofreading and suggestions!

And special thanks to my wife Sarah for all of her support and understanding.

OTHER BOOKS BY DAVID RHODES

Written In Stone
Blood Trail
Dreams Like Tears
Shawnee Falls
The Last Blue Sky
The Dragon With Three Names

82ND AND CENTRAL AVENUE

It was his first job as job site supervisor for an entire project and he was excited. Though it was just a small apartment building he hoped it was the first step to a tower somewhere, anywhere. He smiled to himself and nodded his head. Now that he was a few weeks into the project he was actually sleeping so even at six in the morning he was feeling good.

As he walked around the worksite he could tell that everything was going well. Sure, it was still just "the big hole in the ground" but in his mind he could see what was coming. The foundation, the pipes and conduit, the steel, then the building rose five stories before him in a matter of seconds. He smiled as the vision disappeared and only the hole in the ground was left; he was happy.

Even the weather was cooperating. The spring temperatures were mild and there hadn't been a lot of rain. Today was supposed to be the same, seventy degrees and not a cloud in the sky. A good work day.

He was used to looking a little different though; blue jeans, a short sleeve shirt and work boots. Most of the time now he had on a tie, slacks and loafers. Loafers! Have to look like you're the boss, Mr. Webster had told him. He agreed and grudgingly did what he had to, but he still wore his old hardhat with all of the old faded stickers. He had to draw the line somewhere.

He walked along Central Avenue and all of the perimeter fencing looked good but he noticed a No Trespassing sign was gone and another one was only hanging by one wire. He made a note of it and a reminder to see if any of the site video cameras showed the theft. The guards at the vehicle entry gate assured him they had the material delivery schedule for the day and they talked for a few minutes about fishing. He had known them for a long time and wasn't going to let 'I'm the boss' get in the way of swapping some lies with the guys.

As he turned onto 82nd he checked the Authorized Personnel Only signs by the employee entry and talked with the guards there. A few jokes later he was walking west on 82nd and the first thing he saw was a lot of the crew standing in front of the cafe. That was a good sign, they were eager to get to work…or to see the attractive waitresses in the cafe. Either way, it worked for him.

The second thing he saw upset him. It was a black tarp-covered load on a flatbed trailer with a partially exposed I-beam. That meant one of the iron deliveries was already on site. The concrete foreman wasn't even due until next week so how could the exterior wall iron be arriving already? He felt his blood pressure rising as he started walking toward the truck when he noticed the third thing.

The flatbed trailer was hooked to a 1970's bright red cabover semi like his grandfather used to drive. Not only that, it looked like it was in good shape, like it hadn't been driven much. Who would be driving that around? The low bed trailer looked a little shorter than normal too. He wondered if it was from the 70s also.

As he got closer to the semi a voice called out from the group by the cafe, "Hey, Boone, honey. Amanda has been asking when you're going to stop by for a cup of coffee."

Boone stopped and looked at the short, heavyset woman standing in front of the cafe as he heard the catcalls and woops from a few of the others. He laughed and called back, "I knew I shouldn't have hired my grandma to work on this job."

As everyone in front of the cafe started laughing, the woman shouted, "Grandma? I'm only ten years older than you and I taught you everything you know. You're lucky I'm here to assist you."

"You're my assistant now?" Boone asked as he got closer to her.

She paused for a moment then replied, "Now that I think about it, I'm more like your partner."

As the laughter grew louder, Boone put his arm around her shoulders and said, "And Dottie, that's why I feel so bad about having to fire you this morning."

"Fire? Me? Sorry boss, union rules say I have to be here."

Boone turned to a short, wiry man leaning against the cafe front window and asked, "Is that true, Digs?"

"I'm sorry to say it is, Boss. She fills too many holes."

"What?" Boone asked with mock astonishment. "The only hole I ever see her fill is the one under her nose."

"Oh, no," Digs replied gravely. "Claiming to be a woman, of obvious advanced years, unknown ethnicity, with numerous textbook mental and medical problems. If you fired her Human Resources would be all over you."

Dottie glared at Digs then said, "You know after we pour the foundation for this building everyone will be asking 'where's Digs?' And I'll just say that I hear he's holding up well."

Digs laughed and told Boone, "You heard her, right? She just threatened me."

Boone took off his hard hat as he rubbed a hand through his dark brown hair and replied, "No, I think she was just stating fact."

Dottie nodded as everyone laughed then Digs called out, "Boone, I think Mr. Webster just got here. Maybe I should talk this over with him."

Boone looked over as Mr. Webster got out of his car but he was more interested in the three dark colored cars that pulled up behind him. As people in suits got out of them Boone wondered if there was going to be an inspection of some sort.

Mr. Webster waved at him and shouted, "Boone, come here for a second." As Boone joined him Mr. Webster continued, "Boone, this is Agent White of the Secret Service. He has something to talk to you about."

Boone turned to the agent who shook his hand and started, "Boone, it is nice to meet you. I'm sorry I have to cut to the chase so quickly but we are in a hurry."

"I understand," Boone told him.

"Here's the problem. President Powell is in DC and at this moment should be heading down State Street to a breakfast meeting. Unfortunately, there has been a massive pile up on State so we are in the process of using Central Avenue, back behind us. We're running point and didn't think there would be any problems until we ran into your work, and the construction that's going on across the street from you."

"Yeah, Taylor Construction started on that about nine months before our project," Boone said. "And I understand what you mean about the traffic. We have a lane blocked and Taylor blocks one and sometimes two depending on their deliveries."

"That's right," Agent White agreed. "So, the local police department is going to stop traffic here on 82nd as the president goes by, and also make sure whatever opening we have on Central is clear. I'm going to leave a couple of agents onsite here because of the bottleneck and then we'll be out of your way."

"What timeframe are we looking at?" Boone asked.

"He'll be here in fifteen, maybe less, and the whole motorcade will be through in about two minutes total."

"That's no problem, is it, Boone?" Mr. Webster asked.

"None at all, sir. Oh, should I keep everyone back here?"

"No, that's not necessary," another agent said.

"Oh, sorry," Agent White spoke up. "This is Agent Winters. She and Agent Russell, who is already walking back toward Central, will be staying here until the president is through."

Agent Winters reached out to shake Boone's hand and advised, "You can call me Kaly." As he shook her hand he noticed she was a few inches shorter than him and had a firm grip. She was wearing a dark blue suit with the jacket unbuttoned so he could see the holster on her right hip. He also thought she was attractive and wondered if she ever let her tightly pulled back hair down.

Then he realized he was still shaking her hand and quickly let go with a, "Yes, ma'am."

As the Secret Service vehicles and Mr. Webster drove away she continued, "If you are ready, let's move to Central Avenue."

As they started walking Boone turned and shouted to the group of workers by the cafe, "You can come up and watch the president drive by if you want to." A few fell in behind Boone and Agent Winters but most walked back into the cafe.

Dottie shouted back, "We don't have to work over for this, do we?"

"No, Grandma," Boone replied. "But you do have to work for a change."

With a laugh Dottie flipped him off and Agent Winters asked, "That wasn't really your grandmother, was it?"

Boone smiled and said, "No, just one of the crew."

Then Dottie called out again, "Honey, don't let him tell you he's six feet of solid muscle or a millionaire in disguise when he asks you to dinner." Then she cackled loudly and ducked into the cafe.

Agent Winters paused for a second then asked, "Are you sure she's not your grandmother?" As Boone laughed, she looked over at the worksite and asked, "How much longer before you start pouring concrete?"

"Just a couple of days. You know about this kind of thing?"

"My dad runs my grandfather's construction company in Cleveland. I never was interested in it, but you do pick up things when it's always being talked about. How did you get in the business?"

"Started when I was fifteen. Running errands, odd jobs, manual labor, that sort of thing for Webster Construction. I had a knack for getting things done so I kept getting moved up the ladder. Mr. Webster thought highly of me and paid most of my way through college and grad school so I could really learn the business. When I graduated I came right back to where it all started."

"Now you're minding it instead of grinding it," Agent Winters said. "As my grandfather, and father say," she added quickly when she saw Boone's quizzical look. "In other words, you're the boss."

Boone laughed and said, "I had you the first time, I was just wondering where you got it from. I'll have to remember it." He paused, then asked, "How did you get interested in the Secret Service?"

"Movies, TV shows, the news, you name it. I just thought it was fascinating, guarding the most important person in the world. Did three years for a small police department just outside of Cleveland then I…just a moment, Boone." She turned her head slightly to the left then after a short pause spoke into a hand mic, "Got it. Five minutes out. Right. We'll be in place." She smiled at Boone and told him, "Things are rolling. We'll be out of your way in about ten minutes or so."

"No problem, Agent Winters, and I hate to tell you, but I didn't know the president was in town."

"Truth be known, the president may not even know where he's at today. He's that busy. But I am sorry we're slowing you down." Then she added, "And please, it's Kaly. Call me Kaly."

"Okay, Kaly. You're not causing any problems…especially for the crew. They get to start late today."

"So how many stories is your building going to be?"

"This one is going to be five and…" Boone trailed off as he heard a clanging sound behind him. As he turned to look, Kaly did too, but everything appeared the same. Then the flatbed trailer moved side to side just for an instant. "Did you see that?" Boone asked.

"That load is shifting," she said. "Do you need to -" she stopped abruptly as an I-beam fell from under the tarp and clanged loudly onto the street.

Boone could feel his blood pressure going up again. First, the truck shouldn't have even been there. And second, it had been loaded so poorly the material was unstable. He was going to tear into someone about this. He began walking quickly back to the truck when he saw the two police officers who were going to stop traffic on 82nd on their radios. Then the crew came out of the cafe. Digs looked in his direction and gave him a wave as he walked to the truck. A few others joined him and Boone could see them shaking their heads.

Okay. Things could wait for a few minutes while he watched the president go by. Besides, he was enjoying talking with Agent Winters…Kaly. He walked back to where she was standing and she said, "Well, I'm sure that's a problem, but I'm sure you'll say you can delegate it to someone else so you can ask me out."

Boone felt himself turning red and wondered if anyone would miss Dottie if she disappeared as he stammered, "I, I'm sorry about Dottie. I'm not like that, really. I'll -"

Kaly smiled as she cut in with, "Boone, I'm just teasing you. What I'm saying is that unless you have other obligations it would be fun to go out tonight. I'm off duty in a few hours and we seem to have a few things in common to talk about. And hey, it will be on the government."

Boone smiled back and told her, "I do not have any prior obligations and since the government is paying for the dinner, it's like I have to go. Right?"

"That's right," Kaly agreed. "Let me give you my card and I'll write down -"

Then the sound started.

It was behind them and Boone thought it sounded like the loudest Buddhist tantric chanting he had ever heard. It was a very low bass sound with pops and bursts as if it was being bubbled through water. It was actually vibrating his legs and arms and he could feel the hair stand up on the back of his neck. He turned to Kaly and asked, "What is that?"

She shook her head and as they turned toward the semi truck they saw the tarp begin to move. Not opening up as if another I-beam was about to fall out, but up and down in different places. Then it began rolling and being pushed and pulled in different directions at the same time. The movements got faster and faster and suddenly the tarp was exploding up and away as some type of animal fought to stand up on the trailer.

Boone couldn't understand what he was seeing. A Komodo dragon? No, it was too big, much too big. Its movements were quick and fluid and as it grew taller the low bass sound increased until it was almost unbearable. And then the monster stood before them.

Boone felt like he had fallen into a nightmare, looking at an unbelievable living thing that he had only seen representations of in movies and documentaries. Documentaries about dinosaurs. He had no doubt that, as unbelievable as it seemed, he was looking at a *Tyrannosaurus rex*. Beside him he heard Kaly whisper, "No. It's impossible."

Time slowed as the beast cautiously stepped from the flatbed trailer and onto 82nd Street. It was huge, at least fifteen feet tall, maybe twenty, when it raised its huge head up and every inch of thirty-five feet long. Its scaly skin was a mottled black and brown with a few patches of a dull yellow. The eye ridges were red and there were black quills sticking out of its back from its head to the base of its powerful looking tail. Boone wondered why he couldn't see the *Rex's* teeth sticking out of the side of its mouth. Then he realized that it was completely quiet.

When he looked down from the *Rex's* head he was surprised to see all the workers who had come out of the cafe just standing still, as if they were frozen in place. But as the *Rex* slowly turned his head in their direction they began screaming and running back to the cafe. That brought the *Rex* back to reality and it leaned down closer to the one person who hadn't run, Digs. The deep bass sound grew louder and Boone began running toward Digs and the *Rex,* shouting, "Run, run."

But it was too late. With a sudden lunge the *Rex* flashed its teeth with a quick snap and most of Digs disappeared. Most of him. The *Rex* lifted its head and shook it from side to side as it swallowed. With a sudden turn it faced toward Boone and took a tentative step forward. Boone skidded to a stop and as the deep bass rumbling started again he turned and ran back toward Central. Partly to get away from the *Rex*, mostly to help Kaly who was shouting into her microphone, "Can anyone hear me? Stop the motorcade. Do not come down Central."

There were gunshots behind him and Boone looked over his shoulder to see the police officers who were going to stop traffic firing at the *Rex*. They were near the construction fence but the *Rex* did not pay them any attention. It suddenly darted toward the cafe and the whipping of its tail shattered a street lamp pole like a twig. The officers dove to the ground and then ran west on 82nd, their guns seemingly ineffective against the giant animal. Boone could hear the sound of breaking glass but the *Rex* couldn't get its head inside the front of the building. After a few seconds it turned its attention back toward Boone who was now back with Kaly.

"Let's go," he shouted but she stepped toward the *Rex* and fired at it with her handgun. It shook its head like it was fighting off an insect attack and kept coming.

Kaly looked at Boone and said, "I had to try."

"Well, let's try running," he shouted and she shook her head.

"Can't," she told him. "The president's here."

Now it was his turn to be brought back to reality as police motorcycles, their sirens screaming, shot past him. He could see down the street that other motorcycles and cars had gone past him and he hadn't heard them at all. And none of them had heard Kaly; no one in the motorcade knew what was happening.

Boone turned back toward the *Rex* and saw that it had stopped. Maybe being shot was affecting it, or maybe the motorcycles were too confusing. He thought things were going to work out...for two more seconds. Then he saw the dry van trailer sitting in front of the Taylor Construction site begin to shake.

A crashing sound from the trailer told Boone and Kaly that something big wanted out of it. "Not again," Kaly shouted as suddenly something burst through the thin trailer side wall. There was no mistaking this time, not even for a second, what it was. A *Triceratops*. Boone had always thought of them as a giant rhino but it was so much bigger. Twice as big it seemed with the largest head of any animal he had ever seen. It was twenty-five feet long and at least ten feet tall at the top of its neck frill. Its scaly skin was a dull brown with patches of green mixed in and the head a uniform dull brown. But it was the four foot long horns that held his attention.

The screeching of brakes brought him out of the two seconds it took to take in everything about the *Triceratops* as a car tried to swerve and miss the animal. It would have made it if the *Triceratops* hadn't lunged forward and tipped it on its side with a flip of its horns. A limo entered the intersection and the *Triceratops* whirled to face it. Its frill was now mottled with a dark red pattern. The limo slid sideways into the massive lowered head and as it spun away from the animal its roof was ripped off leaving two people lying in the roadway and another slumped in the back seat.

The *Triceratops* was injured by the collision that had knocked it down. But it staggered to its feet as the low bass sound grew louder and the *Rex* suddenly appeared. It was distracted for a moment as another car screeched to a halt just a few feet from it and then reversed as fast as it could. Boone couldn't take his eyes off the *Rex* but he heard the crash that told him the car had just run into something behind him.

Kaly shouting into her hand mic brought him back to his senses as she asked, "Can anyone hear me? We have agents down at Central and 82nd and we have, we have...we have dinosaurs."

Then she turned to Boone and said, "That's the president in that car. I have to try and get him."

"There's a couple of dinosaurs in the way," Boone told her.

He thought she looked sad but determined when she looked back at him and said, "I didn't say I was going to make it."

Then two things happened at the same time. Kaly started moving, running behind the *Rex* to get around it, and the *Rex* charged the *Triceratops*.

Boone couldn't remember why he was following Kaly, it was just a snap decision. Boone's concentration moved back and forth between staying with Kaly and trying to make sure he wasn't killed by one of the dinosaurs. More than once a tail either flew over their heads or landed in between them. He could hear jaws snapping, bellowing, grunting, stomping, scraping and some noises he couldn't describe. The fighting that he actually saw was right out of…nothing he could reference. No movie action scene could do it justice. He could only decide it was right out of 66 million years ago.

Boone couldn't remember arriving at the limo, it had just happened. Kaly was sitting in the back seat with the president and shouting, "Sir, sir, can you hear me?" It was a few seconds and then his eyes opened and he took a large breath and nodded. She pulled her hand mic up and shouted, "Yes, yes, all of that is correct. Agents down, multiple accidents at this location. The president may be injured and -" Her voice went up several notches as she shouted loudly, "Yes, I said dinosaurs; there are two of them. I -"

Kaly and then Boone saw the president's eyes grow larger as he looked past them, toward the area they had just run through. They also realized it was quiet. Not a sound. Deadly quiet. They turned slowly and there was the *Rex*, blood dripping from its jaws as it towered over the fallen *Triceratops*. But it was staring straight at them.

"Why is it looking at us?" Boone asked quietly. "It just ate Digs and killed its next meal. I mean, it has a lot to eat right there, right?"

"Look at its right side," Kaly said. "It looks like its arm is broken and it may have an injured leg. Maybe it's in pain and isn't thinking about eating. Maybe it's just mad."

As the president leaned forward he unsnapped his seatbelt and suggested, "Maybe we should discuss this someplace else."

Kaly slid across the seat to the door behind the president and slowly opened it. "Are you good to go, sir?"

"I'm good to try it anyway," he replied.

Boone joined Kaly and they never took their eyes off the *Rex* as they slowly helped the president out of the car. As they continued backing away, the president advised them, "My left arm doesn't seem to be working right but I can keep moving and I could go faster."

"Going faster seems smart," Boone suggested.

As they began backing away from the car they could hear sirens getting closer but Kaly started feeling uneasy out in the open. "Where are we going?" she asked.

Boone swung his head around and was surprised to see how close they were to the vehicle gate to his building site. "This way," he said as he tugged on them. "If we just disappear maybe it will start eating and the cavalry will get here and we can -" The *Rex* began its low bass noise again and Boone finished with, "I hate it when I'm wrong."

As the *Rex* took a step toward them they turned and ran for the gate. The president asked, "Should we get in the guard shack?"

"Not if we want to live," Boone told him. As they ran through the gate, Boone glanced back and saw that Kaly had been right. The *Rex* seemed to be having trouble with its right leg and wasn't moving as fast as he had feared. As he entered the worksite he saw that Kaly and the president had stopped to wait for him and he shouted, "Go, go. Head toward the worker entrance at the other end of the site. I have a plan."

As they turned and ran, Boone headed toward two vehicles that were parked in a ten yard wide storage area that ran the length of the excavation. One was an excavator but he wasn't sure if that would do what he wanted. Instead, he climbed into the dozer cab. He wanted ramming power. As he started the vehicle the *Rex* entered the site and paused for a moment. Boone ducked down and hoped for the best. He didn't think the *Rex* would be interested in the dozer just because it was making noise but if it was, he may have made a mistake. But the *Rex* was focused on the two forms running away from it and it started after them.

Boone flipped the safety levers off and pushed the left toggle forward but kept his foot on the decelerator. As the *Rex* got in front of him he honked the dozer horn and the *Rex* stopped and looked at him. Without thinking he lifted his foot off of the decelerator and after a second of slowly moving he slammed the left toggle forward as hard as he could. As the dozer picked up speed the *Rex* froze for a second and then twisted sharply as it attempted to avoid the collision. It didn't quite work; the dozer struck the *Rex's* leg with a glancing blow but didn't knock it into the hole.

Faster than Boone was prepared for, the *Rex* spun back at the dozer and bit down on the ROPS protection bars and began shaking the dozer back and forth. Boone couldn't believe how strong the animal was but he was already backing the dozer up as fast as he could. There was a screeching metal ripping sound as the cab roof tore away and debris rained down on him. He looked up and all he could see was a giant wide open mouth. He instinctively ducked down and that was when he saw the debris was actually broken off pieces of *Rex* teeth.

He backed up for a few more seconds then stopped to see where the *Rex* was. It was to the right of the dozer and facing slightly away from it. He would have to drive forward and turn and Boone knew he couldn't move and react as fast as the *Rex*. But he couldn't let it get to anyone else either so he started forward, turning toward the animal. Instead of flanking him like Boone feared, the *Rex* lowered its head and came straight at him and he instinctively pulled back on the right lever to raise the dozer blade. The collision impact caused Boone to let go of the throttle lever as he was thrown forward. The *Rex* howled in pain as the blade hit its injured leg and arm. But now it was really mad and the deep bass rumbling grew in intensity as it pivoted and came at Boone from the right. But just before it reached the cab a shadow passed over it and then it was reeling from being struck by something from behind and above it.

Boone backed away from the *Rex* again and he looked over to see Kaly was in the excavator. She had hit the *Rex* with the excavator's bucket and it was actually staggering and shaking its head. Kaly started easing the excavator forward and began bumping into the *Rex,* causing it to stumble back in front of the dozer. Boone started the dozer forward and when it hit the *Rex* it crumpled and he was able to start pushing it toward the hole.

The *Rex* had other ideas though. It began trying to climb onto the front blade but its right leg was sticking up under the huge piece of steel. Boone thought this was great until he got to the edge of the hole and instead of dropping off the blade, the *Rex* was caught in the dozer blade. As the blade extended past the edge of the hole, the entire body of the *Rex* was hanging off the front of the dozer like a macabre deadweight.

Boone stopped the dozer and tried to reverse it but it was too late. He could feel it sliding closer to the drop off and knew the dozer's internal counterweight wasn't going to be able to stop the tip. He pivoted in the seat and looked up and saw the roof, though crushed and mangled, had a hole he could fit through. He pushed up and out as fast as he could but he was still partially inside as he felt the dozer start to fall forward. With a last push and kick he found himself spinning free and then landing hard on the ground. He hoped he had not followed the dozer into the hole.

He tried to push up and a wave of pain racked his body. A second later he heard Kaly beside him saying, "Stay down, Boone. You hit hard, something might be broken."

Boone could feel his head clearing and replied, "I don't think so. I just had the wind, and maybe my breakfast, knocked out of me." Then he asked urgently, "Where's the dinosaur?"

"In the pit."

"Dead?"

"Well, it did have a ten ton bulldozer land on it."

Boone actually laughed as he got to his feet and replied, "Well, I'm going to be in trouble now."

"What? Why?" Kaly asked.

"That dozer probably cost $75,000 and every paleontologist will be wanting to know why we didn't throw a net over that thing and drag it to a zoo."

Now Kaly laughed as she slipped under his right arm to help steady him as they walked and said, "We? I was bringing the net back so we could catch the little darling. But, I promise to visit you in prison, at least -" She looked at the hand she had put around his back and continued, "I got blood on my hand, you've got some kind of back wound."

"Is that the only place I'm bleeding?"

She looked up and replied, "You've got a laceration on this side of your head and several blood spots on your face. You may have more, I can't tell."

Boone just nodded and asked, "Where's the president?"

"We ran into a couple of agents and I turned him over to them. He's probably at a hospital by now."

"Thanks for coming back to help." Boone looked down at Kaly and added, "I really mean that. It had me without you."

"Hey, we have dinner plans, remember?"

Boone smiled and advised, "By the way, that was the bravest thing I ever saw."

"Well, I did have the big bucket in front of me."

"No, I mean heading toward the president when those two giants were fighting to the death."

"I actually didn't think I would make it."

"That's why it was so brave."

"Why did you follow me?"

"We have dinner plans, remember?"

As they both laughed, police officers, paramedics and people in suits began flooding through the pedestrian gate. As the medics stopped to help Boone, an officer kept running past them and as she did she shouted, "You two are the craziest people I've ever seen. Thank you."

Kaly was suddenly ushered away by agents toward one of their cars. Even though she argued that Boone should come with her he found himself standing by an ambulance near the cafe. He glanced at where Digs had been standing and was relieved to find that there was a large tarp covering the area and it was surrounded by orange cones. Dottie came up and Boone saw she had cuts on her face, probably from the window glass breaking when the *Rex* tried to stick its head inside the cafe. Tearfully, she said, "I can't believe

Digs is gone. We were always joking and kidding each other. He was a good friend and…and I just can't believe it." Then she lifted her hands and cried, "But what can you believe today?" Then she added, "I'm glad you're okay, boss." Then she walked away.

Boone looked at the other workers who were standing nearby and said, "This has been a hard day for all of us." He looked down at his watch and continued, "And it's not even 9:30 yet. You're probably going to have to talk to the police and maybe the Secret Service. But, when you can go home I'll talk with Mr. Webster about seeing that you're paid until we start up again. I'll also let you know what Digs' family plans will be."

Everyone voiced their appreciation and as they started gathering together he started to get into the ambulance. Then he stopped and stared. The paramedics followed his gaze and saw he was looking at nothing. As Boone continued on into the ambulance he realized he was the only one who understood. The flatbed trailer was gone. What happened to it?

He thought about that and all of the other events from the morning as he was being poked and prodded by the ER doctors. It was late afternoon when he was told they were finished with him and that there was a room at the hospital for him. "A room?" he asked as he sat down to get dressed.

"Yes, sir. It's being paid for by the government."

"Uh, am I free to go home if I want to?"

"Yes, sir. You do not have any life threatening injuries. They're just appreciative of what you did."

"I'm glad," Boone told the doctor. "But I think I'll sleep better at home."

"No problem, sir. Get this pain med prescription filled as soon as you can and I'll be sending your information to your doctor for follow up. And sir, I saw what you did on TV and I want to let you know it has been my pleasure to treat you."

"Uh…okay. Did you say you saw me on TV?"

"Oh yes, sir. You pushing that *Tyrannosaurus* into that giant hole was something else. And you got out in just the nick of time. I know you are going to make it, but I still tense up every time I see it."

As Boone stood up, every muscle in his body seemed to knot up in pain but he just smiled and shook the doctor's hand and asked, "What's the best way out of here and where is the closest Metro station so I can get to my truck?"

"Actually, I can't let you drive because of the meds we gave you. There is a Secret Service car standing by for you, though."

They stepped into the hallway and a young man in a suit walked up to them and said, "Good evening, Mr. Christopher. I take it you are wanting to leave the hospital?"

As Boone turned to follow the Lobby signs the man asked, "Are you prepared to talk to the media about what happened today?"

"I'm barely able to believe what happened today," Boone replied. "Why?"

"Sir, there are about a hundred reporters in the hospital lobby right now. If you would like to speak with them I'll lead the way. If you do not want to speak with them I'll take you another way."

"Another way, please," Boone said.

"Yes sir. By the way, I am Agent Martinez and it is a pleasure to meet you. We will be taking a few flights of stairs and then jump into a nondescript van at the hospital underground delivery entrance and be on our way."

"Thank you, Agent Martinez. I certainly appreciate your help."

"Again, it is my pleasure and may I say you are one brave man."

"Don't forget Kaly, Agent Winters," Boone pointed out.

"We haven't," Agent Martinez assured him.

"And," Boone paused for a second then continued, "and how many were killed or hurt today?"

Agent Martinez looked at him for a couple of seconds then replied, "One civilian, your friend, and two agents. Five other agents were seriously injured. Fortunately, no police officers or civilians were harmed. Well, other than you."

"I was afraid it was going to be more than that."

"It may very well have been if you hadn't pushed the dinosaur into that hole. Wow. Never thought I'd ever be saying that."

They went down two flights of stairs and were in the van within three minutes.

"What will you tell the media?" Boone asked.

"That you were taken to an undisclosed location at your request to recover from your ordeal and will be meeting with President Powell in a few days to receive his thanks. A press conference will be held then and you will answer a few brief questions at that time."

"Well...okay then."

Agent Martinez laughed and said, "We've done this a few times so we know the drill. Also, we'll help you get ready for the press conference by assisting you with a response that you could just read, or prepping you for a Q and A session. Your call."

"Thanks and we don't seem to be heading toward my house or my truck."

"No sir, we are not. Your house has a large camp of reporters in front of it hoping that is where you will show up. But, you are booked into the penthouse suite of one of our city's finest hotels. Two days and three nights, all expenses paid."

"I don't really feel as if -"

"Sir," Agent Martinez cut him off as he turned down a ramp and stopped by another service elevator. "You saved the life of the President of the United States and probably the lives of many others. Let us do this for you." Agent Martinez smiled and continued, "Besides, we're here so you might as well go up and get something to eat and have a good night's sleep."

All Boone could do was laugh and agree. A few minutes later he was in the suite which was actually bigger than his house. He stood still for a few seconds trying to breathe in the reality of everything when he heard a noise coming from another room. Then a door opened and Kaly walked to him and said, "Did they have to threaten you to get you to come here?"

"Well, not exactly. But it wasn't what I wanted to do."

"I told them you would just want to go home but I do agree the media took care of that. So, just look at this as part of the craziness that happened today and let it go at that."

"I can do that," he told her.

"Great." She pointed over his shoulder and said, "You have half of the suite with your own living room, bedroom, bathroom and balcony. I have the same for my half and they meet in the middle here at this large entryway that connects to a dining area and another balcony."

Boone nodded his head as he smiled and said, "Okay, I can tough it out here for a few days." Then he asked, "Why are you here?"

"Well, I'm in the middle of writing the longest and strangest case report I've ever written and it's taking some time. So, it was decided I needed to be kept away from everyone too. I've had EMT training so I told my bosses I could look after you to make sure you didn't die before the press conference in addition to writing my report. I also need to interview you about your perspective of what happened and get that into a report. I will also help you write a written response for the media or toss you some of the questions that they will ask so you can have intelligent sounding responses."

Boone laughed and replied, "Just that last part will take more than a couple of days."

Kaly laughed with him as she added, "But none of those are the most important reason why I'm here."

"What is? My safety?"

"No, silly," she said as she took his arm. "We have dinner plans, remember?"

REPETITION

Boone woke up and wondered where he was. It was 6:30 and he was in a nice room, great bed, but not his. Then he remembered everything and wondered how he could have forgotten. Dinosaurs, Digs, and a kaleidoscope of images that blurred together in a blend of reality and the surreal. A monster rising up before him then falling into an abyss under a ten-ton bulldozer. Of snapping ten-inch-teeth and Kaly's smile. Oh, yeah, Kaly.

They had watched television for just a few seconds when the video of Boone jumping out of the bulldozer as the *Rex* disappeared into the pit came on. Boone watched for a few seconds then turned away and they went to the dining room. It was a great dinner, short but full of conversation that wasn't about what had just happened. She was interesting and, for some reason, she seemed to think he was too. When he stood up and found his muscles weren't working right, she had helped him to his room. After saying goodnight, he had fallen across the bed and now he was back up to speed. He smiled, and his face hurt. He tried to sit up and just dropped back onto the bed. Pain will do that to you.

Inch by inch he forced himself to sit up and swing his feet over the edge of the bed. He slowly stood up and found that he could just barely walk, stooped over and thinking he was going to lose his balance at any moment. He worked his way to the bathroom and found a stack of clean clothes, jeans and a pull over shirt. The hot water felt good, and it was the longest shower he had ever taken. As he dried off he looked at himself in the mirror and understood why he was so sore. There were bruises on top of bruises. A few scrapes and scratches he could see, and he still felt the tear across his back.

He dressed slowly and walked to the main suite room. He felt better and at least he was walking upright instead of staring at his feet. He heard Kaly laugh and as she walked out of her side of the suite she said, "I am surprised you are up so early."

"You're up early too."

"Yes, but I didn't get body slammed by a bulldozer."

"I guess it's just habit. I'm always up early."

"How are you feeling?"

"Like the bulldozer won."

Kaly slipped an arm through his and walked him to the dining room. Plates were set on a large table, so they would be directly across from each other. There were also several covered dishes, and she explained, "They brought me too much breakfast so if you like pancakes, eggs and orange juice you're welcome to them. If not, we can get room service to bring you whatever you like."

"No, that sounds good," Boone replied. "Especially the juice. I am very thirsty for some reason."

"Your body is probably wanting to wash out all of the medicine they gave you yesterday. Which reminds me, did you take your pain pills yet?"

Boone shook his head and replied, "I don't know if I have them and unless I have to, I won't take them anyway."

"I understand, I'm the same way," Kaly told him. "But, you saw the video; you hit the ground hard. I'm glad you didn't break anything but surprised you didn't. Remember, you can see the external bruising, but you can have internal bruising including bruised organs like the liver, spleen or kidneys."

She felt his head and continued, "You don't seem to have a fever. You didn't throw up when you got out of bed and you're not feeling dizzy, are you?"

Boone laughed and said, "No, Doc, but if you're interested I have a boil on my -" Then he froze as his face turned red and his mouth dropped open. Kaly shrieked with laughter as Boone tried to stutter out a few words and then he started laughing too.

A voice behind them said, "Mr. Webster, I think yesterday was too much for both of them. They've gone crazy."

Kaly and Boone turned around as Mr. Webster answered, "Agent White, I believe you are correct. Obviously, crazy." Then he smiled and shook Boone's hand and then quickly said, "I'm sorry," as Boone winced with pain.

"That's okay, sir. I'm almost 100 percent."

Agent White shook his head and said, "Mr. Webster, I can't believe you were right. I thought there was no way Boone would be up this early."

"He's pretty tough," Mr. Webster replied.

"He certainly is."

"Hey, what about me?" Kaly asked. She looked down at her right hand for a moment then added, "I mean, I think I broke a nail yesterday and…and I almost twisted an ankle."

There was a second of silence then everyone started laughing. Mr. Webster shook her hand also and told her, "Don't worry, we think you were pretty brave too. It took both of you to handle that *Tyrannosaur*."

As everyone sat down, Kaly asked Agent White, "Sir, do you need us for something?"

"No. I mentioned to Mr. Webster I was going to look in on you this morning, and he wanted to come along. We're both concerned about you two, and I want to make sure we are on the same page as far as physical and mental health are concerned. So, bear with me as I ask a few questions."

"Kaly, how are you feeling physically? Do you feel the doctors checked you thoroughly and you received the treatment you should have?"

"Yes," Kaly replied. "Everyone at the ER was great, and they went out of their way to help me. They kept me informed about what had happened, what was happening and what was going to happen. There were absolutely no problems."

"How about you, Boone?"

"Well…I'm pretty sure everything was okay. I really only remember bits and pieces after I arrived, and I started getting treated. I'm sure it has to do with the meds I received. I do think everyone treated me well though. The doctor at the end was very nice, and so was your agent that brought me here."

"I'm glad to hear that both of you were treated well, and I can assure you that you were given the best treatment available." Agent White paused for a second then continued, "I'm sure Kaly remembers from her training that anytime a person is involved in a stressful situation, a disaster, a traumatic incident…" Agent White shook his head and paused for a second before he continued, "And who knows where what happened yesterday fits. Just one, all of them, or did yesterday create its own category? But, whatever it was, we are concerned about your mental health as well as your physical well-being.

"You both quickly realized you were involved in extraordinary circumstances. Neither of you have ever trained for what happened, so you were forced to jump into a mindset that allowed you to handle things the best you could. Fortunately, for the rest of us, you chose quickly and correctly. You saved the president and took out the threat.

"But, being exposed to those types of situations and having to deal with them causes mental trauma. Especially the way you were right in the middle of things, probably thinking you might die at any moment. The closer a person is to the center of the storm, so to speak, the higher the possibility of mental health problems.

"Now being fit mentally and physically before an incident does help a great deal in recovering from these types of incidents. I've reviewed Kaly's job evaluations and training records, and I also know she passes our physical fitness testing without any problems. But, I don't know about you, Boone. Mr. Webster tells me you are energetic, always on time, a great problem solver and a positive influence on your workers. So I get the feeling that mentally you are pretty squared away. What physical activity do you do?"

"Well, I've always thought you had to be in pretty good shape for the job and life in general. I work out pretty consistently by running, lifting a few weights, stretching, and mix in some yoga. I also have been involved with Small Circle Jujitsu for several years so when you put it all together, I feel like I'm in pretty good physical shape."

Agent White smiled and said, "I agree. But, and Kaly knows the drill but you don't, we are always concerned about post traumatic stress disorder. Kaly will be meeting with our departmental mental health interventionist, as our policy requires for a critical incident debriefing. Mr. Webster tells me that before you moved into management you would have seen a similar caregiver through your union rules. Our interventionist, Dr. Porta, said she would be happy to speak with you also. In fact, she seemed quite eager to do it. You don't have to, you can go to someone else, but we are offering it to you for what you did yesterday."

Boone smiled and replied, "I appreciate the offer, and I look forward to speaking with Dr. Porta. I understand the dangers of PTSD. I do want to point out though that people keep talking about what I did. But it was Kaly, Agent Winters, who led the way. She saved the president, and I just helped. We both took out the dinosaur and put it in the pit. It was a team effort."

"I understand," Agent White replied. "But you are getting a little more recognition from the general public because that was her job. Don't get me wrong," he added quickly as Boone started to speak, "I am her biggest fan. She will receive all of the honors that are due her. But you are just an ordinary guy who stepped up and, well, stepped into the center stage. You're everyone's hero."

"I don't want to be a hero," Boone said quietly. "I truly feel I did what anyone else would have done in my place."

"Then just tell the people that," Mr. Webster said. "Be who you are, let people know they would have done it too, so everyone will feel better about themselves."

"I liked that, Mr. Webster," Agent White told him. "I really did."

"I did too," Boone admitted. "I'll do what I can."

"Excellent," Agent White said. "Now then, before we leave, a few dos and don'ts to remember over the next couple of days. Don't watch more than a few hours of television and continue talking and joking like you were when we came in.

"Kaly, I know you completed a preliminary case report of this incident before you were taken off duty. Do not start writing the official report until tomorrow morning, or later if you want."

"I know," she replied, "wait at least two sleep cycles."

"Why is that?" Boone asked.

"Glad you asked," Agent White said, "since it also pertains to you. You see, people tend to think of their memories of an incident running like a video. But that's not how it works. Different things are stored in different parts of the brain and are pulled up by you as needed. But, the trauma of the event will create chaos with those memories as you access them. They may be out of order; you can forget things or add in things that did not happen but seem very real. If you wait two or three sleep cycles, your brain begins to return to normal and your memories become more accurate."

"Thanks," Boone told him. "That's useful information."

"You're welcome, Boone. Also Kaly, remember that you fired your duty weapon, and there will be a departmental investigation into that. I will -"

"What?" Boone interrupted. "How can Kaly shooting at a *Tyrannosaur* possibly need investigating? She was trying to protect everyone."

"It's okay," Kaly told him. "All Secret Service use of firearm incidents are investigated so the public can see we are held accountable for our actions. I had a reason to fire my weapon, and I hit the target. I'm sure my use of force will be ruled justified and there won't be any problems."

Boone looked at Agent White and said, "Just make sure I'm called to testify."

"I will," Agent White told him. "But, and I can't be official about this, I don't think Agent Winters has anything to worry about either." Then he continued, "Boone, we will need a statement from you also. You can write it or Kaly can take the statement from you. And just like Kaly, sometime after tomorrow."

Agent White stood up and continued, "Drink lots of water, limit your alcohol, get your sleep, take your meds and keep your contact with people outside this room to a minimum. Don't keep reliving things; let your mind sort things out and put them in perspective for you. Oh, yes, if you feel different in any way, like you're losing a grasp on things, let us know. You were there for us, and we will be here for you.

"And one last thing, the White House meeting with the president and the press conference. They will be the day after tomorrow and probably in the evening. You will both be expected to say something, as long or as short as you like. You do not have to answer questions, Boone, but Kaly, it would be nice if you did."

"I'll make us look good," she told him.

"You already have," he told her. "Now we'll let you get on with your day." Mr. Webster gave Boone a quick hug and said, "Stay gone as long as you need to, and I'll let you know about Digs. We'll take care of everything for you. As a matter of fact, Dottie has almost convinced me you're really not needed at all."

Boone laughed and said, "Tell her I miss her too. Tell everyone I miss them." Mr. Webster nodded and then they left, and Boone sat down and was silent.

"Is that a tear I see in your eye?" Kaly asked.

"Yeah, the hero cries."

"That just makes you human, doesn't it? Well, that, and the boil on your ass." As Boone laughed she continued, "I told you last night I had two brothers in construction. Do you think we all sat around and talked about unicorns and elves?"

"I get it. You're one tough lady."

"And you're a gentleman." Then she hugged him and continued, "But you're still my hero. Now I'm heading back to my room to work on my report outline. I keep remembering things."

"I think I'll head back to my room, drink some water, and lay back down again. I'll see you in a while." He walked slowly back to his bed and after his water he lay down and thought about Kaly's hug. And then he fell asleep.

Across the hall Kaly had a problem continuing her case report outline. She kept thinking about the hug too and wondering what Boone had thought about it. Then she finally got mad at herself and got back to the outline. Mostly.

When Boone woke up he hoped it was noon and not midnight. He hadn't wanted to waste the entire day sleeping. He sat up and took a deep breath and let it out slowly. Oh yeah, the pain. His back felt like it was on fire, and for a brief moment, he thought about the pain meds, then he dismissed them. Pain meant he would go slow and not hurt himself again.

He hobbled into the main room, and when he saw it was empty, he went into the dining room. Kaly was sitting there working on her computer, and he saw that the plates were now set up so they would be sitting next to each other. Again, there were other covered plates, and she told him, "I'm not sure what we've been sent, but it smells good."

As Boone sat down he winced and Kaly asked, "Are you hurting a lot?"

"About the same as before," he told her. "But my back is talking louder this time."

"Lean forward just a little and let me take a look," she told him. As he did she lifted his shirt and poked and prodded for a few seconds, then said, "You're still bruised of course, and will be for several days or maybe even weeks. All sorts of fun colors back here. There is some swelling, but the abrasions I can see aren't too red, so I think you're healing okay. Nothing is bleeding through the main bandage, so I think everything is okay there too. Now lean back again."

He slowly moved back to an upright position as Kaly pulled down his shirt in the back and up in the front. "Hey, just as colorful here and several more abrasions. Again, I think you are healing like you should be. But looking at your back and chest I can see why you weren't hurt as badly as you could have been. You don't show it, but you have quite a muscular torso. It probably saved you from a lot worse injuries."

As she pulled down his shirt, Boone said, "You know I charge the ladies in the neighborhood five dollars for a show like that."

"Do you do that to your construction customers too?"

"Do what?"

"Overcharge them."

"You are quick," Boone laughed.

"I told you, I have brothers. I had to be able to keep them in their place."

"I give up," Boone replied. "Let's see what there is to eat, and tell me more about your family."

Kaly talked for a while then said, "Your turn. What about your family?"

"My father passed away several years ago and my mom just two years ago. I was an only child so no real close relatives. A few cousins spread out here and there and that's about it."

"No wife or girlfriend?"

"No, just work." Boone paused and asked, "What about you?"

"I've called my mom about five times now, and she's spreading the news to everyone else. That's all the calls I've made." As Boone thought about that, Kaly continued with, "So, jujitsu. Have fun with that?"

"I do, and no, I don't want to go a couple of rounds with you. I'm sure you're ahead of me there too."

"Well, my brothers have taught me a thing or two over the years."

"Such as?"

"Well, I do know an interesting knock out that I've used a few times."

"Good to know," Boone said as he pretended to inch away from her with a smile. And it was a great smile, Kaly thought. As she tried to think of something to say, Boone continued, "Do you want to watch a movie? I know we're not supposed to watch anything about us but surely there is a movie channel."

"That sounds like a plan," Kaly agreed as she helped him up and then kept her arm wrapped around his as they walked into the main room.

They sat down together on a large couch, and as Boone turned on the TV, Kaly wondered if she should give him some room. Before she could think anything else the dinosaurs were on the screen, and Boone changed the channel as he said, "Sorry about that. I'll go to the channel list and -"

"Stop," Kaly shouted. "Go back. That wasn't us."

"What?"

Boone changed the channel, and they stared in amazement at a *Stegosaurus* calmly eating plants as people stood about 100 feet away taking photos of it. The news crawl at the bottom of the screen read, "RIO DINOSAURS, ATTACKS SIMILAR TO DC."

A voice narrated the scene. "And this is the calm after the storm. This massive animal, a *Stegosaurus*, is eating plants here in Tijuca National Park as Brazilian Army personnel stand by with weapons ready, but not actively engaging the dinosaur. It is at least twenty-five feet long and maybe twelve feet tall at the top of its back plates. Fortunately, it has not used those huge spikes on the end of its tail.

"The dinosaur is not considered a threat at this moment, and we are told that scientists are working with the Brazilian Armed Forces in hopes of capturing the animal instead of killing it. This is a dramatic difference to what has been happening for the last hour here in Brazil's second largest city."

The scene cut to a mountain that looked like a tooth sticking straight up toward the sky. Boone recognized it as Kaly said, "That's Sugarloaf."

The narration began again with, "The following video may be disturbing to some."

Two huge, bird-like forms were flying above the top of the mountain and as the scene panned back two others could be seen. "Oh my god," Kaly gasped as the two began attacking a cable car that was moving agonizingly slowly toward the mountain. It was rocking back and forth, and suddenly a figure fell from it, and one of the flying forms dove after it. The other grasped the side of the car and stuck its head inside repeatedly until it emerged with something in its jaws and flew away.

The narrator could be heard taking a deep breath as they continued, "It appears that at least one person was possibly killed in that attack and maybe others. We have had no word on the occupants of the cable car, which, as you can imagine, was severely damaged and is still in the same place. We can only hope that there are survivors, and they will be rescued soon.

"I am told the creatures are *Quetzalcoatlus*, some type of flying dinosaur. You could see how big they were compared to the cable car. Wait," the voice shouted. "I can hear jets, yes, you can see three of them on your screen. The Brazilian Air Force is on scene and, oh!" Two of the animals disappeared in splashes of crimson and spiraled out of sight. The jets quickly reappeared, and the announcer was shouting, "There they go, the other two are falling into Guanabara Bay. Let's hope this puts an end to today's dinosaur attacks which began about an hour ago at Mauá Square. For more on what is happening there now let's cut to Miguel."

A new reporter began speaking rapidly, "As you can see behind me the Mauá Square is not filled with the usual tourists. Instead, there are police officers and Army personnel investigating the unbelievable dinosaur attacks that began shortly after noon. These dinosaurs, five in all it is believed, were different from those that attacked Washington, D.C. yesterday. They walked on two legs, were about six to seven feet tall, covered with light brown feathers, with sharp curved claws on their hands and feet and razor sharp teeth.

"Similar to the D.C. attack, they suddenly emerged from the back of a delivery van that was parked about a half block away from this popular tourist destination. As you can imagine the Square was packed, and the dinosaurs immediately began attacking, and I'm sorry to say, killing and possibly eating some of their victims. A preliminary report states that twenty people were killed and dozens of others were injured, some with life threatening injuries.

"Police officers arrived within a minute of the attacks, and though they shot and killed at least two of the dinosaurs, four officers were killed and at least seven others critically injured. As other officers arrived, they stayed further away and used their rifles to kill three more of the animals. Authorities are studying video of the incident to confirm all of the dinosaurs have been accounted for. Businesses are being searched to make sure -"

A scream cut Miguel's words short as the camera quickly moved off of him and toward a doorway about fifty feet away. One of the dinosaurs that had not been killed was standing there; a figure lay still at its feet. The sudden movement of the camera had attracted its attention, and with blinding speed, the animal rushed toward it. The image blurred as the camera was jerked to the right and down. A loud noise, like a shot, was heard and then Miguel's voice, now speaking Portuguese, was heard. Another voice answered, and a few seconds later the camera view showed Miguel again. His eyes were wide open with fright, and he was breathing heavily. Miguel pointed to a building behind him and said, "Here, within sight of The Museum of Tomorrow, we have come face to face with the prehistoric past. Yesterday it was Washington D.C., today it is Rio de Janeiro. What is happening?"

Boone turned off the television and asked, "What is happening?"

Kaly shook her head and answered, "Yesterday was hard enough to explain. But now, twice? It doesn't make sense. None of it makes sense."

They both jumped as Kaly's phone rang. She answered and after a few seconds said, "Sorry, it's too late. We just saw it." She paused, then continued, "Okay, we'll try," and then hung up.

"Let me guess," Boone said. "Forget the second one, focus on the first one, and don't turn on the TV again."

Kaly laughed and replied, "Add in a few colorful words, and you have it."

"How do we do that? My heart is racing."

Kaly thought for a moment and said, "Let me interview you about yesterday. Just the major points, like you were creating an outline. We'll talk about it again tomorrow, and I'll get you into the finer points then. Doing the outline today will at least get us focusing on our incident instead of Rio."

"Agreed," Boone said. "Just let me know when you're ready."

Kaly got her laptop, and they sat down at the dining room table. "Just talk normally," she told him. "I have a voice to word program that is pretty good, and I can clean it up when we are finished. Start whenever you want to."

When Boone finished, Kaly looked thoughtful. "Did I mess up?" he asked.

"No, I'm just trying to figure out something. You said the truck that the *Tyrannosaurus* jumped off had disappeared."

Boone laughed and said, "Don't worry, I'm not going crazy. I remember what Agent White said about remembering things, so I suppose I had things wrong."

"But, you don't. As you were led away, I saw where the ambulance was parked, and it was right next to that rig. You would have seen it."

"So, now I'm *not* seeing things."

"Let me check something," she said quickly as she began typing and then scrolling on her laptop. It took her several minutes and then she told Boone, "Look at this. It's a still shot taken from one of the officer's body cameras that were by the truck when the *Tyrannosaurus* first came out. The truck is there and so is a fence post with an old cup lying next to it." She tapped her keyboard as she continued, "This is a dash cam view from a police car that pulled up after you had just gotten into the ambulance. What do you see, or not see?"

"No truck."

"The dash cam shows the police car stopped right next to the ambulance. Look, you can see the fence post with the cup. So sometime between me looking back at you, walking to the ambulance, and you getting in the ambulance, the truck just disappeared."

"That's unbelievable. Who took it?"

Kaly leaned in close to Boone and whispered, "I didn't say anyone took it. I said it disappeared. Watch." She started reversing the video and suddenly the truck appeared. One second it wasn't there, and the next second it was just as Boone remembered seeing it.

He jerked his head forward and told Kaly, "Play that again, slowly."

She started tapping her laptop and frame-by-frame the video moved forward until the truck just vanished. Then she played with it, going back and forth several times until Boone leaned back and asked, "What does this mean?"

"There's something else," Kaly said. "Rusty, Agent Russell, he was standing by on the other side of the street waiting for the president."

"Yeah, I remember; he was already walking that way."

"That's right," Kaly said. "He's missing too."

"What? This just gets weirder and weirder," Boone told her. "Have we both gone crazy?"

"No," Kaly replied. "I'm calling -"

Her phone interrupted her, and she told Boone, "It's Agent White." She answered and began, "Sir, we've just discovered something. The truck the dinosaur was on just disappeared. I mean it - Okay, but - Okay, right now." She stood up and said, "He says get the TV back on, we might as well hear about it now instead of later."

They stood up and rushed into the main room, and as the picture came on, they saw the crawler SYDNEY, AUSTRALIA THIRD DINOSAUR ATTACK. They sat down on the couch in disbelief as a woman narrated, "This video has been streaming for about an hour now and indicates that the recent dinosaur attacks are not limited to the ground and air. We're not sure which ferry the people were on, but they were heading east through Sydney Harbour and are north of Millers Point. As you've heard so many times over the past two days, portions of this video may be too intense for some viewers."

A video of what was obviously a view from a moving boat of some type started. What sounded like a young girl's voice said, "Hey everyone, I wasn't too happy about getting up early this morning, but I have to admit that the sunrise and reflections underneath the Sydney Harbour Bridge are pretty spectacular. I can make some great prints and artwork from this." A dark shadow moved across the video, and the scene blurred and then refocused with the camera pointing at the deck. As it moved side to side and up and down, a quick view showed at least a hundred people were on the ferry.

As one voice called out, "What was that?" another shouted, "Look at the dolphins." The camera was brought up, and Sydney Harbour was filled with hundreds of dolphins jumping out of the water as they streamed west past the boat. As other fish joined in, the water foamed white like rapids. Sailboats had their masts snapped and some were being overturned. About 100 yards away two people in the water began calling for help, and the crowd on the ship began shouting, "Help them," as the ferry turned to provide assistance.

As a woman shouted, "There's a whale out there," a long, dark object moved slowly between the swimmers and the ferry then sank out of sight. The water began to calm, and the swimmers were within fifty yards when the water exploded, and a huge, writhing shape rose straight out of the water, taking one of the swimmers with it in its huge mouth. The shape hung for an agonizing moment above the other swimmer then crashed down on them with a large splash.

Screams of terror came from the people on the ferry as the boat abruptly turned which caused the camera view to move toward the sky and then back down. The view swept the water, and as a lone dolphin jumped fewer than fifty feet from the ferry, the terrible shape reappeared. As it rose from the water it was close enough that everyone could see the diamond-shaped scales on its black and light gray body. It twisted and coiled as the dolphin it had just missed slipped past its huge mouth, and its great body smashed down on the ferry stern. There were screams and calls for help as the camera bounced and rattled off a ladder the person carrying it was climbing. When the bouncing stopped the video angle was pointing down at the deck as the giant anmal wriggled off of it, leaving behind dozens of smashed bodies. Then the girl's voice could be heard shouting, "Mom? Dad?" followed by sobbing.

"We don't know what that was," the narrator said while the crawler now read: HUNDREDS DEAD IN SYDNEY DINOSAUR ATTACKS. "But it is still in the Sydney Harbour."

The scene switched to a large grassy area as a new commentator said, "Meanwhile, rescue crews are searching vehicles on Macquarie Street and the grounds of the Royal Botanic Garden after an attack by three *Tyrannosaur* type dinosaurs." A few seconds of the three dinosaurs chasing people was shown and then the narrator was saying, "These are the only images of the dinosaurs to surface so far. Some are speculating they may be *Australovenator*, but no one knows for sure. All of the animals were eventually destroyed but not before they attacked many vehicles and early morning park patrons.

"We have also heard that a dinosaur of some type caused an explosion at a service station just west of the downtown Sydney district. The servo was destroyed, and the animal and several patrons were killed. I want to stress this has not been confirmed, but we do have news units rushing to the scene. We will keep you updated on all of the early morning events as we receive more information."

Kaly turned off the television, and they walked out onto the dining room balcony. On any other day they would have enjoyed the warm day, but as they looked down on the streets below them, they saw very few cars, and no one walking on the sidewalks. "Everyone is hiding," Kaly said.

"Or watching their doors with loaded guns," Boone replied. "I can't figure any of this out. Can you?"

"No, and I'm calling Agent White again." Boone knew when the phone was answered because Kaly immediately began, "Sir, the truck in Washington just disappeared, and I heard that Rusty was gone too. Are there - no I've not talked about this with anyone, I - he's the one that told me about the truck so yes, he knows about it." There was a long pause and she answered, "Of course we won't talk about this with anyone, Sir. I understand, tomorrow at noon." She hung up and told Boone, "Change of plan, we need to finish our reports today and be ready to leave tomorrow. Too much is happening."

"What did he say about the truck and your missing agent?"

"He already knew. He says they're trying to get a handle on things right now, and oh, yeah, there is a nationwide curfew of 10pm and a strong movement toward activating all military units and declaring martial law." She looked down again on the nearly empty street below and asked, "What can you attribute to the sudden appearance of animals that have been extinct for millions of years?"

Boone shook his head and said, "I can't think of anything."

"Well, apparently we're the only ones." As Boone looked perplexed she continued, "So far some of the public suggestions are; atom bomb radiation, hydrogen bomb radiation, the Russians, the Chinese, Jesus is returning, God has given up on us, God is mad, a time traveler left an open portal, dinosaurs were never really extinct, it's a government trick, the president is up to something, it had to be the Canadians, and I guess a few hundred more.

"The fact is, every law enforcement agency is trying to solve a puzzle that flies in the face of logic. How can you solve something like this?" She took a deep breath and advised, "At least we don't have to worry about it, and we won't have time to think about it because we have work to do."

"That's a good thing," Boone agreed. "I want to understand all of this and since I can't, it's driving me crazy. Let's get to it."

It was after 9pm before they felt that both of their reports covered everything that had happened. "Done," Kaly said as she closed her laptop. "Our reports have been submitted, and I pity the person who tries to say we missed something and to do them again."

"I agree, and I'm also hungry. You?"

"Starving," Kaly agreed.

A few minutes later they were eating on the dining room balcony, and as the evening before, they talked about everything except what was going on in the world. Their mood lightened for a few minutes as they laughed and joked. Then Kaly took a deep breath and said, "I hate to be the one to break things up, but I need to get to bed. I don't know what tomorrow is going to bring."

"I understand," Boone told her as they walked into the main room. "Tomorrow and possibly many days after."

"Yes," Kaly agreed as she started to turn away, then she turned back to Boone and hugged him. It surprised him, but he quickly recovered and hugged her back. They stood locked in each other's arms for several seconds before saying "Goodnight," and walking to their rooms. As they each lay in bed they thought about the hug and wondered why the world had to pick this particular moment to go crazy.

The next morning started with a nice breakfast that was interrupted by another call from Agent White. Kaly answered and Boone heard, "Really?...not really...yeah, just the high points...you don't say...yes, we can make that happen...okay, bye."

Kaly looked at Boone and started, "I was going to say, 'you're not going to believe this', but with all that's happened, you will. London was visited early this morning by a swarm of tiny something or others, one of those big club-tailed things, and of course a carnivore of some type. Death and mayhem followed, and I figured you didn't need to see it on the TV?"

"I've seen enough of it," Boone agreed.

"Oh, I forgot to mention, one of those giant long neck ones is grazing and swimming in King George's Reservoir."

"You know," Boone started, "it is interesting that so far, each city has been attacked by different dinosaurs."

"I wonder what that means?"

"Something to someone," Boone replied. "What else did your boss have to say?"

"We're leaving early, and the car will be here in about fifteen minutes. Fortunately, we don't have much to pack so I guess we're ready to go."

Boone nodded and got his old clothes and put them in the bag where his new clothes had been in. Kaly joined him a few seconds later, and as they started toward the room's door, Boone paused and said, "You know, I need to say something to you."

"I hope I haven't -"

"You haven't," Boone cut in. "I just wanted to say…well, this is usually not me, but considering the way things are right now I…I decided to reinvent myself today." Kaly started to say something, but she could tell Boone was having a hard time saying what he wanted to say so she just listened.

Boone took a deep breath and started, "I'm sure we're getting ready to go in different directions, so I wanted you to know that over the last three days, starting before the craziness started when we first met, I have felt an interest in you. So I was wondering, or hoping I guess, that sometime in the near future, when all of this is done, you might like to get together or something. Or not. I'm sorry, I'm not very good at this. I just thought -"

"Yes," Kaly replied. She gave him her business card and continued, "I would like to get together with you again. I was getting ready to give you this before everything started. I find you interesting and between the real world interruptions I thought we were connecting. I like talking to you, so call me anytime; don't wait until things are back to normal. And, don't be surprised if I call you. I really like talking with you."

As Boone mumbled something she continued, "And I think we missed something last night."

"What?"

"That was our second dinner date. Don't you think you should have kissed me goodnight? I'm feeling a little sad right now."

She moved in closer, and they kissed. As they parted, Boone asked, "You just kissed me; wasn't I supposed to kiss you?"

"What a smart man," she told him as they kissed again.

A few minutes later they were walking through the mostly empty hotel lobby and onto the street. There were two cars waiting for them, and as they split apart, Kaly shook his hand and as she squeezed several times said, "Boone, thanks for all of your help." And under her breath she added, "Call me tonight."

THE WHITE HOUSE

Dennis Powell woke up and glanced at the clock - 7am - and he hadn't been awakened early with news about more dinosaur attacks. Maybe that meant London would be the last. Maybe. There was still the cryptic message that he, and many other leaders around the world received; INSTRUCTIONS SOON; YOU WILL BE CONTACTED; JURASSIC SWORD.

He hated this. Tax hikes, union problems, global warming, government fraud allegations, worldwide mistrust between countries, politics, these were things he could understand. But not this dinosaur mess. Two years of a relatively calm presidency gone in one unbelievable morning. He shook his head. Why did this have to happen on his watch?

He moved slowly as he sat up; his arm had just been badly bruised, but he had other pains in his body. Once again, he thanked fate that he had not been thrown out of the car like the two Secret Service agents. One was dead, and the other still in critical condition. He'd take the bruised arm and be glad that was all that happened to him. That also reminded him that tomorrow afternoon he was going to honor the fallen agent, Agent Winters, and the construction guy. Without them, people would be talking about him in the past tense.

He glanced around the room for his slippers then walked over and opened the drapes and let the early morning sun in. He looked to the left from the second floor bedroom window as he did every morning. Past the Truman Balcony rose the majestic Washington Monument. He smiled; it felt like his anchor during troubling times and even more so today. He'd been attacked by dinosaurs. *Dinosaurs.* And so had three other cities around the world. How could that even happen? No one had any idea, although everyone had ideas. He couldn't help smiling about one suggestion; yeah, the Canadians did it.

It looked like another beautiful spring morning, and he thought about stepping out onto the balcony for a few moments but remembered the Secret Service and the Capitol Police were not going to allow that. Too exposed to…what? A *Tyrannosaurus* in the backyard? Better safe than sorry, he told himself.

Fortunately, Beth was in San Francisco. Nothing had happened there other than the expected media storm surrounding the First Lady. She had called him several times to check on his safety and assure him she was okay. He was glad she was safe, had not been attacked, and was on her way back. But, it made it easier for him to look at the problem without her close by. And that's all anyone had been able to do, look at the problem. It was hard to find a solution for something that was unexplainable. He glanced back toward the top of the Washington Monument half expecting to see a *Pterodactyl* or something perched on it.

There was a rustle of paper behind him, and he turned around wondering what the noise was. He was amazed to see a bearded man sitting at a desk in the corner of the room leafing through a newspaper. He hadn't been there ten seconds before. The man was wearing a dark blue cowboy hat, dark blue coat, and dark blue pants that had a gold stripe down the leg.

As President Powell exclaimed, "What the - " the man swiveled toward him, and he saw the blue clothing was actually a dirty Civil War union army uniform with gold leaf patches on the shoulder straps. The coat was partially opened, and as the president's eyes swept across the belt buckle with US stamped on it, he was alarmed to see the man was armed with a sword, knife and an old pistol.

The president instinctively darted toward the bedroom door, and the man sat back in the chair and said, "Ya cain't git out the door and yu'rn phones ain't a workin' neither."

The president stared in amazement as his hand kept passing through the doorknob; he couldn't grab it. The same thing happened when he tried to pick up the hotline phone next to the bed. The only phone he could hold onto was his cell, and it just had static on it. Finally he gave up and turned to the man and asked, "How did you get in here? How did you get past security? What's going on?"

"I do need to 'splain myself," the man replied.

The president sat down on the bed and began breathing quickly. "Relax," the man told him. "I ain't here to hurt ya."

"Then why are you here? Why can't I touch things? Why…" the president froze then continued, "Do you have something to do with the dinosaurs appearing?"

The man leaned forward and started, "Now yu'rn -" then he laughed and quickly added, "I am so sorry. I'm talking like I'm still in 1864. Let me start over." He took a deep breath and said, "I do not have anything to do with the dinosaurs appearing. But, I am here because of them. I believe you need my help, and I certainly need yours."

"Then why do you have those weapons?" the president asked angrily. "Why don't we talk in the Oval Office? I can get my staff -"

"We can't do any of that, Mr. President," the man interrupted. "I need to explain things to you in private, so you can wrap your head around what I'm telling you. No interruptions by staff people and having to explain myself ten times. It's going to be hard enough just getting you to understand."

The president tightened his jaw a couple of times and then said, "Okay, it seems I have to listen to you. What do you need to tell me?"

"This is the most important part we have to get through so I'll just lead with it. Let you think on it for a minute, ask questions, then get down to the nuts and bolts of things. Before we can have a meaningful conversation you have to understand that I'm a time traveler."

For several seconds it looked like the president had frozen in place. Then he tried to speak but nothing came out as he moved his lips. Finally he managed, "A what? What are you saying?"

"My name is Winston Adams, no relation to any presidents; my friends call me Win, and I'm a time traveler."

As the president's face reddened, he said tersely, "I thought we were going to have a meaningful conversation."

"Okay, we're making progress," Win said. "I'm going to assume you're 'a what?' was your denial phase, and now you are angry. I've let people continue on to acceptance, but we don't have time for all the ups and downs and thinking you're going crazy and on and on…so now I just show people. Look out your window again."

"Is this some kind of a joke?"

"See, you sound angry, so I'm guessing that's where you're still at. But I'm also not sure if your question is some type of bargaining. So, just look out your window again, and we'll go from there."

The president pushed himself up and with a couple of glances back at Win walked to the window and looked down at the grounds then gasped. "What kind of stunt are you trying to pull? This is not funny. Bring it back."

"The balcony hasn't been built yet," Win said quietly. "Look down at the drive. What do you see there?"

"How did you get those cars there?"

"Okay, sir, now turn around and look at me." As the president turned, Win continued, "Thank you. Now then, what year did those cars seem to be?"

"I don't know, 30s or 40s. How did you get them there?"

"Okay, take a deep breath and look again."

"There aren't any cars down there now."

"Look up."

As he did, the president stopped and actually took two steps back. Then he pressed his face to the window and asked, "It's so wide open, where are all the buildings? And, is that…is that…"

"Yes. that is the Washington Monument being built. Did you know it was stuck at about 150 feet for twenty years because of lack of funds? That's just amazing to me. The area around it was used to graze cattle. They didn't start building the monument again until 1876. It's about 400 feet tall now."

"What year is this?"

"It was 1883 a few seconds ago; now it's today again."

President Powell looked out the window at the completed monument then slumped back on the bed. "I don't know what to say. Is this real?"

"What time did you wake up?"

"About 7am."

"What time is it now?"

"It's, it's still 7am."

"That's right," Win said. "The reason it's still 7am, and you can't touch certain things in the room, is because I have us in a time flux. This room is in the same second it was when I entered, and I will keep it that way until I leave. That way no one is wondering why they haven't seen you yet or who's talking to you. It's just us with all the time we need to discuss things."

"Okay," President Powell replied. "Are you going to talk about the dinosaurs?"

"I am."

"And, you said you needed my help."

"If I am going to be able to help you, I will definitely need your help. And, of course, this has to be kept between us and a very few select individuals."

The president shook his head and replied, "Do you think I'm going to start telling everyone about the time traveler I just met in my bedroom?"

"Probably not," Win agreed. "But, I'm concerned that if the person behind these attacks thinks that we have any way of catching them, they will disappear and start all over again. Also, they would probably eliminate any threats to them. Meaning me."

As Win paused, the president asked, "Before you begin, I just have to know, why the Civil War uniform?"

"Good question, sir."

"I think under the circumstances you can call me Dennis."

"Thank you, Dennis, and please call me Win. I hope we'll be friends by the time all of this is over. But to your question, the White House in 1864 is, of course, in the same spot it is today. Though the White House was completely gutted and modified in the early 1950s it was basically rebuilt with key rooms in the same locations.

"In 1864 anyone, and I mean anyone, could walk into the building and try and gain an audience with Mr. Lincoln. Back then it was part of the presidential job, but I know for a fact he found it tiring. He'd look at me with those tired eyes, and I would announce, 'Ladies and gentlemen, Mr. Lincoln needs to leave you for a few minutes to address an important matter. He will return shortly.' He'd try and hide a smile and we'd walk down the hall -"

"You *knew* President Lincoln? Abraham Lincoln? You spoke with him?"

"Yes sir…Dennis. Traveling to 1860 was one of the first things I did when I could travel. I studied the people, the military, and of course, the White House. Of course, I didn't know I would be using the White House one day but, and I'll let you in on a little secret, this isn't the first time I've done it. But, maybe more on that later.

"Anyway, I met Mr. Lincoln in late 1861 when I walked into the White House just to see what it was like. I was dressed like I am now, not a general that everyone would be asking questions, or a colonel which for some reason generals like to yell at, just a major. I was minding my own business when Mr. Lincoln surprised me by just walking right up to me. He shook my hand and asked me about myself. I told him I was Win, and he said 'I like that name; it's what we have to do'. He also asked if I was named after General Scott, so of course I said yes. He liked that too. I told him I was with the 37th Massachusetts Regiment, and we were building a fort near Washington. He thanked me and then went on about his business.

"I didn't go back into the White House for a few months and like before I wasn't there to see him. But, suddenly there he was shaking my hand again and unbelievably he remembered me. He said, 'Win, and we are", and he laughed. He asked me what I was doing, and I told him I had been transferred to the 11th Vermont Regiment by General Halleck and asked to help with his staff because of my knowledge of Washington. Then he told me how tired he was meeting with everyone all day, and I told him I'd help him out. That was the first time I told everyone he had to leave for a few minutes.

"We walked up to his office; it's called the Lincoln Bedroom now…of course, you know that, and he kicked off his boots and leaned back in a chair and stuck out those long legs. I can still see it. Then he told me a few stories, stretched and smiled, and said it was time to get back to work. As we walked downstairs he asked me if I could help him out again sometime, and I told him I could. So, about once a week or so he'd look up and see me and get a big smile on his face."

Win looked down at the floor and was quiet for several seconds then continued, "Anyway, I went into the White House and up to

Lincoln's office this morning and travelled to Lincoln's Bedroom then just walked down the hall to meet with you."

"Thank you for that story," Dennis said.

"Of course. Now then, first, I know who is behind the attacks."

Forgetting the pain in his arm Dennis jumped up and shouted, "What? Who?"

"My brother, August Adams."

"All right. Let me out of here, and I'll let everyone, FBI, CIA Secret Service, Interpol...everyone know."

"That's actually impossible, sir."

"Why? Name, date of birth, pictures of him. Someone will find him."

"Well sir, he hasn't been born yet."

"What?"

"Dennis, please, sit down and relax. Remember, we're talking time travel. I mean, I haven't even been born yet."

Dennis ran his hands through his hair and replied, "Okay, when my head explodes it will be your fault. Okay...okay. We know who it is, so how do we catch him?"

"I believe he has made at least three mistakes which I'm hoping will lead to more information and then finally to a lot of answers."

"What mistakes?"

"First, I believe, and I don't have all of the information yet, but I believe all of the dinosaurs we've seen are from North America. They are from different geological time periods, but from North America. August, or more to the point, the people who work for him, have gone back in time in North America and captured the animals. Then, through various means, they shipped them, trucked them, whatever, to different parts of the world to appear in our time. Since I knew the animals were from North America, I didn't have to search the entire world. If this is true, then I know exactly where his base of operations is."

Excitedly the president said, "So all we have to do is look for shipments in the last days or weeks from the U.S. to London, Rio and Melbourne and see when something as big as these animals went out."

"Well...no," Win shook his head.

'No?"

"You're still not thinking *time travel* yet. They could have shipped the animals in 1924 and then had the crates placed in a building that is still in those cities today. Then they activate their time travel from whatever year it was, and they open the ball, sorry 1860 talk, they appear here in the present time. Just like I did just now from the 1864 White House."

"But, shipments from North America during a completely unknown time period are going to be impossible to find."

"Precisely. That is why the second mistake may be the most important. We saw their vehicles disappear."

"What do you mean?"

"I'm not sure if you've been told this yet, but the Secret Service confiscated a video from the police that shows the truck the *Tyrannosaurus* was on just vanished. One second it was there, and then it was gone. Now I think that truck was still drivable, but the trailer the *Triceratops* destroyed, it wasn't going anywhere, but it has disappeared too."

"How does that help?"

"It gives us something to look for here in Washington, on Central Avenue to be specific. We just have to figure out when we would find it."

"I don't follow."

"The trailer was badly damaged by the dinosaur breaking out of it. My guess is that the bad guys saw how badly damaged it was, and they left it behind in whatever year they were in. We just need to have a records search done for an abandoned, wrecked trailer found on Central Avenue in the 1950s."

"They didn't use computers back then," Dennis pointed out. "I doubt if anyone has taken old abandoned vehicle reports and made electronic records out of them. Plus, what year are you going to start in? It could have been anytime."

"I agree. But the information about the truck is that it was from the late 50s and looked pretty new. So, I'm going to start in, say 1955, and work forward. But, that's where I need your help."

"How so?"

"I have a team of specialized people who help me solve these types of problems. They are highly motivated and can adapt to any type of situation. They -"

"Wait a second," Dennis cut in. "You have a team? For these types of problems? You've done this before?"

Win paused before answering, then said, "In the future, the powers that be create this unit to stop people from altering the known timeline. The problems have never been as severe as this before, and though we've only had to explain to a few people from the past before about us, we know this time is different. We believe you will keep this quiet because you're trustworthy, and also, like you said, who would believe you?"

"Okay," Dennis said. "What do you need from me?"

"Access to this time period's most powerful computers and information centers. We cannot use technology from our time without alerting August that we are here. Any changes in your grid would be picked up immediately. So, my people need clearance to enter buildings and use equipment, whenever they need to. Also, supervisors need to be in place who know this is a national security matter and handle any employee complaints or questions. This has to be a no questions asked operation. Later, if we are successful, you can say you had help from an intelligence agency and people can guess which one all they want.

"Oh, unless you want me coming back wearing my uniform and waking you up, I'll need a pass to enter the White House anytime I need to. I also need clearance to move around the building without question. Is that possible?"

"It is," Dennis answered. "I will have to speak with the people I know in person; I don't want this going out in an online meeting. I will cancel everything I have today and get this done by the end of the day. You should be operational tomorrow morning."

"Dennis, with all due respect, I'd like to be operational before midnight. The sooner we start the better, and, if there is another attack my people will have live access to critical information."

"I'll get it done," Dennis assured him.

"I almost forgot, I want Agent Winters and that construction guy. They have what no one else on my team has; experience with dinosaurs."

"I'm sure I can get Agent Winters for you, but the guy is a civilian. He'd either have to come voluntarily or we'd have to arrest him."

Win smiled and said, "Invite him to a meeting and let me explain things to him. I'm sure he'll want to be part of this. He seems like the type."

"He was definitely the type to help save my life," Dennis said. Then he said, "You mentioned three mistakes by your brother. All the animals are from North America, you might be able to trace the damaged trailer…what was the third one?"

"August thinks I'm dead."

"Why?"

"Because he tried to kill me."

"Well, you have got to tell me more about this," Dennis said.

"My brother was part of TIM. That is, Time Immersion Management. A very big part. He was the leader of this group before me, and because of his abilities, we were able to stop a lot of problems. But, one day I found out that the list of incursions we were working on was not a complete list, several incursions were missing. Someone was keeping information from us. When I started checking into the incidents, I found out they all involved technology that could be used for time travel on a large scale.

"I took the information to August, and he was astounded. He told me to keep my findings secret because it was obvious one of the people above us was manipulating things. So, we began checking, and everything we looked into led to a dead end. But one day we met, and he excitedly told me he had found everything. He told me about an abandoned mine in North Dakota that was being used to build undetectable time portals.

"I jumped at the chance to go with him to get the evidence and expose the person responsible. We went to North Dakota and were able to get past the guards and deep into the mountain. It was just as he had told me it would be. Inside the mine there were offices filled with computer banks from my time, your future. We had discovered a vast enterprise to do something big in this time. This wasn't going to be a simple incursion for old coins or precious metals. I wasn't sure what it was going to entail, but I did notice they had pictures of dinosaurs in their meeting room. I told August we had all we needed, and he said not yet and suddenly the room was full of people wearing guns and calling August 'sir.'

"I was dumbfounded, shocked. When I asked him why, he took me for a walk through the rest of the mine, which he had purchased in the late 1800s. He showed me all of the new technology he had invented and the dinosaur pens. He told me he was going to use all of it, the old and the new, for the good of mankind. I asked him what he meant, and he explained that mankind had become too self-centered and lacked higher values which should distinguish us from animals. We were petty, and self-righteous, with delusions of grandeur. We were de-evolving, going in the wrong direction, and he blamed this particular time period.

"When I asked him what he proposed to do about it, he just laughed and said that humanity needed one leader, just one. That way decisions could be made impartially and without political agendas. When I asked condescendingly who this great leader was going to be, he laughed and said I could mock him all I wanted to, but it was obvious it should be him. Only he had the mental capacity and ability to rule the world. But, then he paused and said he wanted me to be part of his plan. He didn't say what I was going to do, and I'm sure he was just trying to placate me.

"I asked him how he was going to accomplish this, and he told me he would first show the world what he could do. He would make it clear to everyone he could time travel and wreak havoc anywhere in the world he wanted to with extinct animals. This would convince everyone they should do what he asked. If there were countries, or groups of people that didn't follow, they would become extinct also."

Win paused as he shook his head, then continued, "He was very proud of how things were organized. How the animals were tranquilized and kept asleep in specialized containers during any transport they had to make. Only period trucks were used to haul the animals, and if they needed to be shipped, it had to be when there were lifting systems capable of moving heavy containers."

"I'm still not clear on how it works," President Powell said.

"It sounds complicated, but it's not," Win started. "Let's take the animals that appeared in Rio, for example. First, they were captured by one of his animal teams, and I have to admit I don't know all of how that happens. I assume medicated food to reduce the risk to his workers, but that's just a guess.

"They are transported to the mine and -"

"Wait," President Powell interrupted. "Do they use trucks, or...or, what?"

"They do use some trucks with hoists," Win replied. "But they have to use helicopters to lift the heavier animals onto the trucks. Cranes move too slowly, so they are kept near the mine to lift the animals into caged areas."

"If there are trucks, then there are roads?" President Powell asked.

"Yes, a limited number that lead to sites where they lure animals to them. Like I said, I'm unsure of the process, but rotting animals or the smell of certain plants I'm sure would be enough of a lure."

"Okay, what happens next?"

"The sedated animal is transported to a warehouse in New York. And sorry, I have no idea where it is. This transportation can occur during any year from the mid 50s to now. They spread the shipments out, so that a convoy of trucks doesn't leave the mine site all at once. No one thinks twice about a single truck driving down a road.

"Once they are at the warehouse they are medicated again and a decision made for what will be the best date to ship them out."

"You mean they weren't just shipped to Rio or London last week?"

"Well, that is possible. Though even now a very low percentage of shipping containers are ever closely inspected; August wouldn't want to take any chances. The animals would have been sent back in time when inspections weren't like they are today. Also, if you're shipping something on a boat, it's nice to know what the weather is going to be like for the voyage. My brother would not be happy if a storm caused a delay in an animal getting somewhere.

"So, the Rio containers were shipped and stored in a building that is still present today. Then, the animals were sent to the future, that is now, and teams there use nondescript vehicles to distribute the animals and then leave the area. The workers then return to North Dakota."

"So, if I have this straight," President Powell began. "There could have been four or five groups of workers taking the dinosaurs to Rio. They all left North Dakota in different years, maybe even different decades. Once they were in New York, the animals were possibly shipped in other years or decades, depending on ship availability, storms, whatever. So, they arrived in Rio spread all over the calendar, then were all forwarded to the same day...and were sent out like package deliveries."

"That's how I understand it," Win agreed. "I have to admit, his team studies every aspect needed to ensure that the animals arrive at their destinations unharmed. And, those destinations are all warehouses or buildings that were present at the earlier date as well as the target date. It involves a lot of real-time hours, but no actual time as far as August is concerned. With the right knowledge, and the right amount of money, he could...no he can, take his dinosaurs anywhere he wants to because it has already happened as far as he is concerned."

"He could have shipped a dinosaur in 1965 that will terrorize someplace tomorrow," President Powell noted.

"Yes," Win nodded. As the president looked out the window, Win continued, "I feigned interest and asked August how it all worked, especially since the mine would not be present in prehistoric times. He told me the mine we were in, at least various parts of it, was present 70 million years ago. He had mapped out what parts of the mine moved, disappeared, grew in size, or got smaller. Then he put in travel units. So, when you are moving around you don't notice changes because you are automatically transported to the correct time when a portion of the mine can be used."

"So, it would seem to be one large open cave if you walked all the way through it?"

"Yes," Win agreed.

"What else did he tell you?"

"He reminded me of the sword of Damocles, and I asked him what that had to do with his plan. He laughed and said he was going to hang a sword above the world. He called it a Jurassic Sword, and he asked me what I thought."

"Jurassic Sword?" Dennis asked sharply.

"Yes, why?"

"Because many of the leaders of the world have received a mysterious electronic communication that simply said, INSTRUCTIONS SOON; YOU WILL BE CONTACTED; JURASSIC SWORD. No one has any idea what it means."

Win nodded as he said, "Well, that makes me 100% sure it's my brother." Then he paused for a moment before continuing, "I could sense he was starting to understand I wasn't on board with Jurassic Sword, and I began to figure out how I could play a hand he didn't know I had. I had brought a timepiece with me; that's something we use to coordinate our time travel. I didn't know who we might run into; I had it just in case.

"I was walking in front of August, and there were lights behind us that cast our shadows on the mine wall. As I saw him raise his arm, I knew I only had one chance, not to be there when the gun went off. I almost made it." Win raised his hat and Dennis could see a thin scar that ran along the left side of his head that looked like a misplaced part in his hair.

"He never had anything to do with guns and fortunately I think this was the only time he fired one. It was painful though, and when I fell to the floor, August saw the blood and was sure he had taken me out of the picture. He didn't take the time to see if I was alive or not. He walked away, and he shouted to someone to let the *Rex* out for a snack. I heard some laughter and could feel the heavy steps of something big getting close to me. I looked up, and I don't mind telling you that seeing that gigantic animal almost made me freeze and not use my timepiece. But just as it lunged down, I squeezed the timepiece with all my strength, but I also instinctively raised an arm in self defense. At least that was all it got.

"I kept time hopping until I found the mine empty. I was able to make my way out without being seen. I met secretly with another TIM member and explained what had happened. They took things from there and I just kept moving from one time period to another. I couldn't risk August finding me and finishing what he started.

"Then, I heard what was happening here, now, and I knew it was Jurassic Sword. I had tried not to believe him when he first told me about his plan, but now there is no denying it. My brother is killing people, innocent people, so he can make the world what he thinks it should be. He has irreparably altered the timeline and must be stopped before he damages it any further."

"This would be an unbelievable story if the proof wasn't being demonstrated all around the world," Dennis told him. "And, he shot you, his own brother and fed you to a dinosaur. He's a mad man."

Win stood up and nodded as he said, "It is an unbelievable story, especially to me. I never thought August would do something like this. But, power can make people do crazy things, and the ability to time travel, well, that's very powerful. I would caution you, Dennis, to remember how smart my brother is. When he contacts all of the leaders, just listen and don't speak. Also, don't slip and say his name to anyone, he has help in this time and we don't know who it is. Since I'm the only person who could have told you who he is, he'll know I'm still alive. Because you are right; he is a mad man."

As Win turned to leave, he said, "So, now I'm heading back to 1864 to get out of this uniform. It's made out of wool and is terribly uncomfortable, but I was afraid if I used modern material, it might be more comfortable but look wrong to the other soldiers." Then he clicked his boots together and continued, "And these things, President Thomas Jefferson wore them, and somehow they caught on, and they issued them as footwear for the army. Now I'm talking about a shoe with a straight flat, no left or right shoe, just straight. Can you imagine that?

"So, before Jefferson Davis became President of the Confederacy, he was the Secretary of War for the United States. And just before the war he improved the boot with left and right flats. So even though I have a pair, and I'm a Union soldier, I'm still wearing what's called a Jefferson boot. And no matter what the name, it's still uncomfortable."

He shook hands with President Powell, and as he turned to leave, the president asked, "I was just wondering, did you talk to Abraham Lincoln on the day he was assassinated?"

Win took a deep breath and shook his head as he answered, "No, but it was hard not to. But, I decided that it wasn't worth the risk of changing the timeline. I didn't know how he might interact with me, if I would cause him to be late or something. You know General Grant turned down Mr. Lincoln's invitation to go to the theater that night. What if he had insisted I go instead? No, I stayed away until I just couldn't take it anymore. So, I hid in the shadows in the trees across from the White House, and I could see him walking toward the carriage, and yes, I wanted to stop him.

"He was halfway into the carriage when a man ran up to him, and Abraham stepped down to talk to him. I had the delusional thought for a moment that something had come up and that he wouldn't go…but of course he climbed back into the carriage. As they drove away, I thought about going to Ford's and standing outside, but I decided I wanted to remember him alive, with that smile on his face."

Dennis said quietly, "I understand. You'll be in touch?" Win nodded, and after he left the room, Dennis started making calls.

JUST ANOTHER DAY

Boone sat in the Neighborhood Diner wondering when his life was going to start getting back to normal. There was going to be a press conference tomorrow, but there were still dozens of reporters outside of his house. So, there wasn't anything for him to do except sit here until he could call Kaly later. Hopefully she would be able to meet him someplace, maybe someplace out of the way. Everyone who had come into the diner had done a double take when they saw him and came over to talk to him. He knew all of them, but he was already tired of talking about what happened and having his picture taken. He had thought about a motel room, but he just wanted to go home.

His phone buzzed, and though he was disappointed it wasn't Kaly, he was happy to see it was Mr. Webster calling. He answered, "Sir, it is good to hear from you."

"How are you doing, Boone?"

"As well as can be expected I guess. Still sore, the scratch still hurts, but mainly I can't get in my house."

"Boone, you're the only person I know who would call a wound that took about 100 stitches to close, a scratch. And, what's this about you can't get in your house?"

"The media is still out front. I know they are just doing their job, but I just don't feel like running a gauntlet."

"Boone, I wish you would have told me sooner. We own condos in several parts of the city for visiting executives to stay in. Big enough to get lost in, full kitchen, access to a pool, hot tub, and I don't know what else. Just tell me what part of town you want to stay in, and I'll give you the address of the closest one. Don't think for a second you are putting the company out in any way. We take care of our family, and right now you are the member who is most in need. You've got to let me help you here."

"I will, sir, and thank you. I'll call you later and let you know what works best for me. And, you know, about the dozer. I know insurance will cover things, but I am really sorry -"

Mr. Webster started laughing and said, "Which dozer are you talking about? The one you used to push the dinosaur into the pit or the brand new one they gave us?"

"New one?"

"That dozer company's name has been on every newscast since it happened and will be for at least a few more days, if not weeks. Literally a million dollars worth of publicity for them. They've taken over getting it out of the pit, so they can put it on display in their showroom. And, they're giving us a top of the line dozer to replace it. 200,000 dollars I think is what it costs. So Boone, one more thing for you to stop worrying about."

"I guess so," Boone laughed.

"And another thing, or five," Mr. Webster continued. "No one knows how to contact you, so they've been calling us. I know you're not interested but talk shows, the morning news, the evening news, local and national, and even commercial offers have been coming in. Whether you like it or not you're famous. If you and that Secret Service Agent could sing and dance, I bet they'd book you in Vegas."

Boone laughed loudly and replied, "I'm amazed, I really am. Another reason not to go home, or learn how to dance, I guess."

After a moment of silence Mr. Webster continued, "Boone, there is something else I need to tell you. The memorial service for Digs is tomorrow and, though the family loves you, they've asked if you could not attend. They don't want their private gathering to turn into a media storm. They said they would rather have something private with you later, like a barbecue, something that you and his family used to do. They hope you are not upset."

"Please tell them I am not upset and that I understand completely. Tell them he'll be in my thoughts, and I will call them when things have quieted down."

"I told them that was how you would feel about it, but they were worried."

"You're the best, sir."

"You won't say that when I start cracking the whip again," Mr. Webster chuckled. "But until then, take it easy, see that mental health person, and don't come back until you're ready to. No, change that, don't come back until they say you're ready to. And call me for the condo information."

"I will, sir, goodbye."

As Boone disconnected the call, he ordered a piece of pie, and his phone started buzzing. Again, he was disappointed it wasn't Kaly but surprised it was Agent White who asked, "Boone, how are you feeling today?"

"I am fine, sir."

"Do you feel up to meeting with someone to discuss the incident and possibly do some follow up?"

"I have been expecting your call about the mental health evaluator, sir. I am ready to -"

"It's not that," Agent White cut in. "We may have a lead and need your help."

"Sir, I am ready to help anytime you need me."

"Where are you now?"

"I'm at the diner by the construction site."

"I'll have a car there for you in about fifteen. And Boone, thank you."

As Boone finished his pie he wondered what information the Secret Service had and who they suspected. He stepped outside and walked down the street, away from where Digs had been killed. An SUV pulled up beside him, and as the rear window came down, he smiled as he heard Kaly ask, "Hey, big boy, need a ride?"

As he climbed in he saw the driver was Agent Martinez and asked, "Is this what she usually does all day?"

"No, sir," Agent Martinez replied with a smile. Then he added, "Usually just part of the day."

"I can't wait until it's time for your evaluation, ex-Agent Martinez," Kaly laughed. Then she asked Boone, "What do you think this is about?"

"I have no idea," Boone said. "Don't you have any information?"

"Only that we are meeting with a scientist of some sort, maybe a paleontologist. He has some information on some of the dinosaurs, and I think he wants to get some firsthand information about them from us. He told President Powell we have the firsthand experience he needs. Also, he might have some kind of lead to the bad guy."

"Coming from the top," Boone pointed out. "I can give him pretty vivid descriptions of everything."

Kaly nodded and agreed, "Unfortunately, I can too."

"I thought we were going to meet with the mental health person," Boone said. "Any idea when that's going to happen?"

"I do have a tentative timetable for things," Kaly replied. "Let's see, meet with this guy for an hour or so and relax the rest of the day. They were very adamant about that. That reminds me, you were at your worksite; you weren't working today, were you?"

"No, I couldn't go home because of the reporters, so I came in for a piece of pie."

"Pie?" Kaly exclaimed. "You walked out of there without pie for me?"

"And me," Agent Martinez noted.

"Did you hear something?" Kaly asked. "Sounded like the voice of an ex-agent?"

"What if ex-Agent Martinez bought some pie after this meeting?" Boone asked.

"Well, that would be better than ex-Agent Martinez *not* buying us pie after the meeting," Kaly pointed out.

"There will be pie," Agent Martinez laughed as he pulled onto a drive that led up to a small, light gray building. It had a parking lot on two sides of it and houses close by in all directions. A small, faded sign above a glass door read Custom Furniture. "And, here we are. My instructions are to wait for you here. I hope he has good intel, Kaly."

"I do too, Ricky. Be back in a few."

"He seems like a nice guy," Boone said as they walked toward the warehouse entrance.

"He is," Kaly agreed. "I like everyone I work with. Keeps the job fun even when it's boring."

As they walked through the door, they were immediately greeted by a man with a bushy beard and long dark hair who said, "Welcome, welcome." As he shook their hands, he continued, "I have been looking forward to speaking with you. Unfortunately, it will be about the terrible events you went through, what you saw, and what you remember. Please, come in and sit down."

They found they had entered a room, about fifty feet square with a ten-foot ceiling. There were four sets of stairs leading up from each corner of the room, and along the wall across from the entry were three bright red doors. The left one was marked WATER, the middle OUTSIDE, and the third LAUNCH. The room was partially furnished with only a small rectangular table and three chairs in the middle. The man sat on one side of the table and Kaly and Boone on the other.

"I assure you, this will not take long," the man started. "But where are my manners?" he continued. "I'm Win Adams, and I know you are Kaly and Boone. Is it okay if I call you by your first names?"

"Of course," Kaly answered.

"Good. And I would like you to call me Win. Also, would either of you like something to drink? Or eat?"

"No, thanks," Boone said.

Win quickly continued, "Then I'll just jump right into things. First, Boone, do you remember seeing the trailer the *Triceratops* came out of while you were walking on Central before everything happened?"

Boone thought for several seconds then replied, "I can't say for sure, but the trailer probably was there. The street in front of the Taylor site had three trailers in front of it, but I can't tell you anything about them."

Win asked Kaly, "Did you see the trailer when you arrived?"

"Yes. As we turned onto 82nd, I noted there were three trailers, a smaller silver one with no markings, and then two standard-sized trailers, one light blue with a red star on it and the other was white and had black horizontal lines."

Win nodded and asked, "Did either one of you feel the smaller trailer was suspicious, out of place, anything?"

Boone shook his head, and Kaly answered, "No."

"Good, good," Win told them. "Now then, Boone, in your detailed description of events you mentioned -"

"Wait," Kaly interrupted. "You've seen our reports?"

"Yes," Win told her. "I've been given clearance by the president and everyone in the Secret Service chain of command down to Agent White. I hope that doesn't concern you. It was vital that I have the access so I can assist you."

"No," Kaly assured him. "It just surprised me, and I thought we were here to assist you."

Win nodded and replied, "I hope we can help each other." Then he told Boone, "Tell me about your suspicions regarding the semi and trailer parked on 82nd."

"The main thing was how old it was. You don't see forty-year-old rigs hauling things, and it looked new, not brand new, but I'd say it didn't have too many miles on it."

"And you saw it as soon as you walked out onto 82nd from the worksite?"

"It was hard to miss."

"Do you think it would be possible that some of the workers who arrived early and were in the diner saw the truck?"

"Yeah, definitely," Boone replied.

"In your narrative you listed the people who were outside, and you thought you could see a couple more inside. But you didn't know all of their names?"

"Not full names, no. I mean Digs and Dottie worked with me the longest, then there were the brothers Jerry, Mikey and Dave. Big Ray and Tom were there and every project you usually get a few new people on. I think they were Carlos, Nick, Bobby, Trey, and…Sammy. Those were the ones I saw for sure. I'd bet there were a few more in the diner that I didn't see."

"Thanks," Win said. "And I have talked with Dottie. She told me she was the first one to arrive, and she swears the truck was not there when she went into the diner. When everyone else started showing up and drinking their coffee outside, she noticed the truck had arrived. Said it was about five minutes before you walked up."

"Did she see anyone around the truck?" Kaly asked.

"No, it was parked and empty as far as she could tell," Win replied. "And the truck was already there when your team arrived?"

"Yes," Kaly answered. "And all I noticed was that it was a truck with a covered load. I couldn't tell you anything about how old it was."

"Where was Agent Russell?"

"Agent Russell was in the car with me, Agent White and Mr. Webster."

"And both of you noted the last time you saw Agent Russell he was walking back toward the intersection of Central and 82nd?" After they both agreed, he asked Kaly, "Is he still missing?"

"Yes."

"What do you make of that?"

"I don't know," she replied. "No one found a body, and he hasn't called in. And no one has said they kidnapped him or anything."

"What do you think that means?" Win asked.

There was something in the tone of his voice that made her say, "I think it means something to you."

Win smiled and nodded his head as he said, "Yes, it does mean something to me. I know both of you have seen the video of the semi disappearing, so, what does all of it mean to you?"

"So, you think the truck disappearing and Agent Russell missing are connected?" Kaly asked.

"I do. But, what do you think?"

"A connection seems reasonable," Boone said. "But, I don't really investigate things."

"I think it's a reasonable assumption too," Kaly agreed. "But I bet the reason we're here is you're getting ready to tell us why it's not just an assumption."

"Possibly," Win replied. "But even with what I know I can't say for sure how the two are connected. But I can tell you why the truck disappeared."

"Why?" Kaly and Boone asked in unison.

"Time travel," Win answered, then leaned back in his chair.

Several silent seconds went by until Boone said, "That's the bossest thing I ever heard."

"What?" Kaly asked in amazement. "You think this was *time travel*?"

"Sorry, I read a lot of science fiction, and it's the only thing that answers all of the questions. The truck and your agent have just disappeared. Unless you're ready to say it was magic, it had to be time travel."

"Boone, I'm amazed," Win said. "You are the only person in all the years I've been doing this who has instantly agreed with what I have said."

"But, I haven't," Kaly pointed out. "There is no such thing as time travel. No one briefed me on this before they sent me over here."

"That's because right now there are only three people I have told about it. You, Boone and President Powell."

"The president bought this?" Kaly asked.

"He did after I showed him a sample of it."

Kaly stood up and said, "Well, you are going to have to do the same for...oh, my god."

The walls to their left and right had suddenly become clear, and Kaly and Boone couldn't believe what they were seeing. Instead of a parking lot and neighborhood houses surrounding the warehouse, there was now thick brush and waving palms all around it. When they looked out the left side, they could see all the way to a blue shimmering lake and the animals in and around it.

They were dinosaurs. They had no idea what they were other than some were 'duckbills'. Others were huge with long necks and tails, and they walked on four legs. Their heads, which looked tiny compared to their busy bodies, moved back and forth through even the highest tree canopies as they devoured vegetation. The 'duckbills' were in the shallow portion of the water or standing close to its edge. They were dark gray with just slightly darker areas around their heads and the top of their legs. Some of the animals on the land were eating shrubs close to the ground while others were stretching up to eat from lower tree limbs.

Other smaller animals, about three feet tall, darted through the vegetation and some were in the trees. Some were green and gray with scales while others had brightly colored strands of wavy string-like feathers.

A shape passing through the tops of the trees suddenly turned into a light brown winged creature that Boone thought was a

Pterodactyl. Its skin looked different in some areas, and he wondered if there was some type of feather making it look darker on its back. It glided down gracefully and skimmed the water with its long beak until it rose majestically, with a fish firmly held in its teeth. It soared up and out of sight above them.

Kaly and Boone froze as a large animal walked out of the tree line on the far side of the lake edge. It stood about ten feet tall on two muscular legs and was obviously a carnivore. All the animals around the lake stopped and stared at the animal which simply began drinking. As it stood back up it eyed the other animals slowly then turned and vanished back into the trees. A few seconds later the other animals returned to eating but still looked around warily.

"Could that thing see in here?" Boone asked.

"No," Win assured him. "One way viewing hologram system. Outside we look like a rock wall. And, even if it did try to get at us for some reason, this station can't be breached by even the biggest of them. We're safe."

"I would like to go outside," Kaly said.

"Okay," Win replied.

"Uh, let's wait a second," Boone suggested. "I need to know why we're going outside. You did see what was out there, right?"

"I want to make sure we're not watching a movie or something. It did look real, but I want proof. Besides, didn't you say this was the bossest thing ever?"

"I did, but getting eaten by a dinosaur is not."

Win laughed and said, "It's safe. We are monitoring the area, and the closest large carnivore is the one we just saw."

"You mean the one that is sneaking through the forest to make Boone a dino snack?" Kaly teased.

"I'm not laughing," Boone shot back as the red door marked OUTSIDE hissed open. They stepped into a smaller room, and when the door behind them closed, another door opened in front of them, and they stepped outside. As the heat, humidity and animal noises swept over them, Boone asked, "Convinced yet?"

As three chicken-sized animals, covered with yellow, silky feathers, with long tails, darted past Kaly, she nodded her head and replied, "Yes." They walked further away from the building, and

Kaly felt the leaves of some shorter shrubs and ran her fingers through the dirt. She looked back at them and said, "This *is* the bossest thing ever."

They stepped back into the smaller room, and when the door closed, a breeze began to blow on them. "We are being medicated and scanned for pathogens, well, at least the ones we know about. So far we haven't had anything dangerous follow us back to our time."

The interior door hissed open, and they walked back into the big room and sat down at the table. While they were out, a glass of ice water and a fruit bowl had been left for each of them. "Is there someone else here?" Kaly asked.

"Yes, Otai operates the time machine which, as you can tell, is the entire area we are in. This is a common area for the TIM, or Time Incursion Management. Otai and I are agents of TIM. He must have felt you would need something after the heat and the shock of all of this."

"He was right," Boone told him.

Boone and Kaly drank and ate for a while before Kaly asked, "What is TIM, and if you have other agents, why did you show us this?"

Win leaned forward and said, "Because, I need you to understand what is happening, and why, and...I need your help with another portion of this investigation. Both of you exhibited the ability to size up a situation and react quickly and correctly when the *Rex* and *Triceratops* appeared. Those attributes are what I look for in team members even if, like you, they will be temporary. And, I think I can reasonably say you won't tell others about what you just saw or, if you help, what we are about to do."

"People think I'm crazy enough," Boone said.

"And I don't want people to think I'm crazy at all," Kaly added. Then she asked, "But what about your other TIM agents? Why don't you just use them for everything you need?"

"Because of the world wide attacks that have occurred, and those that could occur at any moment. You have witnessed firsthand, and seen on your media, coordinated attacks on the world. TIM does not feel they are finished. We are trying to put out the fires of the last ones before the flames of the new ones begin. In short, we never expected anything like this to occur. We don't have enough agents. We need your help."

"What do you want us to help you with?" Kaly asked.

Win explained, "I want to go to the intersection of Central Avenue and 82nd Street on July 6th, 1957." He held up a small cylindrical object and continued, "This will let us time travel, so we can watch the truck and trailer being parked. Hopefully this will let us see who is involved and answer some questions I have about what happened."

"Wait," Kaly interjected. "Why wouldn't we just take them down right then?"

"If the right person is there then I would agree to that. If he isn't, and I doubt if he will be, then we have to let things play out just as they did. If we interfere he'll know we're on to him, and his next attacks I'm sure will kill even more people."

"So, you know who is causing all of these attacks?" Kaly asked.

"I do," Win replied. "My brother."

"Wow," Boone exclaimed. "And if he's not there, we can't interfere?"

"That's right," Win agreed. "We have to preserve the timeline." He looked at Boone and asked, "I understand you lost a friend; are you sure you want to go?"

"To make sure his death means something, yes, I do."

"How do you know it is that exact date?" Kaly asked.

"I began a police records check this afternoon for the damaged trailer starting with the year 1955. We had boxes and file cabinets full of old reports, and we were going to have to sift through spools of old microfiche as well. Hours and hours of work. Then we got lucky. One of the guys who was searching was a retired officer whose grandfather had been an officer in the 50s. Out of nowhere he asked, 'Wouldn't it be funny if we were looking for the baby rhino case?'

"Of course I immediately asked, 'What?' And he explained that back in the summer of 1957 his grandfather investigated a case where a circus had abandoned a damaged trailer along Central Avenue. It even had a dead baby rhino in it. They never were able to discover what circus it had been or who had owned the trailer.

"I had that file pulled immediately, and though the license plate was missing from the trailer, the officer who handled the case wrote down some numbers that were on the back of the trailer. Those numbers indicated the trailer was made just last year."

"A decades old case with modern ID numbers," Kaly said.

"Exactly," Win agreed. "So, now we can track down a sales record for the trailer and actually visit the scene at the time the incident occurs and see who shows up."

"Let's go," Kaly said excitedly.

"I'll meet you outside of the diner by the construction site in about an hour," Win told them. "Boone, we know that the buildings that were demolished for your apartment building were built in the early 60s. Before then, that corner was just a large wooden lot. We'll go back to 1957 from there, set up cameras, and find a good surveillance point. Then we'll see what happens and decide what to do after that."

As they rode back with Agent Martinez, Kaly was wondering how she was going to tell him they didn't want pie after all when her phone buzzed. "It's the boss," she advised. Then she advised Agent White, "Yes, finished with the meeting...we were going to...okay...yes...no problem...I will." She looked at Agent Martinez and told him, "It's your lucky day, Ricky. You need to head straight back to the office, and I need to take care of something else."

As they stopped in front of the diner, Boone told Agent Martinez, "Wait here for a minute." He ran inside and quickly returned with a takeout box that he handed in through the rolled down window. "Ricky, a piece of the best pie in town."

Ricky smiled and said, "Thank you, Boone. Thank you."

As he drove away, Kaly said, "I hope that wasn't the last piece."

"Ours is being set on the table at this moment. I guessed you might want ice cream also?"

"Of course. Do I look like a barbarian to you?"

Just as they finished eating, Win walked past the front window, and a minute later they were all walking toward a white panel truck parked near the construction gate. Win stopped and told them, "I parked here to block the view from the diner in case anyone just happens to be looking out. Unless there is a person on this sidewalk walking toward us from either direction, we can't be seen. Also, I don't know if there was a sidewalk here in 1957, but if not, this should be a shoulder of the street. Are you ready?"

"This is really going to happen, isn't it?" Kaly asked.

"It is," Win told her.

"Cool," Boone said.

They immediately knew they had traveled because it was darker but still light enough they could see that both sides of the road were wooded. It was warm with a light breeze blowing. Kaly and Boone took a few seconds to look around, and Win said, "It is a little disconcerting, isn't it? One second you are in your time and reality, and the next, you're questioning your sanity."

"What time is it?" Boone asked.

"It's a little after 8pm, so we have about a half hour before it's dark." Win bent down and made a small pile of sticks and told them, "This is where we will need to be, so we reappear next to my truck, and no one will see us."

He reached into a pouch on his side and held up six tubes and said, "We need to get these cameras in place. Watch what I do." He walked to a small tree and held one of the tubes against the side of the slender trunk. A thin line shot out of the back of the camera and wrapped around the tree and back to where it started from and automatically fastened the camera to the tree. The tube was pointed back toward the area in front of the diner, and Win explained, "I want to see who drops off the *Rex*."

Then he started walking toward Central Avenue. They watched and listened for traffic, but there was none on 82nd. There were cars moving on Central though, so they cut through the woods until they were across from where Boone thought the trailer would be parked. "Just to make sure, let's place cameras on the outside edges of the area you think the truck will be in," Win instructed. "Angle them in a little, and that should give us some room in case we are a little off." Kaly went left and Boone right then they met back in the middle with Win.

"Now what?" Boone asked.

"We wait," Kaly said. "Surveillance 101."

"Have you done this often?" Boone asked Win.

"Yes, and I hope this is the usual. Quick in and out with the info. Unfortunately, sometimes I have to be a local so to speak. Period dress and talk, so I don't seem out of place. Carry the right money and try and fit in. I try to keep it short, but every second you are playing a role you can slip up."

"Such as?" Kaly asked.

Win chuckled and replied, "I was on Pier 54 when the *Carpathia* brought in the survivors of the *Titanic*. There were maybe 40,000 people there, and I knew pictures were being taken. Flashbulbs were going off everywhere, but I just wasn't cautious enough. If you look close enough at the pictures you'll see me in one of them. I was foolish, very foolish. Fortunately it was the only time that my image was captured. After that, I stayed away from the cameras."

"But you still went to famous events?"

"Of course. What else can you do if you are a time traveler? You go see what really happened."

As the sound of a large truck approaching got louder, Kaly said, "We need to stay behind these bushes so this time traveler will do what they are supposed to."

Win nodded, and they listened as the truck was parked on the spot that was behind them near the diner. They couldn't see who had been in the truck, but they heard their voices as they walked along 82nd toward Central Avenue. It sounded like a man and a woman, but they couldn't tell what they were saying.

A few seconds later, they heard another truck, and within a minute, a blue semi-tractor pulling the silver trailer arrived. Two men got out of the truck and quickly unhooked the trailer and pulled the truck up to where a man and woman were standing on 82nd. Though they knew it was going to happen, both Boone and Kaly started when the silver trailer disappeared.

"How long until -" Boone was cut off by the sudden reappearance of the now torn apart trailer.

The four people near 82nd Street started toward it when one of them commanded, "Get back to your truck and see if it is damaged too. If it isn't, get it out of here. " As the man and woman ran out of sight, the same voice shouted to the driver of the blue semi, "Turn your rig around and let's get some light on this mess."

A man ran up to the trailer and turned on his cell phone light to look inside. When he did, Kaly whispered, "That can't be..." As the lights of the blue semi got closer, she whispered excitedly, "It is. That's Rusty, Agent Russell. I think everyone thought he had been taken by the bad guys somehow."

"But now we know why he is missing," Boone whispered back. "He's one of the bad guys."

As the semi driver jumped out of the truck, Rusty said, "What a mess. We can't hook it up; we'll have to leave it."

"We can hook a phase unit on it and come back later," the other man suggested. Then he used a flashlight to look inside and exclaimed, "Hey, the little *Tri* is still in here."

Rusty replied, "Yeah, I saw that. Let's throw some wood in there and light it with a flare. I think these trailers are aluminum or something that will burn. There won't be anything left of it."

"Are you sure? It looks like steel to me."

"Don't worry about it. I want to get out of here before any traffic comes by." As Rusty spoke, the flatbed tractor trailer drove by and out of sight and he added, "Come on, let's go. We'll follow them."

"I don't think there's enough wood -" the other man started, but Rusty lit a flare, and tossed it into the trailer. He climbed into the truck and shouted something to the driver. The other man just shrugged, got in too, and drove away.

"What now?" Kaly asked.

"Nothing," Win said. "We know the trailer doesn't burn, and there's no big 'Dinosaur Found' headline because they think it's a baby rhinoceros. I was hoping one of them might be smoking, so we could maybe get some DNA off a cigarette. But, I didn't see any of them do something we could take advantage of."

They collected the video cameras as they walked back through the woods to 82nd Street. As Kaly pointed out, "Still, we know Rusty was involved. If he shows up, claiming he was kidnapped or something -"

Win interrupted with "Yeah, that would be great. But..."

"But?" Kaly asked.

"The trailer that was left behind is a loose end and my brother doesn't like loose ends. We'll get some good intel through facial identification of the others."

They found the pile of sticks and were instantly back on 82nd Street. Kaly asked Win, "Were your questions answered?"

Win shook his head and replied, "Not all of them."

"Like?" Boone asked.

"Why didn't they unhook the 50's semi before sending the trailer to the future? I know the trailer is old also, but it would have been less noticeable than the semi."

"That's right," Boone agreed. "And, if the cover had been on tighter I wouldn't have seen the steel. I would have just thought it was another type of delivery and not paid a lot of attention to it."

Win paused before getting into his truck and smiled as he said, "I want to thank both of you. I know this has been the strangest day of your lives, but I'm hoping it was also the most interesting day of your lives. I wanted to take your measure today and you rose to the challenge perfectly. Right now, in this time, I trust you two, the president and Otai. Everyone else cannot be told anything because we do not know who is working for who. Look at Agent Russell.

"With time travel, my brother could have planted his agents years ago to rise up through the ranks of whatever political party or military department he thought would be of use to him. I will say though, that August does not tend to think that way. He usually just responds to things as they happen because he knows he can just send someone back in time and change the outcome to his liking. I hope it won't bother you; I may be asking for your assistance again."

"I think I can speak for both of us when I say we are ready whenever you need us," Kaly replied.

"Count on us," Boone added.

Win smiled and said, "Thanks. I'm meeting with the president tomorrow morning and I'll report what we have found out about the trailer. I think my brother is addressing the leaders of the world even earlier. I'm sure it will not go well for them. Hopefully, they will all understand the gravity of the situation."

Kaly put her hand on Win's shoulder and said, "President Powell will understand the situation, and I'm sorry your brother is involved. I hope everything works out, and again, we're here for you."

Win just smiled and nodded his head, and as he drove away, Boone asked, "How can the top three strangest and interesting days all come in a row like this?"

Kaly thought for a second and agreed, "I see what you mean. The world got weird, weirder, and now this. I'm not sure if I count anything that has happened as interesting though."

"Is that what you tell all of the guys you kiss?"

"What?"

"That they're not interesting."

Kaly laughed and replied, "Oh, a little get even. I didn't know you had it in you." Then she kissed him and asked, "Does that let you know I find you interesting?"

They hugged, and Boone said, "It does." As they walked toward his truck he pointed out, "You know, I just realized that it's still early in the day, but we've taken two time travels that lasted over three hours in real time though only a few seconds in this time."

"It does feel like it should be much later," Kaly agreed. "By the way, I have a nice couch in the hotel room I am staying at. You're welcome to bunk there since you still have the media on your lawn."

"I would, but I think I'm going to be sleeping in a condo tonight. You're welcome to bunk there if you like. I hear it has a pool and a hot tub."

"Of course I'll stay there," Kaly said. "Because of your wound I've got to make sure you don't get in the pool or hot tub."

"Wait. What?" Boone asked.

They both laughed as Kaly said, "You big baby."

AUGUST ADAMS

As he sat at his desk, he gently rubbed his temples with the first two fingers of each hand. All he had to do was simply follow directions; prep the items, then position them to cause the most chaos and destruction. Correctly. That's all.

The *Rex* worked perfectly; fear, running, screaming, guns firing, people dying. Too bad it didn't get the president; that would have been an unplanned bonus. It would have stopped the United States government for hours.

The *Triceratops*...it was supposed to wake up first. That would have brought things to a standstill. Depending on how the situation was handled, there would have been onlookers, police, and a multitude of media. Add in the playful calf and the area would have been packed with people.

Then the *Tyrannosaurus* would have come out of that trailer like a prehistoric jack-in-the-box. There would be screaming, running, and hysteria as the huge predator began attacking everything that moved. How many people would have been killed or maimed?

The *Triceratops* would have reacted violently causing even more death and destruction as it fought the *Rex* with hundreds of people all around. The police, and probably the Army, would have been forced to kill the animals in a hail of gunfire as the world questioned the unbelievability of what had just happened.

What could have been.

Instead, the tranquilizer dosage was wrong, and the two animals fought each other too soon. The chance to really cause a spectacular scene that would have changed the psyche of the world had been wasted. That the *Rex* died so spectacularly did make up for what it should have achieved. But not enough.

And leaving the trailer behind, and using that old semi. What was that moron thinking? All he had to do was follow directions.

He stood up and walked over to the mirror that was hanging between the large dinosaur mural and the beautiful painting that he had stolen and replaced with a fake from the Ackland Museum. The sword.

As always he thought he looked rather average. Just under six feet tall, short brown hair, brown eyes, clean shaven, and a face that didn't make any woman turn and look at him when he walked into a room. No, what made him above average, far above average, were what he called the three Is that described him; intelligent, inventive and intense. They had made him what he was today; the man who would be known as the savior of the world.

But that would be in a few minutes. Now he had to take care of the trailer stupidity, and he suddenly knew how it would help him during his speech. He sat back down at his desk and said, "Send him in."

A few seconds later Agent Russell walked in. He was nervous; he knew that mistakes were not tolerated, and he was wondering what was going to happen. Still, he tried to project confidence as he asked, "You wanted to see me, Mr. Adams?"

"Please, Russ, how many times have I asked you to call me August? Have a seat."

Looking a little relieved, though still apprehensive, Russ replied, "Thanks."

August went straight to the point with, "I'm sorry we're meeting so early, but tell me about the trailer."

Russ dropped his head and replied, "I thought that's what this would be about. Well, it was damaged by the adult *Triceratops* and couldn't be moved. I thought it would be best if we just burned it. The cops in that time didn't have as many investigative tools as they do now, and if we burned it, I thought it would just look like there had been an accident."

"But it didn't burn," August pointed out.

"No, no it didn't," Russ stammered. "But, I checked the newspapers, and what I thought would happen did. They just towed it away, and I'm sure it's rusted into nothingness by now since it was in such bad shape."

"You're sure?"

"Well, well pretty sure. That type of metal wouldn't have been able to stand up to the weather around there for very long."

"But you were told to bring it back, and Joey suggested you put a phase unit on it. Why didn't you?"

Russ glanced to the side for a second then answered, "I thought I heard a car coming. I felt it was necessary to leave at once. I made the call on site since I was in charge."

"You were in charge," August agreed. "So you can also explain why the *Triceratops* woke up late and the *Rex* early? Were they given the correct dosages?"

"I'm, I'm sure they were, sir. We were in a hurry though and - "

"Why were you in a hurry?"

"The other team, Julie and Mark, were saying 'let's go', and -"

"The other team?"

"Yes, sir."

"Thanks for that information."

Russ smiled for a second; it was always useful to blame things on other people. But he was back in the hot seat again when August asked, "What about the infant *Triceratops*?"

"Well, sir, the infant was dead, so there wasn't any reason to bring it back. Those things are so heavy I figured we'd have a hard time moving it from the trailer. I didn't think anyone in the 50s would know what it was and so...and they didn't. The newspaper reported it was a rhinoceros. They thought a circus truck had been damaged. It all worked out."

"It did," August agreed. "But I have to tell you I am disappointed. You were given a specific set of instructions which you should have carried out. You are well placed in the Secret Service and a valuable asset, but this will not happen again. Do I make myself clear?"

"Yes, sir, I mean August. It won't happen again."

"I know it won't," August replied. Then he asked, "Are you prepared for part two? Ready to go back?"

"I am, yes, I am. I was kidnapped, I have the story, I won't let you down."

"Again, I know you won't." As August stood up Russ knew he needed to leave, and as he stood up also, August asked, "Could you do me a favor?"

"Anything, August."

"Give this envelope to Patre on the way out, would you?"

Russ glanced down at the red envelope and said, "Of course," and left.

August thought to himself that things had a way of happening for the best. Yes, it would be an interesting lesson for everyone. Well, everyone except Russ.

August sat back down at his desk and gathered his thoughts for a few seconds as he watched the time count down. It was always important to be precise. With a wave of his hands over 250 view screens appeared in front of him. They ran from wall to wall and floor to ceiling. As the person in the view screen spoke, their screen grew larger so August would know who was speaking. At the moment many of the screens were getting larger and smaller as most of the people demanded to know what was happening and why they had been forced to attend the meeting.

They all stopped abruptly, however, when a small, bright green dinosaur jumped on August's desk and began chittering. It was less than ten inches tall, walked on its back legs but would occasionally drop down to its fronts legs to balance. August dropped a small piece of apple on his desk, and after a quick smell, the animal grabbed the fruit in its mouth and jumped off the desk.

"I believe I have everyone's attention now, and I will immediately address the question that everyone has," August began. "Yes, I am responsible for the recent dinosaur activity. Now I need everyone to listen closely to what I have to say or there will be more attacks." He paused for a second, and when no one spoke, he continued, "And by the way, I will not appear in any of your facial recognition programs, so don't get distracted by trying to find out who I am. I will tell you.

"I am August Adams, and I haven't been born yet. You see, I am a time traveler." Those people who began talking again quickly grew silent as the dinosaur reappeared on his desk. He stroked it, and it nipped at his fingers until he tossed another slice of apple onto his desk, and the creature grabbed it and ran away again. "You are the leaders of the sovereign nations, independent nations, independent areas and disputed territories of the world. Which one of your countries has the ability to produce dinosaurs?"

After a moment of silence, August continued, "Each of you is here because you are the leader of your people. I am speaking to each of you on an equal basis to allow each of you to make your own decisions about what I am about to say. Believe me, it is very important that you do so.

"I know it is very early to very late for some of you. But, I have also invited the public to watch this meeting. Every person in the world who wants to is watching you right now and will judge your actions. So please, allow me to continue without interruption.

"You see, recently I had a moment of clarity as I realized the truth about our world. And it frightened me as I'm sure it will frighten you also when I explain it. This realization made me ask myself what was wrong with the world, why the world was like it is, where the world was surely heading, and finally, was there anything that could be done about it? Many of you have probably done the same, but you don't have the strength to be honest with yourself about what you know to be true. Fortunately, I do.

"Let's begin with what's wrong with the world, and the list is far longer than what I will discuss now. First, there is general mistrust and hatred between many of our world's countries. I venture to say that when each of you think about what is wrong with the world, you included at least one country, and probably more. I am not here to say you are wrong.

"Global warming is stressing our ecosystems to the breaking point. There is more pollution which affects the air we breathe and is slowly increasing our daily temperatures. Weather patterns are changing, and the severity of storms is increasing. As a result, there is more human illness and death as well as an increase in wildlife extinction.

"The oceans and its fragile life chain are faced with higher acidic levels, and the sea level is rising as our polar ice melts. Soon, cities will begin disappearing under water as our continents shrink. We will lose valuable living space in a world that continues to become more and more populous.

"What is the quality of life for our world population? Hunger affects almost ten percent of the people and is rising quickly in countries in Asia and Africa, and for far too many countries hunger is a byproduct of the ravages of conflict. Many children are stunted, too small for their age. Yet in other countries, adults and even young children are obese.

"Literacy rates are rising but not fast enough, and illiteracy is still prevalent in Africa and Southern Asia. Why? What if the person who could cure cancer is in one of those countries where people are starving and not receiving a proper education? Why are our educators, those who guide our future generations, underpaid?

"I understand the desire to visit the moon and Mars for possible colonization, but what about our homeless here on Earth right now? There are 150 million worldwide. What is being done for them other than a dinner on Thanksgiving and Christmas? How many people experiencing homelessness have to die before it is fully recognized for the problem it is?

"The basic human rights of equality, freedom from discrimination, the right to life, liberty, and personal security, freedom from slavery, and the freedom from torture and degrading treatment are routinely politicized by many, and completely ignored by others. Why do some people feel it is okay to traffic people for profit? Hate because of skin color, gender, sexual orientation or religion?

"I am not against guns. But why is it not apparent to everyone that using a firearm is not the correct way of solving a problem? Why are some people blinded by their fanatic loyalty to gun ownership that they can't see that not everyone should be allowed to carry a gun?

"We still have war, in this, the 21st century. What is so important that we have to kill each other over it? Usually some petty dictator wants to show how important they are, and it costs innocent civilians their lives.

"Why are some political groups who stand for hate, oppression, and killing those that don't think like them still in existence? Why are there gangs of people who murder and run drugs that ruin people's lives? Why are the same people allowed to commit most of the crimes over and over again?

"So, let's see, what's wrong with the world? Everything. Why? Societal indifference from political leaders like yourself to the ordinary person going about their day. What happens then? Too many people die in a world full of people who simply want to turn away and pretend everything is okay.

"Where are we headed? If we don't change our ways, if we don't make the world a better place, we are doomed to self destruction. Be it through a global war, pandemic, or man made weather problems, we will simply cease to exist.

"That brings me to what can we do? We must realize that inaction to cure any of the world's problems is a crime. And it starts with each and every one of you. The leaders of the world have failed the people they are sworn to protect and faithfully serve. Up to now. From this point on, if you do not try and fix the problem, then you are a criminal. And criminals must be eliminated.

"When I was young, I had a simple way of ending crime that amused my friends. I would tell them that all first time offenders had to eat all second time offenders. It always got a laugh, but no one could deny that the problem would be solved, and crime probably wouldn't last much longer. But of course in a world where leaders are afraid to really try and stop any of the above problems, that wasn't going to happen.

"Until now. You see, I have the way to make that happen. I can make sure that second time offenders do get eaten. Literally. I have -"

"Have spoken too long," a woman shouted out.

Her screen immediately enlarged, and August smiled and replied, "I agree, Madame President. Please, tell me what you are thinking. What are your suggestions?"

"You are talking to us like we are children. Lecturing us like we are students in a classroom instead of the leaders of the world that we are. You cannot tell us what to do and how to act. I have my ports watched and my borders patrolled now. You cannot sneak your pets into my, or anyone else's, country now. You are an empty threat, and you will be hunted down, *Mr. Time Traveller*. What do you say to that?"

As her picture now filled everyone's screen, August just leaned back in his chair. Then he placed his fingertips together and took a deep breath and let out a sigh. Then he told her, "Your regime takes bribes from drug cartels, money launderers, sex traffickers and much, much more. Some of your police are corrupt, and those that aren't have found that it is in their own best interest to look the other way when someone is murdered or kidnapped. Your people are hungry and poor while you have grown fat and rich. Sooner or later I'm sure you would have done something to warrant further attention from me, but it is fitting that you are the first, so you can be an example for the others." August then leaned out of the video frame as he said something that could not be heard. Then he smiled at the woman.

As she stood up and sneered, "An example of wha -" she was suddenly cut off by bursts of automatic weapons firing and loud screams. "What is that?" she shouted. But the only answer she got were shots and screams growing louder as they got closer to her. There was a noise behind her, and she spun around and raised her arms, but they couldn't protect her. The dark, blurry shape crashed into her, and she fell to the floor screaming until she suddenly stopped. A small trickle of red that had splattered her computer screen slowly trickled down until the view cut back to the shot of all of the leaders.

"That did not have to happen," August shouted loudly. Then he took a deep breath and continued with a lower voice, "That did not have to happen. But, it should now be clear to even the most fervent disbeliever that I am what I say I am. And I can do whatever I want. Whenever I want. Wherever I want. And now, I am going to discuss what is to be done to help our world."

He leaned forward and started, "I am not interested in removing any of you from your positions as head of your countries. Some of you, like the late Madame President, will do that yourselves. But, I now expect all of you to immediately begin addressing the problems I mentioned today, and any others that you may think of.

"I do not want to stop the exploration of the stars or any meaningful science. That would put people out of work. But don't spend money on some projects to the exclusion of trying to find a way to create a better world to live in.

"There are people in the world who are billionaires many times over. You need to begin distributing your money to projects that need it. Surely you can live on one billion dollars, can't you?

"Tax laws need to be restructured. The rich need to pay their fair share of taxes. The poor don't need to pay any.

"Criminals need to get their full and fair due, but if everyone has enough money to buy whatever they need, then we should have fewer criminals. Gangs, hate groups, and career criminals will go out of business on their own, or be put out of business.

"I do not expect the police to do any more than what they are supposed to. But laws need to be changed to stop recidivism and give criminals the sentences they deserve. And I have to ask, why do we have so many people experiencing homelessness when our criminals live in climate controlled rooms with meals and medical attention supplied by citizens who work hard for their money?

"I do not want to hear about committees, filibusters, or hesitation. You have forty-eight hours to start implementing solutions, so fill your committees with people who do, rather than talk. If you make mistakes, as I'm sure you will, you are now a global team; not adversaries. I will tolerate mistakes made in good faith. I will not tolerate lying, waiting for others to get things done, or trying to avoid hard decisions altogether. If you do, this is what you can expect."

The screen cut to a man lying in the corner of a room that was surrounded by thick metal bars. A loud horn startled him, and he slowly began moving and then sat up. He rubbed his head and then looked around and quickly jumped to his feet. August's voice began, "This is Agent Russell of the United States Secret Service. Some of you may recognize him from his employment with the United States Secret Service. He has a wife, three children, and I'm sure many friends who know him as Rusty. He has been in my employment for many years now, and that should be a caution to the rest of you...where else am I already embedded? Agent Russell made many mistakes recently. He cut corners, lied, he tried to blame others. In short, he made some mistakes that I could not forgive."

As August stopped speaking, Agent Russell's voice could be heard asking, "Can anyone hear me? Hello...hello? Anyone?"

"Rusty, do you hear me?"

"Yes, sir. I mean, August. I hear you. Can you let me out of here?"

"Rusty, I can't do that. You see, the whole world is watching you right now. I have explained that you let me down, made mistakes, and now you must be an example for them."

President Powell cut in with, "Mr. Adams, August, excuse me please. Couldn't you just turn him over to me? I will make sure he is punished."

"I am sure he would receive some type of punishment, after you have questioned him about my organization. I'm sorry, Mr. President, I can't do that."

"Please," Agent Russell shouted. "Please, I won't say anything. What do I know? Nothing, nothing at all. Please let me out of here." There were two soft bell tones, and he began screaming, "No, no, not that, not them." He turned around to look behind him, and then he tried frantically to climb up the bars, but he kept sliding back down. Eight shadowy shapes appeared in a long hallway behind him. They ran on their two rear legs and had long, tooth filled open mouths. Each was about six feet tall, with gray feathery arms, and as they got closer, their long foot claws made a distinctive clicking sound on the hard concrete floor. As Agent Russell shouted "Maggie" over and over, one of the creatures jumped at him feet first and then the others exploded into him.

The screen stayed on Agent Russell for another few seconds and then August was back on. "Damocles wanted to live the life of Dionysius II because he believed it to be wondrous and full of everything he had ever wanted. As he ate at the king's table, he suddenly noticed that a sword hung above his head. From that point on Damocles could not enjoy the riches and servants that he thought every king deserved.

"So, I want each of you to understand; you should not feel you deserve your power and all that goes with it. Instead, you must understand it is the people of the world who give it to you, and I now hang a sword above your heads. A Jurassic Sword if you will, and it is hanging by a thread.

"I will take one question."

A woman quickly asked, "Sir, I do not mean to offend you, but why did innocent people have to die in your attacks?"

"Mrs. President, I am not offended," August replied. "That is a fair question, and I must say it was a tough decision to make. But I finally realized I could not just attack the heads of state. The general population of every country would just say it was your problem and go about their daily lives. They had to be involved, they had to have a vested interest in what your decisions were going to be.

"So, I had to help them understand they are threatened too. That if you refuse to change the world, or if you drag your feet, they will pay the price. That means they will expect you to start now and make progress. If you don't, then maybe I won't have to remove you, they will.

"You have forty-eight hours."

August waved his hands over his desk again, and all of the screens disappeared. Immediately a door opened, and three people walked in and sat down at a large, round table in a corner of the room. August joined them and opened with, "I think that went well, especially the examples. Unfortunately, there will be those who think they can bargain their way out of any further problems. After all, it is what they have been doing all of their political lives. We will have to show them we do not bargain.

"There will also be one or two countries who think they can fight against what we have begun. A government may not seem to be leading the opposition, but they will be. An attack or two though will have their people up in arms, and we will be speaking with new leaders.

"And, I expect some resistance from some of the gangs from South and Central American cartels, and possibly America. They will not give up their money without a fight. They will not understand that soon everyone will have enough money, and they can start new lives. They will want to hold on to all of their power, and we will be forced to show them they can't. Gina, what is happening right now?"

A woman with short, jet black hair and lipstick opened her laptop and put on a pair of reading glasses. She nodded for a few seconds then said, "Most countries have started addressing their people. They are telling them they will begin within the hour to find working points to solve the problems you outlined. A few leaders are stepping down, citing old age or family commitments, certainly not their inability to get things done.

"Existing alliances are forming think tanks, scientific study groups, sociological boards, and anything else they can think of to show they are following your request. I think most of these countries are sincere in their desire to get things rolling. Some countries are reaching out to form new alliances though not everyone is talking to all of their neighbors yet. That could take a little time.

"There are a half dozen countries vowing to fight back, at least that's what they're saying publicly. I'm sure some of them want to appear strong for as long as they can. Two of the countries though have mobilized their armed forces and seem sincere in their willingness to resist you.

"Many gangs are saying they will fight also. Most, however, don't have any strength behind their words. But there are core groups in Russia, the United States and Japan that are heavily armed and have been able to stay active for decades in their countries. They are vowing to fight until the end. Unless there is a shift in their thinking, they will have to be dealt with."

August paused for a second and then asked, "What would be your suggestions, Patre?"

He was a large man, well over six feet tall, and very muscular. He always wore a gun on one hip and a large knife on the other. He was the only person that any of them knew who had survived a dinosaur attack. He smiled and replied, "It would seem the place to start would be the countries that refuse to acknowledge their fate. But, I would point out that gangs believe they are their own countries, with their own laws and consequences. They believe they can withstand anything.

"I would suggest then, that all three gangs, a former Soviet organized crime group, the Americans in Southern California, and the Japanese, be completely obliterated. Both countries that have mobilized against us should be taught a painful lesson which should make the others see the light. It will require a massive effort on our part, but nothing that we are not capable of."

"Yang?"

He paused for several seconds before answering, and everyone knew he was formulating a plan, a five move checkmate. He slowly replied, "Yes, yes, I see it. The small, fast moving animals for the Columbians in their thick jungle area. For the United States, the same but also add in *Triceratops* and *Stegosaurus*. Maybe an *Ankylosaurus to*o. Heavy duty animals that can take out houses and apartments if they are provoked.

"The Russians need all of the previous plus some well placed big boys like *Tyrannosaurus* and *Allosaurus*. They will have missiles and heavy weapons, so add in some sauropods too. They'll focus on them and won't see the smaller animals until it is too late.

"For whatever country you decide on, choose the one with the loudest supporters. Put in everything from A to Z, and don't stop until an hour after they plead for mercy. As you said, August, the citizens of the world must understand they have a part to play in all of this also."

As Yang finished, Gina added, "August, I would like to make a suggestion, collar control on the American animals at least."

"I think you are right," August agreed. "And…the Colombian and Japanese animals as well. These are gangsters and drug dealers, but we want to protect innocent bystanders to some extent. Warn the area you are going to attack. If the dealers back down then they will appear weak and never bother us again. But, to the best of our ability, I don't want to see women, children or law enforcement officers being killed by any of our animals. We let everyone know we will protect the innocent. What's our timeframe?"

"It will all be over within three hours," Patre said.

As everyone left, August stood up and walked over to a small picture that hung on a wall that was kept in the shadows. It was hung so he had to bend over to look at it. He wanted it that way, so he would grow tired of looking at the picture and walk away. The picture itself didn't show much, two adults and two teenage boys looking at the camera. It had been a warm day, they were all wearing tee shirts and shorts, and they were smiling. Everyone looked happy.

But, it was what the photo didn't show that was important. Behind the forced smiles was an alcoholic genius father who expected, no demanded, his children be geniuses too. And when they were, he nearly broke them as he drove them to be something he would be proud of.

The mother who turned her back on her sons when they needed her the most. How else could she find the time to make sure she claimed her rightful place in society? Surely not by being there for her children, protecting them from their father, making sure they received the love they so craved.

As parents, they had failed miserably. At least when they died a few weeks after the photo was taken, they had left their sons the money they had never spent on them for anything. Fortunately the brothers were smart and had used the money wisely for education and knowledge. They had been inseparable.

Then the invention. Time travel. They embraced the new technology and stayed together at first as they explored its potential. Within a year though they had gone their separate ways. Why visit Abraham Lincoln when you could travel to the future and learn so much more? He decided to go to the future and let them know about time travel. Win was afraid the timeline would be destroyed. He didn't understand that it wouldn't be destroyed, the two of them could just reshape it.

Now that more people knew about time travel, both of them helped start TIM. And he was immediately glad he did. It helped him learn more than he ever would have, and he began saying 'We have to protect the timeline.' He didn't want anyone figuring out what he was really doing.

But of course Win realized something was wrong. No one else even had a clue. So, he had fed Win just enough information to take him in different directions while he finished his plans.

Why didn't he see what was needed? Why had Win been so weak? A slap to the face got a person's attention. A shock could bring them back to life. That's all he had been suggesting. The deaths of a few of the seven billion people who populated the Earth was a small price to pay for mass awareness that their leaders were inept. Or worse, criminals.

August shook his head. It was Win's choice, but the wrong one. He couldn't leave him around since he knew about his plans. So, if he expected the people of Earth to be strong then he had to be too. There was one last meeting, one last explanation to Win, one last rebuff, and a bullet. August shook his head and stood up. His back hurt, so he knew he had looked at the family photo long enough.

The door behind him opened, and he"turned to see Gina walking in followed by Patre. As they sat down at the table he joined them and asked, "And?"

"It couldn't be better," Gina told him. A screen came on just as a newsman was saying, "These images are graphic and may be hard to watch for our viewers." Across the bottom of the screen, the words Hundreds of Alleged Drug Dealers Dead in Japan. Video showed bloody bodies, and parts of bodies, covering roadways and parking lots. Weapons lay scattered among the dead along with thousands of empty shell casings.

There were also dinosaur bodies. They were about twelve feet long from nose to tail and would have stood six feet tall. Around many of these bodies were at least a dozen or more human bodies. The newsman was continuing, "This Japanese paramilitary organization had vowed that nothing could stop its alleged gang activity. Obviously, they were wrong.

"The animals, between 70 and 100 of them, suddenly appeared both inside and outside of what has been described as the headquarters for this gang. And they appeared at the exact moment that a meeting between the heads of various factions of the gang were present. Many are saying there were no survivors of the meeting.

"All of this has to be corroborated by law enforcement, but it appears to be the first strike by August Adams. As everyone will remember, it was just hours ago that the mysterious savior of the world, as he is being referred to, said that drug dealers and gangsters needed to stop their illegal activities. This is graphic evidence of what August Adams will do to those who refuse to stop.

"But, apparently August Adams showed concern for innocent victims in the area. Supposedly residents were warned of the attack which allowed many to leave the scene. And, there are several eyewitness accounts of animals being killed by an exploding neck restraint when they turned on an innocent person. Indeed, I have been told that all the dinosaurs that appeared today are now dead. How this dramatic event, the taking out of a heavily armed gang in a matter of minutes, will affect others who are boasting they will stand up to the dinosaurs remains to be seen."

The screen cut quickly to a newswoman in mid sentence, "...both dinosaur attacks happening simultaneously here in early morning Los Angeles and just outside of Moscow in the early afternoon. The videos are just as disturbing as those from Japan with the attacks leaving a thousand or more dead. It is interesting to note that the Los Angeles area received a warning, but Moscow did not.

"The three attacks were obviously coordinated by August Adams in his plan to stop all criminal activity in the world with dinosaur attacks. Though it is still unclear whether his deadly plan will work, there are a growing number of people who seem to think it is a good idea." The video cut to people waving signs reading, AUGUST IS RIGHT.

"It should also be noted that, as in Japan, there have not been any reports of innocent people being killed by the attacking beasts. The animals are now dead and the long process of investigating the scene by the police, clearing away all of the bodies, human and animal, and identifying the dead has begun.

"Here in Los Angeles statements, released under condition of anonymity, indicate all of the dead identified so far are gang members with violent arrest records. But many are still asking why should August Adams be judge, jury and executioner? Here is our own law expert, Raymond Will, with his thoughts. Raymond?"

"Thank you, Misty. First, Mr. Adams, I hope you don't mind criticism of your action plan. And if you do, well frankly, I don't care. I am in an undisclosed location, inside a completely sealed room inside a well guarded building. The only things inside these four walls are the chair I am sitting in and the desk I am sitting behind. I have taken these precautions because I'm not sure about your stance on free speech yet. I do not want to suddenly meet one of your dinosaurs."

August looked at Gina and asked, "Is this live?"

"It is."

"Make it fun, and while I'm talking to him."

Gina smiled and replied, "Already did."

Raymond Will continued, "It is true that many of the people who died today may have been criminals. Maybe the worst sort, committing the worst crimes. But no one person should be the judge, jury, and executioner. No one should have that much power. Legal systems, the world over, are set up to make sure that the accused are tried by impartial decision makers, not someone who has already made up their mind.

"August Adams cannot be allowed to continue his summary executions. He cannot be allowed to threaten the world with -"

As August cut in with "I agree with you one hundred percent," Raymond jumped. As he looked around, August continued, "I should not be judge, jury, and executioner. I have been forced into this position, and when the world has taken the actions that are needed, I will simply disappear, taking my sword with me.

"And don't worry, Mr. Will, I am in favor of free speech. You may think I'm wrong, doubt my motives, and you may speak your mind anytime you wish. You are not a criminal. You are simply trying to be a voice of reason, and I thank you for that."

As a small dinosaur with a white, feathery head, and green and red body stripes suddenly jumped on Raymond Will's desk he rolled his chair back in astonishment. "Remember," August said, "she likes apples."

The screen went blank, and August laughed loudly. "That was fun," he told Gina. When she sat down without saying anything he immediately asked, "What's wrong?"

Patre spoke up, "I'll tell you what's wrong and then you can feed me to the 'saurs'. Watch." A screen appeared showing a man lying on a floor as a *Tyrannosaurus* approached. As the animal's huge head bent forward it blocked their view, but they could hear the snapping of the jaws, see the head shake back and forth, and then rise up as it finished swallowing an arm that dangled grotesquely from its mouth. There was nothing left of the man that had been on the ground.

"My brother being eaten," August said calmly. "I've watched it a few hundred times."

Patre shook his head and said, "No, it isn't. I have slowed the video and enhanced the image of the man. Watch carefully." As the head lowered they could barely make out the darker image of the man's clothing. And then it disappeared.

"Again," August repeated quietly five more times. Then he looked at Patre and said, "He traveled."

"I'm sorry," Patre said. "I should have been in a better position to see -"

"No," August told him. "I have known for some time that Win was not dead. But, obviously you have received some information or we wouldn't be looking at this, right?"

Patre smiled nervously and said, "He was seen in D.C. Win spoke with the Secret Service agent and the construction guy that killed the *Tyrannosaurus*. At this time, we don't know what they talked about. Win was also seen leaving the White House; again, no way of knowing what was talked about or with who. We can -"

"No, you don't need to do anything, Patre. I believe my brother will come to me. He thinks he can stop what I'm doing, but he is wrong."

MEETINGS

Boone opened his eyes and again tried to remember where he was. It slowly all came back to him; he wasn't in the hotel any longer; he had called Mr. Webster and arranged to stay in the condo. But first he had taken Kaly to her room, so she could pack some things and then she bought a swimsuit. His eyes got a little wider as he thought how good she had looked in it. Then he remembered how she had laughed at him again because he couldn't get in the hot tub because of the bandaging on his back.

He was lying on his left side, so he started to roll over on his back when he bumped into something. Was he up against the wall? He tried to turn again and something moved beside him. In a second every dinosaur he had seen in real life and on TV flashed through his mind, and he spun quickly around to see what it was.

He was met by, "If you need more cover just say so". Then Kaly sat up on an elbow and asked, "Or did you need me to scoot over?"

"I…uh…well…uh…good morning," was all he could somehow get out.

Kaly sat up, and he could see she was wearing a tee shirt and pajama bottoms. She put a hand on his shoulder and said, "I am so sorry. I didn't know this would embarrass you. I'll leave you to -"

"Please, no," he told her as he took her hand. "You surprised me, that's all. I mean, I'm surprised you're here, but it's not a bad surprise. I actually like that you're here, even though it surprised me."

Kaly put a hand on his lips and said, "I get the feeling I surprised you."

Boone laughed and told her, "I'm just not used to waking up with a woman next to me and then it was you and…well, uh, good morning."

She leaned forward and kissed him and said, "Let me guess, you can walk on a beam twenty stories up, but you have problems talking with us girl types."

Boone nodded as he agreed, "Yes. I have always been quiet and a little shy."

"You didn't seem to have too much trouble talking me into a bikini last night," Kaly laughed. "You men are all alike. All 'ooh, I can't get in a hot tub or a pool because of a little scratch on my back…but I can watch you'." She pretended to slap him on the arm and asked, "So how could you talk to me a couple of days ago and every other second we've been together?"

"Well, I've been trying to reinvent myself."

"What do you mean?"

"I've done it several times during my life, and I'm sure you have too. When I was young, I had to figure out what I needed to do to make friends instead of staying in the house and reading. I wanted to be somewhat personable in high school, you know, go to games and dances and stuff. I had to work around the guys for Mr. Webster, so I had to figure out what I needed to do to fit in, then make it happen. Then there was college and dorms and living off campus and mixing in. I constantly had to figure these things out. When I knew I was going to be put in charge of projects, I had to understand how to handle people. I could have just settled on ok grades, made a few friends, followed instead of taking charge, but each time I accepted the challenge and reinvented myself."

"But not with girls?"

"No, but lately I've been thinking about my life differently. I don't mind being alone, but lately I have minded being lonely. I have decided I would talk more with women, ask them out, take rejection and keep at it."

"How has that been going for you?"

"Well, you're the first."

"Why me?"

"If you said no, it wouldn't have been a surprise. You're a busy career woman, you are always on the move, you are attractive, so I thought you probably were in a relationship. Lots of reasons why I could tell myself later that the reason you said 'no' wasn't because you didn't like me. I guess I have to protect myself a little."

Kaly put her head against his arm and said, "Wow, that's a lot of baggage. And the reason I know is because I carried some of the same baggage. Now I was never shy, and being around my brothers brought me in contact with a lot of different people. Most of whom I thought were idiots. But I could never connect with you guys. I had dates, I went to the prom, but no big deal. My mom even told me it was okay if I was a lesbian. But, I liked guys; I just couldn't find one that I was attracted to. I thought we connected before you asked me out, and to tell the truth, I was thinking about asking you out.

"So what I am saying is, I'm a woman, but you can talk to me. I'm your friend, though I think we may be headed for something more. Don't be shy around me. Be yourself."

"Okay, I will. So, I have to ask, why are you in bed with me?"

Kaly smiled and answered, "Last night was great. We started with practicing for your media session then laughed and talked about everything from our lives, but never about the dinosaurs. I know we have been through a lot together, but we were really connecting last night through things we have done.

"So, after I walked you to your bed, checked your dressing, kissed you goodnight, and went to my room…I found I missed you. I got ready for bed and just laid there thinking about you. After an hour I got up, got in bed with you, snugged up tight, and then I didn't feel lonely."

"That's nice," Boone said. "But I do feel like I've been used just for my snuginess."

Just as Kaly hit him with a pillow, her phone buzzed. She answered, "Hello, sir…That's because I got up early and met Boone. He still needs some coaching before the…oh, I see. Yes, sir.

"Well, we are off to the races," Kaly told Boone. "A car will pick us up in thirty minutes to take us to breakfast at the White House. There will also be a meeting there along with the award presentation."

"That means I need to go home for a few minutes to get a suit and -"

"I think all of that has already been taken care of," Kaly said. Then she pushed him back onto the bed and added, "Besides, I need one more minute of snug before we get up."

As she drew close to Boone, he murmured, "Maybe two."

Thirty minutes later Agent Martinez arrived, and as they got in the car he said, "What a terrible way to start a day."

"Fill us in," Kaly told him.

He glanced at them quickly then asked. "You didn't see Rusty get killed?"

"What?" Kaly shouted.

"August Adams made an example of him for doing something wrong. He said Rusty had been working for him. No one believes him though."

"I can't believe it," Kaly said quietly.

Agent Martinez nodded his head as he said, "One more thing for all of us to get through." The car was quiet for a few seconds then Agent Martinez continued, "But, you two will have other things to do today. The itinerary is eat, listen, and smile while you receive your awards. But I'll bet the listening part will be eye opening. Government leaders quitting, governments shutting down, some people angry about the dinosaurs but a growing movement to accept what is happening because in the end the world will be a better place. Oh, and I think you will be listening to one meeting and then taking part in another…or maybe the other way around. The president has some type of expert coming in to speak with him and both of you."

"Us?" Kaly asked.

"Yeah, I think it's the guy you met yesterday. You must have made a good impression. By the way, Boone, are you ready for the reporters? We can still change to reading a script."

"As the time gets closer I'm sure I'll think about changing my mind. But I think I want to answer some questions to get the point across that what this guy, August, is doing, is wrong."

Agent Martinez nodded his head and replied, "I can see that, but remember, there are a lot of people who will disagree with you. It's snowballing, and it might just run a course that can't be stopped."

"I guess that's not that hard to believe," Boone said.

"Since yesterday there has been virtually no crime reported, anywhere. I mean world-wide. Everyone is afraid they'll rob someone and end up eaten by a dinosaur. I don't know; it's going to be interesting. But you'll know before me probably because here we are."

The car turned into an east White House gate and stopped for the Secret Service Police. An officer asked, "Hey, Ricky, everything going okay?"

"Yes, just dropping off two for breakfast with the president."

The officer dropped down for a quick look, stood up, and quickly looked again. "Wow," he said with a smile. "It's an honor." Then he waved them through.

"That was nice of him to say that about me, wasn't it?" Agent Martinez laughed.

As Kaly groaned, Boone replied, "You got us here through the D.C. traffic, so yes, I am agreeing with you." Then he turned to Kaly and asked, "That wasn't too much was it? I mean, he probably believed me, didn't he?"

"You too?" Agent Martinez asked as he stopped the car. "I'm deeply hurt."

Boone laughed as he got out and asked, "Aren't you coming in with us?"

"No, I have real work to do this morning."

"That means he's going to breakfast," Kaly said.

"It's true," Ricky agreed.

"The cafe has a great sausage and eggs breakfast," Boone pointed out. "Tell them it's on me."

"In that case," Ricky laughed as he drove away, "I'm having the steak and eggs."

"That does sound good," a voice said behind them, and they turned to find the president smiling at them.

As they both replied, "Sir," in unison, photographers began gathering around them.

President Powell shook his head and told them, "Neither one of you can ever call me 'sir' again. Both of you must call me Dennis." He looked at Kaly and added, "Even when you are on duty. Understood?"

Kaly was still for a second then managed, "Yes, Dennis."

The president laughed as he stepped between them and put his arms around their shoulders, saying, "Let's get some photos out here on this beautiful day."

After a few minutes they were led inside and down a hallway to a small room. As they walked in they saw a table with five place settings. Win and another man they did not know were already sitting at the table, and they smiled and stood up. As the door was closed behind them, President Powell said, "I believe you met Win yesterday and helped him with some surveillance."

"Yes," Kaly answered. "Good to see you again, Win."

"And it's good to see both of you," he replied as he shook their hands. Then he pointed at the man they did not know and introduced him, "And this is my friend, Otai."

Otai stepped up and smiled broadly as he said, "It is a pleasure to meet you, Kaly and Boone. I'm glad to hear you are part of the team."

"Thank you," Boone replied. "It has been very interesting so far."

"Before we get into too many things," the president cut in, "let's get breakfast in here and then we can talk without any interruptions." He pressed a button on the table, and immediately servers came in with trays of food. The president was seated at the head of the table with Kaly and Boone on his left and Win and Otai on his right.

After the servers had placed the food on the table and left, he continued, "Kaly and Boone, this was supposed to be a large event in the State Room with many dignitaries in attendance. But, with everything that is going on, I decided this small breakfast would suit our purposes better. But, I still want to say a part of what I had planned. And that is, thank you, thank you both for saving my life. I will say it again this afternoon when I present you with the medals you so richly deserve. But, I cannot emphasize enough how grateful I am to both of you. If there is anything I can do for you, just ask."

Kaly and Boone said "Thank you" together.

Win laughed and noted, "Boone, you aren't used to being praised, are you?"

Boone smiled as he answered, "I don't mind being told I did a good job; I think everyone likes to hear that. But I think I'm going to hear my name a lot today, and I'm a background sort of person."

"I understand," the president said. "But, think of it this way. You are going to receive a lot of attention today, and for good reason. Your fifteen minutes of fame will be a lot longer. Every day that passes though, will reduce the spotlight as other events take place to occupy everyone. Just get through today, and things will eventually be a lot easier."

"Thank you, sir…Dennis, for that. I'll keep it in mind."

The president turned to Win and asked, "Now, what have you found out?"

"Otai and I have discovered several things. First, and most importantly, we can confirm August was not making things up when he said your Secret Service Agent Russell was a plant working for him."

"How?" the president asked.

Win nodded to Kaly who replied, "As you know we went with Win yesterday, and we assisted with the surveillance of the trailer the *Triceratops* broke out of. We watched as the initial drop was made, and at that time we couldn't identify anyone. When the trailer returned, lights were used to illuminate the damage. Russ, Agent Russell that is, was easy to ID."

Win told everyone, "That's why August had him killed."

"We just heard about it," Kaly said.

"That's right," Win replied. "You were told not to watch any more news reports." He then quickly explained what had happened as Kaly just looked down at the table. Win then added, "Right now I think everyone here should agree that we don't know who we can trust. We cannot afford to take anyone else into our confidence."

The president nodded as he replied, "I agree. This is bad, no…this is terrible news. I'll wonder about everyone I work with now."

"Wonder, yes," Win said. "But don't get paranoid. I doubt if every other person you meet works for August. There might be one or two, so be cautious, but try not to act differently around people. Don't look for clues or everything you see will make you think someone is not who they seem. Otai and I will keep you informed."

"Okay, I'll keep all of that in mind. What else do you have for me?"

"We've connected a few dots; I'll let Otai explain."

"Thanks, Win," Otai started. "First, I want to say that so far each of you has been exceptional during these trying circumstances. Together, I'm sure we will stop August." From a small disc in front of him a holographic screen appeared with a picture of the diner's front window. He moved his hands, and two faces lit up and then enlarged slightly. "Boone, do you recognize these two people?" he asked.

Boone leaned closer and took several seconds before he answered, "No."

"I didn't think you would, but I wanted to be sure," Otai told him. "Now, let's take a look at these pictures." Boone and Kaly immediately realized they were looking at a hologram of 82nd and Central from the night of the surveillance. There were two people standing at the intersection, and Otai enhanced the picture so their faces were larger and brightly lit.

"The two from the *Rex* truck, and the cafe," Kaly said.

"Yes," Otai agreed. "Julie and Patre, part of August's crew. They are part of a dinosaur relocation team."

"But how did they get into the cafe?" Boone asked. "They ran back to their truck and then drove to the corner."

"In your 1957 timeframe, yes," Otai agreed. "But they probably came back early because they wanted to see the show. So, they got back, walked like they were going to eat and just waited. They came out with everyone else when the I-beam fell then ran back inside when the *Rex* started to move. Waitresses in the cafe remember some of the people running out the back door to get away. They didn't appear in any other video, but we think these two ran out the back door, circled around to the truck, and got out of Dodge as fast as they could."

"I understand," Boone told him.

"These two," Otai continued, "and the driver of the other truck, were seen at two of the other dinosaur sites, Los Angeles and London. There are others involved of course and right now we can say there are at least ten people working with, or for, August."

"How do you find people to do something like this? Where do they come from?" Boone asked.

"Where and also when," Otai said. "I was chosen as part of TIM in 1937 when I was an engineering student at Egyptian University."

"1937?" Kaly exclaimed.

Otai laughed as he replied, "Yes. There are others in TIM that aren't from the future."

"There are some from the past," Win explained. "They have the necessary qualities to understand and accept the concept and problems of time travel. You three have done it."

"Yes, but...but how did you adapt?" Kaly said. "I'm not sure I could go into the future and just...just start living like it wasn't anything."

Otai laughed and explained, "The first time I went it was hard. But Win and August took their time with me, and I began to understand. Also, I still spend most of my time in Giza, old and new."

"I've never heard of Egyptian University. Where is it?" Kaly asked.

"It is Cairo University now," Otai told her. "We can talk more about it later perhaps, but right now I have just a little more news."

"Please, go on," President Powell said.

"As Win suspected, a detailed study shows that all of the dinosaurs came from North America. All of the animals were captured in the northern part of the United States. August's group is not working from multiple sites. They have just one, the cave in North Dakota. We just don't know yet exactly when they are working. When August took Win to the cave there was nothing to indicate when he was there."

President Powell quickly asked, "Can you find out?"

"Otai is close," Win replied.

Otai nodded and said, "Unfortunately, I need one, maybe two, more incidents."

"How will that help?" the president asked.

"I will be able to tell how old the dinosaurs are, so we can narrow our 'when' search."

The president shook his head and asked, "How is that possible?"

Otai paused for a moment before beginning, "I doubt if I can explain it without using science you are not aware of yet. But basically, molecular structures generate specific characteristics that allow temporal comparison using quantum kennetvalues." When everyone just stared at him he continued, "We know one number, and we subtract another and that tells us how old *when* is."

"Now we got it," Boone laughed.

Otai smiled and said, "We have narrowed it down to a five million year window. One more, and it will be within a hundred thousand years. Two more, and we'll be within a hundred years, and that's all we need for a quick locate."

"I don't know whether I hope we get two more or not," President Powell said. "I want to stop him, but two more attacks means more people dying." He paused then continued, "The bad thing is people seem to be buying into his philosophy. Kill the bad guys, or who August Adams thinks are the bad guys."

"You can't let him do that," Win said. "This is only the tip of the iceberg. I'm sure August has other plans that will make the world understand he is really a mad man. But by then it will be too late."

"What can we do?" the president asked. "He has the world at his mercy."

"We have to stop him," Win said.

"But how?"

"Otai and I have a plan. As soon as we can find him, we will put an end to him."

"Can I help?" Boone asked.

Win smiled and replied, "You could, but I can't allow it." He quickly held up his hand as Boone started to say something and continued, "I can't allow it because your involvement would link President Powell to our attempt to stop him. If we fail, August would think it was necessary to make an example of him, you, and probably the entire United States."

"If you think you two might fail," Kaly started, "why not take an entire team? Snipe him before he sees you?"

"Those are very good ideas," Win agreed. "But I have to make sure we disarm all of his safeguards."

"Such as?" Kaly asked.

"Who knows?" Win answered. "Does he have to be in proximity to a computer within a certain amount of time or it initiates an attack? Does he have to physically touch something? Do an eye scan? It could be anything or everything. And, if we kill him without knowing his safeguards, we could be unleashing dinosaurs, a plague, or chemical weapons. Right now the what, where and when are too vast to calculate. No, we have to destroy all of his plans before they start."

"I understand," Kaly said.

President Powell's watch beeped, and he said, "I'm sorry, I have to leave. I'm meeting with the heads of several countries to see what is happening with our joint efforts in the areas outlined by your brother. I want to report real progress. I don't…"

"You don't want to be killed," Win continued. "We understand."

"The public will be watching our meeting as well as others around the world. You may all come with me and listen if you like."

"Otai and I will be leaving," Win said. "Again, we can't be associated with you."

As Win and Otai left the room, Kaly said, "And, I think I need to shower, see what I'm going to be wearing for the ceremony, and think about what I'm going to say."

"Yes," Boone agreed. "And I know it's the federal government and all, but I hate you're out the expense of -"

President Powell laughed and said, "No one who saves the president's life has to think about spending money for clothes to wear to a ceremony. You don't have to worry about expenses, and in this case neither do I. Several boutiques have volunteered to dress each of you for the night. They get publicity, and you both get to look great."

"Or at least good enough," Boone replied as he rubbed his face. "It would take a lot to make this look great."

Kaly looked at the president and shook her head as she said, "It's pathetic. He's always searching for a compliment. Boone, I told you we were going to put a bag over your head."

"I can't believe you just said that," Boone frowned. "Especially after I single handedly saved not only the -"

As Kaly took Boone's arm she looked at the president and said, "Don't worry, I'll have his ego under control before the ceremony."

"My ego?" Boone laughed. "You're the one that said your award should be presented on a gold platter. I remember it as if I just made it up."

"You know," President Powell said through his laughter, "I'm an old man and don't see things as clearly as I used to. But, is there something happening here?"

Kaly smiled as she replied, "We'll have to get back to you about that."

As they stepped out of the room, President Powell told them, "Your award presentation is around noon. It's about as close as I can predict things at the moment. I'll see you then." As Kaly and Boone walked away the president smiled. It was nice to think something good might come out of all of this. Then the smile disappeared as he walked down the hallway and up the stairs to his office. He knew his next meeting would probably not result in anything to smile about.

Three hours later Boone woke to the knocking on the door. He looked around and quickly skipped through the hotel and the condo and remembered he was in the White House. He was lying on a bed where he had fallen asleep after putting his tux on. He answered a second set of knocks, "Yes?"

A door opened, and Raymond, the staff person assigned to him, entered. "Sir, just making sure you are ready to go, as you asked."

"Thanks Raymond, I appreciate your help."

"Believe me, sir, it is my pleasure. Also, Agent Winters is waiting in the hallway."

Boone smiled and said, "Please, have her step in."

Raymond stepped out of the way, and as Kaly entered the room, he smiled and closed the door behind her. Boone stood up, and Kaly walked to him and after a quick kiss she straightened his bow tie. "I'm impressed," she told him. "I always had to make sure my brothers' ties were good. Have you worn a lot of tuxes?"

"Not a lot, I just learned how to tie a bow tie, and it stuck with me."

"Well, I must say you are looking very handsome."

"Thank you," he laughed as he took her hand and spun her around. "And I must say you look stunning in that dress. Blue is definitely your color."

"Forget the dress," she told him. "See this necklace? It costs more than I make in five years. You know I was thinking about taking a fork or something from the dinner as a souvenir, but now I'm thinking -"

"I'll take the presidential limo, and we'll speed off and -"

"Get eaten by dinosaurs?" Kaly asked.

"I knew there was something I was forgetting about," Boone laughed.

"Along with the Secret Service, the Capitol Police, helicopters, attack dogs, pit maneuvers, and prison," Kaly added.

"But what a movie," Boone said as they both laughed.

There was a knock on the door, and as Boone said, "Come in," President Powell walked in. He looked tired, far more tired than he should have been after three hours. Boone motioned toward a chair and asked, "Do you need to sit down? Are you alright?"

"No, not really. I…we…Jesus."

"What, Dennis?" Kaly asked.

The president took a deep breath and told them, "The meeting started fine. We've reached out to Canada, Mexico and the seven countries of Central America, and I have to say I think we have made real progress. Enough that everyone involved in the meeting felt it was time to contact South America. We wanted to compare thoughts, ideas, then reach out to Europe, Africa, Asia, and Australia. I don't know what progress they have made, but I'm sure we're probably all on the same page."

As he paused, Kaly asked, "But?"

"South America is, for the most part, right with us. But, Columbia is at odds with the other governments as to what to do. They still feel that if every country resists August Adams, he will lose the ability to control the world. They would not listen to reason. And, and they have paid."

"What happened?" Boone asked.

President Powell shook his head then said, "Just what you would expect. What August Adams promised. We lost contact with them for a few minutes, and then as we reconnected, all we saw was death and destruction. It was terrible, sickening. There was no warning. No one was allowed to get someplace safe, to protect themselves. Hundreds of small dinosaurs, predators of some kind, just appeared all at once in cities large and small.

"It lasted for a half hour. I know that doesn't sound like a long time, but for those poor souls, it was a lifetime. Or the end of a lifetime for many. People running, screaming, and dying horrible deaths. There were…are, bodies everywhere. The government is in complete shambles and any insight they may have had on how to handle our situation is now gone.

"Then August Adams appeared. To him it was just another day, another problem to solve with his ultimate solution. He told us, and the rest of the world, that it was impossible for him to run out of resources. He didn't have to house troops; they lived in the wild. He didn't have to arm them; they were the weapons. And, he didn't have to worry about feeding them; they took care of that themselves. Then he laughed as images of dinosaurs feeding on the people they had killed filled the screen.

"He told us that he hoped this was the last time he had to make his point. Then all of the dinosaurs were killed when he, or someone, blew up their collars. Just before he disappeared he reminded us of how much time we had left."

"I'm glad I wasn't watching," Kaly said. "I can't take much more of this senseless killing. We have to stop him."

"There was one good thing that came out of the attack," Boone told them.

"What?" Kaly asked.

"The *when* of finding August Adams is now within a hundred thousand years for Win and Otai."

"Let's hope it is enough," the president replied. "I hope he was wrong about needing another attack to close in on his brother."

"What about the ceremony?" Boone asked. "Is it still on? Maybe we should just leave."

"No," President Powell said. "Everyone is here, and we are going to have the ceremony. But, I am canceling the dinner just like I canceled the breakfast. I don't want to give August Adams the impression that we are not taking him seriously enough. I'm sorry."

"Don't be," Kaly told him. "The safety of the world is more important than we are. We'll do whatever is needed of us then let you get back to your important work."

"But this is important too," the president replied. "Many other countries have also decided that today is when they will mourn their fallen, and decorate their heroes. The odds you faced, the courage you both showed, along with all of the others, well, it is important that we honor it. People need to take note, not only Americans, but people all around the world need to see how much they are appreciated."

There was a knock on the door, and Raymond stepped in and said, "It is time, Mr. President."

"Thank you," the president replied as he turned to Kaly and Boone and asked, "Shall we?"

He motioned for them to walk in front of him, and they started down a long hallway. As Kaly and Boone glanced at each other, President Powell said, "You could hold hands if you want to."

Kaly laughed and replied, "I don't think that would go over with my bosses just yet."

President Powell stepped up beside her and said, "Then let me help. Take my arm and take Boone's too."

As she did, Kaly stage whispered to Boone, "I think I voted for the wrong guy." They all laughed and were still smiling as they entered the White House East Room. As the people in the room stood and began applauding, the president stepped between them, placed his arms around their shoulders, and they stopped.

"I know you want me to keep going," President Powell said. "But just take it all in. Like I said, from this point on it will get less and less crazy." Then he walked them up to each side of the podium and paused until the applause had died down.

Then he began, "Good evening to everyone who is watching, and to the guests that are here with us. The world has changed so much in the last few days that it is hard to understand what has happened. But, it has not changed so much that we cannot pause for a few moments to honor those who deserve it.

"Around the world, people, people going about their daily lives were suddenly, and violently, taken from their families and friends. I know the "why" has been explained to us, but I do not agree that it was a necessary thing to do. But now, along with all of the other countries who suffered such attacks, we will pause for a minute of silence for those who are gone."

As the room grew quiet Boone thought about Digs and his family. He closed his eyes and saw his friend laughing with Dottie and all the others; they were family. Then he thought about Digs' actual family and how hard the last few days must have been for them.

President Powell broke the silence with, "All of you know the time pressure the leaders of the world are under. So, I only have a few moments to spend with you before I have to meet with others to discuss our important next steps. I will tell you that at this time, I feel we are making great progress toward the goals that have been set for us to meet."

He clenched his jaws just for a moment then smiled and continued, "But now I am going to thank the two people who saved my life. Saved me from a death that no one could imagine before, but which we now live in fear of." Again he clenched his jaws, and Boone knew he was wanting to say something else, but he couldn't.

"Now I know that the Secret Service and Congress will be honoring my two guests. I am also sure that many other organizations will do so too. But, I am starting a new tradition. The tradition of the President of the United States personally commemorating acts of bravery which saved their life, with a special presidential medallion."

An image of the award appeared on a screen to the right of the president and he smiled as he continued, "As you can see it is gold, three inches in diameter, with the Presidential Seal in the middle surrounded by the words Presidential Valor Award. On the back will be the name of the person receiving the award, the date, and the name of the president they saved. Attached to the medal is a red, white, and blue silk neck ribbon. Now, for the inaugural recipients."

He started to open a folder then closed it and began, "We've all seen the video. Dinosaurs are suddenly appearing, not just here, but all over the world. And the courage and quick thinking of

Secret Service Agent Kaly Winters and American citizen Boone Christopher.

"Agent Winters tried to stop the first dinosaur, a *Tyrannosaurus rex,* a killer. But her handgun was no match for the animal. She then tried to halt my motorcade but was unable to do so which resulted in my car driving directly into the path of the second dinosaur, a *Triceratops*. Though it is a plant eater it has four foot long horns to fight off carnivores, and it made short work of the presidential limousine. My driver was killed and a Secret Service agent injured; and I was left unconscious, exposed and vulnerable. That's when Kaly and Boone came to my rescue.

"Now, I'm sure that Kaly has received all types of training in reference to protecting the president. But, I think I can assure you none of it covered prehistoric animals. And, Boone is...no, was, just an ordinary citizen. He has no prior military training or no special life saving skills. I have heard him described as hard working, respectful, a good friend to many and a great human being.

"Yet these two meshed together and immediately took action to save my life. Maintaining their composure, they ran past two fighting dinosaurs to get me away from the accident scene. If they had not, I'm sure I would have been killed. I still vividly remember, and will remember as long as I live, the sight of the *Tyrannosaurus* looking at me...right at me.

"They led me through a construction site, a site that fortunately Boone is in charge of. As we've all seen, and I have watched again many times, Boone jumped into a bulldozer to try and stop the *Tyrannosaurus* as Kaly led me to safety. Then she turned around and ran back into danger to assist Boone with an excavator." The crowd laughed as he asked, "Who knew Secret Service agents had to be able to use heavy machinery?"

He nodded and continued, "Together they forced the animal to fall into the deep foundation pit of the construction area. Boone miraculously jumped to safety as the giant bulldozer crashed down onto the dinosaur, ending the threat to everyone in the area."

President Powell paused as the crowd rose to its feet and applauded. It was a full minute before the crowd stopped applauding but remained on their feet. The president then turned to

Kaly and slipped the award over her head and whispered in her ear, "I hope you noticed it was on a gold platter." Kaly bit her lip to keep from laughing as she shook his hand.

The president turned to Boone who stepped forward, and President Powell slipped his award over his head and whispered, "Just a few more minutes, Boone."

As the crowd erupted in applause and cheering, the president hugged them both and kept his arms around their shoulders as his wife joined them. She hugged both of them and over the crowd noise Kaly and Boone could hear her shouting, "Thank you, thank you so much. Thank you for saving my Dennis."

There were more pictures, but as Boone and Kaly turned to walk away someone shouted, "Boone, what do you think about everything that's happening?"

He paused then looked at President Powell who nodded his head. Boone walked back to the podium and started, "The world had its problems before all of this began. And to some it looks like this dinosaur threat, Jurassic Sword, has made it better. But it hasn't. Who dies next because they didn't agree with August Adams? When does it stop? When only those who agree with him are left? Do they inherit the Earth?

"What happened to free will and opposing views? What will happen to the differences that make life interesting? What will happen when the man who is judge, jury, and executioner begins looking at your country, state, city…or even you, as a terrible threat that needs to be harshly dealt with? Why is he the only one calling the shots? Why aren't the world leaders part of the solution instead of frightened servants?

"It won't stop when the first round of meetings are finished and proposals are made. There will be more and more attacks until the world is worse than it is now. Don't get used to the way things are; they won't be this way for long. Those who enjoy the hunt now will end up the hunted."

There was a smattering of applause and then silence as the crowd was unsure how they should react. Liking Boone's speech could mean that they were disagreeing with August Adams. Boone was right, it could be seen as meaning far more than they were willing to admit.

As they walked back along the White House hallway, President Powell said, "Boone, you certainly laid it out there for everyone to hear. I hope it doesn't -"

"I do too," Boone interrupted. "Maybe I shouldn't have said anything."

"No," Kaly told him as she took his hand. "You heard the response; there was fear in that room. Everyone knew you were right but knew they couldn't show it."

"Kaly's right," the president replied. "We have to make sure everyone understands that all of us are prisoners, and August Adams is a mad warden. Unfortunately, that's as far as it goes right now. There's nothing else we can do."

"So Win said," Boone said. "But I disagree. I want to go with Win and Otai. I know I can help."

"And, I want to go also," Kaly agreed. "We can't just sit here and let this happen. If they have a plan to end it, they will need help, and that's us."

President Powell started to say something, but his wife spoke first, "You know they're right, Dennis. If Win and Otai have a plan, give them some help."

"But Beth, they don't -"

Beth smiled and cut him off with, "*Especially* if they don't want any help."

The president laughed and asked Kaly and Boone, "Do you know the main reason I'm president?" As they shook their heads he continued, "Because of Beth. She believed in me, encouraged me, and worked tirelessly for me. I value her opinion more than any of my other advisors so…I guess we need to meet with Win and Otai again."

Beth kissed him on the cheek and laughed, "I'll see you in a little while." Then she hugged Kaly and Boone and disappeared up a set of stairs.

"Come on," President Powell said as he led them up the same stairs. "Let's meet them in the Lincoln Bedroom."

THE TEAM

As they walked in, Boone asked, "But, this isn't where Lincoln actually slept, right?"

"Right," the president replied. "This was his office, the place where he met with cabinet members and wrote and signed many important documents."

"Like the Emancipation Proclamation," Kaly said.

"That's right," President Powell agreed. "During his presidency many important decisions and meetings occurred here. I sometimes sit down in this chair right here for a while just to breathe it all in." He laughed, "I guess I come here for inspiration."

Boone took a deep breath and agreed, "I can see that."

"Why that chair?" Kaly asked.

"Because this chair is an original. It was in this room during all of those meetings and important moments."

As the president sent a text, Kaly placed her hand on the chair and said, "Wow." Then she jumped as Win and Otai suddenly appeared.

Win smiled and told her, "Sorry, didn't mean to startle you."

"Welcome to my world," President Powell said. "You'd think I'd be used to the way he pops in and out, but it's still a little unnerving."

Win laughed and asked, "What did you need?"

"Let's sit down," the president said. As they all found a chair, he continued, "Well, it seems this room is going to be used for another important discussion. Win, I'll get right to it. I think you need help with your plan. I know you feel confident that just the two of you have a better chance to sneak in, or pop in, and take care of things. But I have some reservations.

"As president, I have been briefed in the past on several clandestine operations, and none of them have gone exactly as planned. They were still successful because of multiple contingency plans that allowed the completion of a task if things took a wrong turn. Because of the overriding importance of your operation, I don't doubt there is a need for more personnel to be involved. If something happens to you or Otai, someone must still stop your brother. But that will not be possible if no one else knows what to do."

Win leaned back in his chair and was silent. A few seconds passed then Otai spoke up, "Win, I think we need a few more also. As long as we use the areas that aren't monitored, it won't matter how many there are. But if there is an accident, or someone sees us and starts to alert the others, help would be useful."

Win was quiet for a few more seconds then asked the president, "And since they are here, I assume that you would like Boone and Kaly to go with us?"

"We volunteered," Kaly replied. "You used us before; use us again."

"But, that was just for surveillance," Win told her. "This will be different. We're going to either capture August, or if forced, kill him. I know you have been trained to use deadly force, but what about you, Boone? Ever thought about having to kill a person?"

"I haven't," Boone admitted. "But, I understand this is a unique situation. People have died, may be dying now or soon, because of your brother. We seem to be at the end of a world I have known about my entire life. It hasn't ended quietly, it's been bloody. So, I'm ready to do what is needed."

Win looked at Otai then asked President Powell, "How many others do you think we need?"

"I think you need to ask yourselves what you think is necessary. I know you just plan to walk in undetected, get as close to your brother as possible, then do whatever has to be done.

"But, what if it takes a while? Do you need food, water, shelter? How close can you realistically get? Do you need a sniper? What weapons do you need? You might have to shoot dinosaurs. Close quarters specialist? Communications? I understand you know the layout of your brother's cave, but has anything changed? What are you going to wear? Do you want med kits? Do you need a computer expert? Night vision? How long will you be gone in real time, not our time which should just be seconds?" The president tried to think of other things but instead just stopped talking.

Otai burst out laughing, "There were some good points there, Win."

Win laughed too and said, "I guess there were."

"Why don't you tell us the layout of the cave?" Boone asked. "Are you going to land, or appear, or whatever it is you do, in the cave? Or, outside somewhere and then walk to an unguarded entrance? What's the plan?"

"Okay," Win answered.

"Wait just a moment," President Powell said. "I had not considered Boone and Kaly for this operation, but I had planned on speaking to you about putting together a team of some type. I have three people standing by who can be here in ten minutes for you to brief. I know for secrecy we weren't going to include anyone else, but these people we can trust.

"I wasn't going to force them on you, but I also figured you'd want to start as soon as possible. I mean, I understand that you can arrive at any time you want in the past, but I want to cut down on the real time here before you leave. Time your brother could initiate more attacks."

"It's the smart thing to do," Otai said, and Boone and Kaly both agreed.

"I seem to be outvoted here," Win told them. He sighed then continued, "I'll use the team, but I do want to make sure everyone knows my plan and my concern about...well, I'll explain when we're all here." Then he looked at President Powell and continued, "Actually, I have thought of one more thing. We'll need a jet to take us to...an undisclosed location."

"Of course," President Powell said. "I'll be right back."

As they waited, Boone asked, "Win, this will sound like an odd question, but I've always read that since Earth is constantly moving through space that anyone going back in time would just appear in empty space. You know the joke, space is littered with the bodies of time travelers. I mean, our universe or galaxy, sorry, I can't remember which it is or maybe both, are constantly expanding. The Earth rotates and orbits the sun and wobbles too, I think. How are you able to land, for lack of a better word, where you are supposed to? And also, why are we just now learning about time travel? I mean, if one person learned to time travel, wouldn't others? And then the next thing you know we've always had time travel?"

Win thought for a second before answering, "After we joined TIM, time travel was enhanced and governend closely. Hopefully, this very public and terrible demonstration of time travel will not affect its discovery moment. The reason is, that when it was discovered, every available safeguard was immediately taken to keep it secret and limit its use.

"As real time progressed, it was decided that time travel could be used scientifically on a very limited basis. To become a time traveler meant you had to undergo rigorous psychological testing to ensure that you would not abuse the powers that would be part of any time travel scenario. In depth warnings were provided on causal loops, the grandfather paradox, the Fermi paradox, and a couple of other paradoxes that your time is unaware of."

Win sighed and continued, "Obviously August figured out how to mask his real intentions during his psychological testing. He also gained everyone's trust right up to the point he abandoned the time travel laws and began imposing his own will on your time. He fooled everyone, and I can only imagine what the consequences of his actions will be once these recent unfortunate events have been controlled and stopped.

"But, the time travel we know now is discovered in the future, and will be again. This timeline can't be changed, it is already happening, so when it is discovered, it must be governed by TIM also. There can't be multiple ways to travel existing at the same time."

"What do you think will happen?" Kaly asked.

"I believe *all* time travel will be permanently stopped," Win told her. "Everyone will think it is too risky to maintain. In fact, all of the steps leading to its initial discovery may be stopped so that time travel can never cause any problems again. That's what I would suggest and support, anyway."

Win looked back at Boone and continued, "Now, in reference to landing in the right spot, I can only speak in generalities because your science has not progressed to the point of understanding the physics involved. Let me just say simply that time travel combines gravitational fields, and how space and time actually interact. I know that doesn't really help, but I think if I actually explained it, even to a group of your scientists, I would just see a lot of blank stares. Other scientific breakthroughs have to occur before the actual ability to travel through time is developed. Anything else?"

"What's the future like?" Boone asked.

Win laughed as he replied, "I can't tell you that."

"Who invents time travel?"

"You do."

As Kaly laughed, Boone shook his head and said, "Now you're just making fun of me."

"That's true," Win agreed. "But knowing anything about the future might make you do something to make sure it happens, which might actually make sure it doesn't occur. Things happen, or not, in their own time, not ours."

"Is he always like this?" Boone asked Otai.

"If you mean wise, then yes," Otai replied as he shook his head no.

Now Win laughed and said, "I have got to get myself a new partner."

"What would that take?" Boone asked.

"Why do you ask?"

"I find all of this interesting. I'd like to work more with both of you. Traveling through time, looking for blips that shouldn't be there, and then figuring out how to correct things. I know it's a team effort, but I could be a helper monkey for all of you."

"You could be a lot more than that," Otai told him.

"Wait a minute," Kaly cut in as she punched Boone's arm. "I received *my* medal on a gold platter, thank you very much. I want to do this too."

Win laughed again as he replied, "I think both of you would make excellent TIM agents. Maybe you could be a team."

"That would be great," Boone said.

"But, I'd be his boss, right?" Kaly asked.

"Of course," Win told her.

Boone hung his head as he laughed, "Why me?"

The room door opened, and President Powell walked in followed by two men and a woman. They were each dressed in gray and green camouflage, had large backpacks, pistols, and carried a rifle. One of the men also had a case that obviously had another weapon in it. The president nodded and said, "Win, you can see I had a team already standing by. They have been briefed that this will be a time travel mission, and they will be following your orders."

He pointed to the man with the extra weapon case and said, "This is Cam. Sniper, combat handgun instructor and master diver."

Cam smiled and replied, "It's good to meet all of you."

The president continued, "Next to him is Vic. Combat handgun instructor, advanced tactics instructor and powerlifter."

Vic nodded and simply said, "Hey."

President Powell paused for a second then said, "Last is Sheila. Special Operations veteran, and both Cam and Vic told me she was especially helpful on a recent mission to a country I can't name."

Sheila smiled and told them, "I want to add it is an honor to meet you, Agent Winters, and Mr. Christopher. That was quick thinking, saving the president like you did. Impressive."

"It was," President Powell agreed. "But now we have to make plans and get all of you on a jet to…I don't want to know," he finished.

"I don't think it will hurt if you know where we're going," Win started. "We -"

"Stop," President Powell interrupted. "As Commander-in-Chief, I am always briefed on every military mission, but I don't want to know anything about this operation. If I should be grabbed by August Adams I won't have any information that can be forced from me. Listen, we can't take any chances. He can literally be anywhere he wants to be. You have to go back and either capture Win's brother or take him out."

The president put a hand on Win's shoulder and asked, "Win, I know you prefer the first, but what if taking him out is the only option?"

"Take out my brother?" Win asked. "I'll do it myself if I have to. We're talking about the destruction of everything we know. August won't stop with what he is asking for now. I'm sure there is more he wants to do, and we can't let him. All I'm asking is, if we get the chance to drop a net on him, hit him over the head, anything that keeps him alive, I think TIM would prefer that."

"What would that help?" Preident Powell asked.

"We have no idea how he did everything without being detected.," Win began. "If he could do it, then that means the ability is there for someone else. All they have to do is figure it out. We get August, we find out what he did, then we can make sure it doesn't happen again.

"There were live dinosaurs in this time period that were never a part of my history as I grew up. If we are successful, the timeline I return to will have this past. Hundreds of thousands, perhaps millions, of people have been killed, injured, or are now living in fear because of *dinosaurs*. We can't let it happen again."

"No way to change -" President Powell started.

"No," Win said. "In fact, we were just talking about it."

As President Powell started to speak, Otai spoke up, "I'm not supposed to say this, but it has been tried before. A timeline has been changed and then reconstructed to the best of TIM's abilities. Of course, it was not torn apart as much as this one has been. But, there were too many variables. An infinite number. So, it can't be done, and it shouldn't be tried."

"Some of us might not be born?" Kaly suggested.

Win advised, "It wasn't that dramatic. But, let's just say, it is possible some small changes would occur."

"Playing with time does seem wrong," Kaly said.

"Many in TIM are now starting to think the same way," Win told her. "Little things add up over the years. Can TIM really say that what should have been the present timeline, the reality before the dinosaurs, is what really was going to happen? It's going to be discussed, and as I said before, I believe that when all of this is over there will no longer be any time travel. But, we'll have to see."

President Powell walked toward the Lincoln Bedroom door as he said, "I've just been advised that the truck to take you to the jet is here." No one said anything as he led everyone down several stairs to a basement parking area. He walked them to a large delivery truck and told them, "This truck makes deliveries every day, so it will not seem unusual to anyone when it leaves. Your gear is in the truck and seating along the sides. Good luck to all of you with whatever you have to do."

As the truck drove away, a man stepped up behind President Powell and instructed, "This way, Mr. President." Absent mindedly he began following the man when he remembered that no one else had walked out with them. He turned to run, but the man reached out and touched him on the shoulder, and they both disappeared.

It was quiet in the truck for a few seconds when a window in the front of the truck slid open, and a voice from the cab shouted, "Agent Winters and Boone, how are we doing back there?"

Kaly laughed and asked, "Agent Martinez, are you stalking me or Boone?"

"Well, it used to be you, but since Boone told me about the food at the I, I'm stalking him now. How about it, Boone? What else is good there?"

"Get the eggs, hotcakes, sausage and gravy breakfast with a tall glass of buttermilk," Kaly told him.

"Really?" Agent Martinez asked. "That's good?"

"I actually don't know," Kaly admitted. "I just want you to flunk the next departmental fitness exam."

"You know, I can feel the love just flowing through the window from back there."

As Cam, Vic, and Sheila laughed, there was a moment of silence and then, "Sorry everyone. I thought it was just Kaly and Boone back there."

"Don't be sorry," Sheila said as she moved up to the window. "Hey," she continued, "you're cute."

"I...I...I don't know what to say to that," Agent Martinez stuttered.

"What's your name?" Sheila asked.

"It's Ricky, ma'am, and I have to close the window now."

As Sheila moved back to her seat she asked, "Kaly, what did I do?"

Kaly paused for a second then said, "You know, I've never seen Ricky with a date or heard him talk about anything other than work. And, he works a lot. He might be a little shy."

"Oh. I didn't mean to embarrass him," Sheila said. "He seemed nice, and he was funny."

"He is nice, and he is funny, and a lot of other things," Kaly agreed.

"He's a nice guy," Boone added.

"Great," Cam growled as he rolled his eyes. "We're probably all going to be dino snacks in a few hours, and Sheila's got the hots for Ricky. A lot of good she's going to be."

"Oh, bite me," Sheila growled back.

As everyone laughed, Win shook his head and told them, "You know, I thought we'd all be tense and nervous about what we're getting ready to do. Instead, you're loose and laughing and making jokes."

"Win, it's like this," Cam started. "Whether it's a bullet you can't even see cutting toward your head, a man standing in front of you holding a ten-inch blade, or accidentally stepping in front of a car...death is going to catch up to you. So, why let fear dictate your life? Stay loose, make jokes, and have fun. Living your life is what makes life worth living."

Win started to say something then he just shrugged his shoulders and said, "I have to agree with that a hundred percent."

The truck slowed then stopped, and Agent Martinez shouted, "We're here, everyone. All you have to do is head for the jet; all of your stuff will be taken aboard for you."

As the back of the truck opened up, they found they were inside a hangar parked next to a small jet. Sheila jumped out and went up to the front of the truck and knocked on the window. As the window came down, she said, "Ricky, I didn't mean to embarrass you. I don't have a filter sometimes on things I say and well, hey, you're cute. I meant what I said. When we get back let's go out and get something to eat and see if anything clicks."

"I well...sure, I think I would like that. And...uh, what's your name?"

"My name is Sheila, and it's a date." Then she gave him a quick kiss on the cheek and walked to the jet.

Ricky was smiling and looking in the sideview mirror when there was a knock on the passenger side window. He quickly rolled it down and Win told him, "Agent Martinez, we're finished unloading the truck. Thanks for your help."

"Anytime, sir," Ricky told him, and with one last quick look in the mirror, he drove away.

The police officers who found the truck later were unable to locate the driver or explain why it was stopped in the middle of an intersection with the engine still running.

As everyone entered the jet they saw Win walking away from the cockpit. The interior of the jet looked similar to others they had been on. There were eight rows of double seats on each side of a wide center aisle. But, the aisle led to an open space in the rear of the jet with a round table and eight chairs. Past the table was a wall lined with cabinets and drawers and open storage areas where several metal cases that had been in their truck were strapped down.

Kaly and Boone sat next to each other with Win and Otai across the aisle from them. Cam, Sheila, and Vic spread out behind them, and as they took their seats, the pilot came over the intercom, "We have been cleared for immediate departure to the Bowman Municipal Airport in southwest North Dakota. Travel time will be just a little under three and a half hours. Please fasten all seat belts, and we will be in the air in just a few minutes." Immediately the jet started moving quickly to the runway. It paused only for a few seconds, the engines powered up, and then they started forward and lifted off easily.

As they climbed, Boone told Kaly, "Well, that was quick."

"I bet we got moved to the head of the line," Kaly replied. "And now I'm starting to feel the anxiety Win talked about. It's really happening."

"It is really happening," Cam said. "But, don't worry. We all get a little nervous at the start of things. Then it all goes away when the job begins. You'll see. You'll adjust, and you won't be nervous at all."

As the pilot advised they could take off their seat belts, everyone stood up and stretched. Kaly smiled at Boone and asked, "Doing okay? How is your back?"

"I'm good," he replied. "Nothing like no rest at all to make stitches feel like they aren't even there."

Kaly winced and started to say something when she noticed that Cam and Sheila had moved to the rear of the jet. Cam was opening one of the metal cases, and as he reached into it, Kaly took Boone's arm and said, "Hey, they brought toys. Let's take a look."

Cam pulled an odd looking green and black camouflage handgun out of the case and said, "Yes, just like Santa, I brought toys. But my toys are for the good girls and boys to use on the bad girls and boys.

"As you can see," Cam continued as he held the gun up, "there are a few modifications to this weapon. Notice that the slide, right where the ejection port is usually located, is a lot wider."

"And, I don't see any ejection port," Vic noted.

"Right," Cam agreed. "This gun has an enclosed rotating cylinder pre-loaded with eight special rounds. When you are finished firing them you slap the top of the weapon and the empty cylinder pops out. Then, you reload another cylinder from the bottom. There is a laser sight, and it doesn't kick like you think it would. It has a special spring and outgas system that takes away the recoil."

"What kind of special rounds are you talking about?" Kaly asked.

"Well, they're explosive rounds. And no, I don't mean they'll blow a dinosaur up. But, they will blow a pretty large hole in one." He pointed at Kaly's holster and continued, "You're a good shot. You hit that *Rex* with all the rounds you fired, but you might as well have been throwing paper wads at it. These will do a lot better. Like I said, they won't blow a tank up like in the movies, but one of these will blow a basketball-sized chunk out of whatever it hits. Add in the hydrostatic shock wave and one or more of these should knock down anything that you hit."

"I've never seen anything like it," Boone said.

"And you wouldn't be seeing it now if it weren't for the dinosaurs. We've got seven of the ten prototypes. They're probably worth a million or so each in design and manufacturing. If we need to use them, and we live to tell someone about it, it's going to be one hell of a field test."

As everyone laughed, Sheila asked, "Rifles too?"

"Each of us will carry a standard issue military rifle," Vic said. "But, I did bring an extra one, and it's special too." He opened a longer metal case and held up what looked like a long black tube with a narrow black polymer stock. "Sorry, I don't have one for each of you."

He held up a six-inch long, thin shaft that was sharpened on one end and asked, "Anyone shot a crossbow before?'

"I had one when I was a kid," Boone told him. "I just shot at paper targets though."

"Well, this is more like a crossbow bolt than a bullet. The pointy part is the business end, with the requisite explosive head. The shaft is made of a special material...I have no idea what it is, and the fletching end contains powder and a primer that develops about 100 pounds of kinetic energy. This bolt will penetrate whatever it hits. Like Cam's handgun, the rifle is designed to reduce any kick to virtually nothing."

"You mentioned the fletching, but I don't actually see any," Boone said.

"They are inside the shaft," Vic replied, "and deploy as it leaves the barrel. I can guarantee this rifle is extremely accurate. Since a rifle is usually for long distance shots, the bolts have a guidance system that will hit whatever you hold your laser beam on. Even a moving target as long as you can keep the laser on it."

"I have got to shoot this," Cam said as he took the rifle from Vic.

Vic held up a magazine and continued, "This holds twenty bolts, and you slap it in the bottom just like you feed in most other gun mags. But," he smiled as he dropped the magazine back in a pouch, "no one gets to shoot anything while we are in the plane." Again, everyone laughed as they walked over to the table and sat down.

Win put his hands together and told everyone, "There are other weapons too. Grenades, mines, something that looks like a mortar launcher, drones, and I'm sure other, uh, toys."

He paused then continued, "I appreciate the fact that we have your special weapons. I sincerely hope we do not have to use them against any dinosaurs. And, when it comes to August, I hope we don't have to use any of them on him."

"Hope is just an illusion of a dream," Vic said. "Don't get me wrong, I hope we don't have to shoot anything either. That means we went in, did our job, and got out. But, looking at things realistically, if things don't go *exactly* as you have planned, we'll have to shoot some dinosaurs. And usually, things don't go as planned. And, I have a strong feeling that we're only going to be able to get close to your brother; we won't get hands on. It's his place we're going into. He's got the advantage."

"I understand," Win said. "It's just that…"

As he trailed off, Kaly said, "It's just that he's your brother."

"Win, we'll do our best," Cam said.

There was another few seconds of silence that Boone broke with, "I feel a little out of place here."

"Why?" Sheila asked.

"All of you have special skills and knowledge about things that will actually help us get August Adams. I have shot a rifle and a pistol…at a paper target. I have shot a crossbow…at a paper target. I've never hunted, and, as I'm guessing about some of you, never been hunted. I've never shot any living thing. I think I'm taking up valuable space."

"Well, you would be wrong," Cam replied. "Each of us has a skill set which includes the ability to rise to the occasion."

Boone smiled and said, "Okay, but really -"

"No buts," Vic interrupted. "This is the truth; I do not believe my first instinct would have been to run past two fighting dinosaurs to save the President. I mean it. A lot of thoughts would have entered my mind, but I'm thinking that particular response would have been a lot farther down on the list."

"It's true," Sheila agreed. "I understand you're modest, you and Kaly. But you didn't run out and around, or jump in one of the other cars for a little protection. No, you just ran within inches of teeth, horns and bad attitudes. You're here because of your warrior spirit. The three of us get things done without being asked and so do you."

"Besides," Cam spoke up, "you apparently know where all the good places to eat are, and we'll need a good lunch when we land."

Kaly punched Boone in the arm and said, "See, you really do belong."

"Thank you, thank all of you," Boone laughed.

"There is other stuff," Win told everyone. "President Powell made sure we have water, food, bug spray, rain gear, med kits, and even a tent. Also, each of us will wear a black and gray camouflage uniform with helmets fitted with special lens shields which will allow you to see without using lights. I think there is helmet to helmet communication also. And, there are probably a few more things I have forgotten."

"He knows we're going to be in a cave, right?" Otai asked. "I understand the uniforms and the helmets, and weapons. But all of the other stuff?"

"The equipment is just standard ops stuff," Cam said. "I get it. When plans go wrong, it's nice to have the equipment you need already onsite."

"You can't ask for it when it's too late," Vic added. "I'll take too much gear over not enough any day. Bring it if you think you'll need it. Correct me if I'm wrong, Win…but though we'll be back within seconds or minutes in this time, we could be there much longer in real time."

"That's right," Win agreed. "But, I think we are all hoping for something quick. A surgical strike, if you will. I don't plan on spending the night."

"Well, a successful surgical strike takes a lot of careful preplanning and perfect execution," Vic said. "I guess now is the time to hear your plan."

"Right," Win agreed. "First, the cave we are heading for is located in a small butte in North Dakota. It is just north of the small town of Bowman. August bought a lot of land in the area and has his people in and out under the guise of paleontological research. There are real scientists who visit the area, and they believe it's just another place to hunt for fossils. The land has a couple of private roads running out to the highway, 85 if I remember right, and no one pays much attention to August's people. They take the animals out on the roads and no one is the wiser.

"The flight plan and passenger list for this jet shouldn't raise anyone's interest, so we'll fly directly into Bowman. We're just another business flying in. Then, we drive east on 12 and then north on 85. Shouldn't take too long, depending on where Boone decides we should eat."

Win put his hands together then continued, "The cave is about three miles from the highway. As we turn off the main road we'll go back to the 1600s and drive as close as we can to the cave entrance. During that time period there will be a very low probability that anyone will see us, and the land should be similar to what it is today. Probably a bumpy ride though.

"We'll continue to the cave, make our way to a small chamber and travel back to his operation site. Since we'll already be in the cave when we start moving we shouldn't set off any alarms. We know where August's office is, we go directly there, and then…and then we do what needs to be done."

There were several seconds of silence before Cam said, "I have a few questions about your plan. First, the *low probability* that anyone will see us. Next, you said we *shouldn't* set off any alarms, not we definitely won't set off any alarms. And finally, we'll be able to go *directly* to his office. I mean, to hear you talk, there is no way there will be any problems. We're just taking a stroll in a cave to kidnap someone. So, now tell us what may happen, no matter how slight of a chance there might be."

"Of course," Win replied. "After all, Vic said earlier that nothing ever goes as planned. So, in 1600 the southwest portion of North Dakota would have been almost completely empty of people. There were Native Americans there; Cheyenne, Hidatsas, Mandans and Sioux, but we're not talking about a huge population. Additionally there were explorers, and the occasional trapper. But, the odds are huge that we will find ourselves surrounded by absolutely nothing.

"If though, through some twist of fate, we should actually appear in view of some Native Americans, hopefully they will think we are trappers. If they see the SUV we'll be in, well, I'm not sure *what* they will think then. I would like to point out that if we are attacked by any people, we cannot harm them in any way.

That would possibly cause a huge change in the timeline that would be almost impossible to straighten out.

"Next, we shouldn't set off any alarms, is as close as I can get because I can't say for sure. But, Otai has worked many times with my brother, even in this cave when it was going to be used for dinosaur study. What do you think, Otai?"

"I agree with Win," Otai said. "Even when we were in places in the past where a person could have walked in on us, August never had any type of warning system. He is arrogant and believes he can talk his way out of any situation. He does not think anyone can figure out where he is or enter his cave system. Hopefully this fault will lead to things going exactly as planned."

Win nodded as he said, "And finally, we should be able to go directly to his office because we know where it is located and how to get there." He paused and laughed as he added, "And, I'm about to show you an immersion program right now that will make you feel as if you are in the cave. Then, all of you will know how to get there also.

"Everyone please remain seated as I start. It can take a while to get used to the perceived motion of what you are about to see."

"Perceived motion?" Kaly asked.

"Yes. You see it will appear like you are moving when you are not. It can really upset your equilibrium and balance. You might even get nauseous."

"Thanks for the warning, Win," Boone said. "Do you think there are any motion sickness pills in all this gear?"

"I don't know," Win said. "But, I'll try to go slow." He reached into a pocket and pulled out what appeared to be a telephone...and the jet disappeared. Everyone jumped and Vic instinctively grabbed the table top. "Oops, sorry," Win apologized.

"Okay, this is too strange," Kaly said as she looked down at the clouds and land below them.

"Strange is not the word I would use," Boone told her. "Terrifying, exhilarating, terrifying, breathtaking, terrifying...and did I mention terrifying?"

"Personally, I had a few other words," Vic said. "But I lost the ability to speak when it suddenly appeared as if we were floating at 40,000 feet, and I realized I was not wearing a chute."

"I've never seen you unable to speak," Sheila laughed.

"Go ahead and laugh," Vic replied, "but I didn't hear *you* say anything about the nice view. What happened, Win?"

As the interior of a cave suddenly surrounded them, everyone relaxed. "Again, sorry. Pushed the wrong button," Win advised. "Now, we are inside the small cavern I've told you about. It's about 100 yards in from the mouth of the cave. Look up, down, to the front, behind you, it is a 360 degree program. This is exactly what you will see when we get inside. Look around for a second. It is smaller than the interior of this jet and is an unused and forgotten part of the cave system. Useless and inconsequential, as far as August is concerned. That's why we will start here."

"Why does it seem orangish?" Boone asked.

"Think of the greenish hue of night vision," Otai answered. "The helmets we'll be wearing produce a light we can see through our helmet shields. But, the light cannot be seen unless you are wearing a helmet. Most of the cave we will be walking through will be pitch black, and we don't need anyone wondering what the orange lights are that are moving around."

"That is correct," Win agreed. "And here is where we will be moving." A map of the cave system appeared in front of them, and as a yellow dot moved through it, Win continued, "It's a walk of about a quarter of a mile. Some of it is quite low; we'll have to be on our hands and knees, but no lower. Again, it is an unused part of the cave system since August's workers can't easily live in it, and neither can any animals."

Win stopped and smiled as he continued, "But, it contains a major component for the success of our venture. The optics relay system unit."

"I'm starting to like this plan," Vic said. "If we can connect to it we'll have real time surveillance capability and be able to devise a strategy and plan of action instead of just guessing."

"Yes," Otai spoke up. "We will be able to see where everyone and everything is. August, his workers, all of the animals. Once we are in the Optics Center we can watch, wait, and create a plan. The Center is just a short tunnel and turn from August's office, close enough we can wait for him to be alone and then grab him."

"Or, shoot him," Vic added.

'Yes, there is that," Otai agreed.

"Could we drop something into the ventilation system?" Boone asked. "If everyone is unconscious it would make things a lot easier."

"True," Win agreed. "But not practical. One, the ventilation system is housed further into the cave network. And second, the cave system is extensive and it would take a long while for any chemical to reach all areas. Plus, the chemical would probably be too diluted to do any good."

"You know, underground caves, dinosaurs, armed guards, other unknown pieces, I was a little uncertain about this mission," Vic said. "But this information makes it sound very doable. I feel better too."

"I don't feel better about it," Sheila told them.

"Why not?" Win asked.

"Because it does sound doable...and it shouldn't. August Adams is one of the smartest men I've studied. No alarms? No protection on the Optics Center? We can just run into his office and grab him without any problems? I don't buy any of it."

"What do you suggest?" Vic asked.

"We need more intel, more time. We need –"

"Tell her, Otai," Win cut in.

Otai nodded and said, "Normally you'd be right. How can anything you hear be a hundred percent accurate? It is, because I know it is. I set it up."

"What?" Kaly asked.

"It's true," Otai continued. "Win had his suspicions about August and confided them to me. We then staged an argument and August quickly made me part of his team. I wasn't sure what to do after I thought August had killed Win. But, to my surprise, Win found me, and I've been feeding him information. So, I made sure there would always be an open door, so to speak; that August didn't know about."

"What about all of the people he has killed?" Boone asked.

Otai clenched his jaw and replied, "I have been mostly on the outside working on other projects for the last two years and was not aware of August's new plans. After the first attack I contacted August, and I couldn't get past his joy of what he had done. When

I tried to assure him that nothing else needed to be done, no other attacks, he told me I was wrong and became quite defensive. I calmed him down, and he told me I'd be called back soon. I feel bad about every attack, and blame myself for not knowing about them and warning Win and the world."

"You can't blame yourself," Win said quickly. "August assigned you other things to do and then formed a new circle just to orchestrate the attacks. If you had spoken up against them, we might be wondering where you had disappeared to."

The silence that followed was broken by the pilot speaking over the intercom, "We're about twenty minutes out from Bowman Municipal Airport. Temperature is a pleasant fify-five degrees, and it will be mostly sunny today. Please be seated and fasten your seat belts. We'll be on the ground shortly."

As they sat down, Win announced, "It appears there have been two more time events since we left Washington. Hopefully no one was killed. But, now I know exactly when we will find my brother."

Boone quietly asked Kaly, "What do you think?"

"Two new time events right when we need them worries me. But, I hope Otai is right, and everything is under control. But I have a feeling Sheila, Vic, and Cam might be right too. I mean, plans have a way of turning into different plans that are made up as you go along."

"Like standing beside an empty construction site waiting for the president to drive by. What could be hard about that?"

Kaly laughed, "Yeah, exactly like that." Then she put her hand on top of his and continued, "I hope it goes the way it's supposed to. I'm in a hurry to know more about you."

Boone smiled and said, "Me too. Let's help take care of this problem and then find a nice dinosaur free vacation spot."

Boone looked out the window to the north, and in the distance he could see a long line of uneven landscape that just for a moment looked like the back of a giant animal rising from the ground.

THINGS NEVER GO RIGHT

They waited until the jet taxied to a hangar and was carted inside before they got out. They were then escorted to a large dirty, gray 4-wheel SUV parked inside the hangar. The crew that moved their gear to the back of the van left quickly without saying anything to them. Vic looked the vehicle over and told them, "Well, this should do the trick. Faded paint, dents in all the right places, get over any rough spots, and the Rocks and Fossils logo is a nice touch."

"Now, let's get something to eat," Vic said.

"But, don't drive straight there, Boone," Sheila instructed.

"Why not?"

"Let's see if we're being followed."

Boone drove aimlessly as Sheila watched constantly out the back windows. After ten minutes she announced, "I think we're good. Anybody else see anything?"

"Yeah, this pancake place we've passed about four times now," Vic growled. "If we don't go in they're going to think we're casing the place."

Soon they were inside sitting by a large window, so they could continue monitoring traffic and pedestrians. There was some small talk, but when their food arrived, everyone got quiet as they focused on eating. When the waitress came over and asked if anyone wanted dessert, Kaly answered, "Flathead cherry pie for everyone."

As the waitress walked away, Otai asked, "What is Flathead cherry pie?"

"The only pie I know that is better than the pie at the cafe," Kaly told him.

"Those could be fighting words," Boone laughed. "How do you know about Flathead cherry pie?"

"Flathead cherries grow around Flathead Lake in Montana. My family vacationed there a few times. We visited other places near Montana, and I found out you could get the pie in North Dakota. And I mean it; it's the best."

"The team is being torn apart by cherry pie," Cam laughed.

"You'll see," Kaly replied as the waitress returned.

Boone took a bite and let out a long breath as he said, "I'm moving to North Dakota...or Montana."

"I can't think of anything better," Cam added.

"I can," Win announced. As everyone looked at him, he told the waitress, "I'll have a second piece please." And everyone else agreed.

They stopped at a gas station after eating so all of them were now in their uniforms. As they drove north out of Bowman, Sheila said, "The road behind us is still clear. Vic, Cam, see anything overhead? Plane, copter, drone...anything?"

"Nothing," they both answered after scanning the sky for several seconds.

"So far so good then," Win said.

"What's the plan?" Boone asked.

"I want you to drive past the two roads that lead out of August's property. Drive north a few miles, so we can get a sense of the landscape. We'll turn around and then just before we turn onto one of the roads that will take us toward the cave entrance we'll go back to the 1600s. Then I'll send up our drone and find a route which will take us as close as possible to the cave. We don't want to have too far to walk once we take August into custody."

"Won't they see us coming?" Vic asked.

"No," Otai assured him. "August doesn't monitor anything in the 1600s, 1700s, or even the 1800s. He doesn't care about buffalo herds or wandering Native Americans, mountain men, or trappers. This area during that time means nothing to him."

Vic nodded his head and said, "Yeah, I keep forgetting about the part where we're going back a few hundred years in just a minute or two. What's the word, Win?"

"Well, Vic, I think it's showtime. There's nothing behind us, and there's nothing in front of us, so I'm hitting the button, and we're going off road."

"What button do you hit?" Sheila asked.

"Oh, that's just a figure of speech. Are we ready?" As everyone said "yes," the road disappeared, and then it was night, day, night in just a few seconds until it finally stayed light. It immediately got bumpier, but it wasn't anything they couldn't handle. All around the SUV was grass that was about a foot tall. It stretched out toward the butte in undulating waves as it covered the rolling topography of the land like a green ocean.

"What time is it now?" Sheila asked.

"About 6am," Win replied

Boone slowed down and told everyone, "I can't tell if there is a ditch or hole or anything that I'm going to hit or drive into that will break an axle or cause us to hang up."

"Stop for a minute," Win told him. As the SUV came to a halt, Win touched something on the dashboard, and a drone lifted off of the top of the van with a loud whoosh. Then he continued, "Let's take a look." They all thought he would open a laptop when suddenly the windshield of the SUV showed the view from the drone.

"That is cool," Boone said.

"It's like we're part of a game," Kaly added. "Boone, start driving and let's see what it looks like."

Boone drove straight to begin with and then started doing some slow weaving. The drone stayed just ahead of the van, and Boone asked, "I guess it is connected to us somehow?"

"Yes," Win replied. "It stays about ten yards in front of us and follows wherever you steer, so you can get some idea of what is in front of you. Let's see if we can stay in some areas where the grass is thinner."

"Uh, can I look out the windshield also?" Boone asked. "It's a little too weird just looking down on us." The drone view slid to the right of the windshield, and Boone said, "That's better."

Some of the grass they were going through was now three feet tall, and they had to slow to a crawl to get through it. The grass was not dense though, so they never had to come to a complete halt until their first problem, an eight-foot drop off. The drone checked along each side of the SUV, and they could see the drop off shrank to just a gentle slope a hundred yards to their left. In just a few minutes, Boone had them back on track heading toward the butte again.

Kaly was sitting behind Boone looking out the side window when she shouted, "Stop; back up a few feet." Boone quickly did and everyone moved to the left side of the SUV to see why they had stopped. There was a large pile of bones including a substantial rib cage partially hidden in the long grass.

"Buffalo," Vic said.

"Yes," Kaly agreed, "but look closer."

It took everyone a few seconds, but then Vic whistled and said, "Look at those old, weathered arrowheads. Someone shot a buffalo with an arrow and, wait - there's an old, larger, spear head. They shot it and stabbed it, and it ran out here and got away from them. I wonder if they went hungry that night."

"Now that was hunting," Cam said. "I wonder if the hunters lived."

"It's how they lived and died," Vic replied. "When there was game they lived, when there wasn't they might starve. We just go to the store. In this time, and for hundreds of years to come, you had to have a set of survival skills that kept you, and possibly others, alive."

"And we complain if there's too much traffic when we drive to the store," Kaly pointed out.

The SUV was quiet as Boone continued to drive and though the ground began to get steeper, there were no major problems for several minutes. As the grass began thinning out the SUV started moving over uneven rocky ground. Boone had to go around small rock formations and then larger boulders. About a quarter mile from the butte he finally came to a rocky slope he couldn't get over. The drone didn't show any easy way to go any further so Boone stopped by a large rock and turned off the engine.

"Looks like this is where we start walking," Win told them. "I have to ask, how much gear do we need to take? Do we really need the tents and all of the food?"

"Probably not," Cam said. "But I'm for taking any type of weapon and explosive we can carry. I can sleep in the open if necessary, but I can't stop a dinosaur if I don't have something that will hurt it."

It didn't take them long to put on their tactical vests, holstered handguns, various smaller packs, and sling long guns over their shoulders. "Make sure you have all the gear you think you'll need and then recheck," Win told them. "As soon as we're ready, we'll start toward the rock face that sticks out from the flatter rocky wall."

Win led the way, and they were careful of loose stones as they walked, so it took them almost thirty minutes to reach the cave entrance. It was up a steep, rocky slope, and they were surprised to find the opening was just a few feet wide and only about five feet high. As they stepped inside the cave, Win paused and told them, "Well, here we are. Part one is finished, and I feel good about it. We weren't followed, and I saw no one as we turned off the highway and disappeared. So far, no major obstacles.

"Now, we make our way to the smaller cavern, travel back until I detect where August is, and then we'll stop. Then we move to the Optics Room, wait for our chance, grab my brother, and then bring him back to present time. You'll go your way, and then Otai and I will escort August to his hearing."

"Sometime in the future?" Kaly asked.

"Yes," Win answered.

Vic waved his hand and asked, "And, by 'bring him back', you mean walking or being dragged out unconscious?"

"Right," Otai answered. He glanced at Win and continued, "And, hopefully alive."

When no one else spoke, Win turned and started into the cave, and everyone followed. It was just like the holograph from the jet including the odd orange color of their helmet lenses. They walked past several large rocks on the cave floor, and in just a few minutes, they reached the small cavern. "Get ready," Win told everyone. "I don't know how many millions of years we'll have to go back before I locate August."

Before Boone could ask what Win meant by 'get ready,' the cavern blurred slightly. At some point Boone was aware that a rock wall had passed through him, or he went through the wall. As the cavern came back into focus, Kaly said, "Well, that was interesting and not at all disorienting."

"What? Oh, sorry," Win said. "I guess I should have warned everyone there might be some slight discomfort. This chamber has always been here, but part of the tunnel walls have caved in or moved over time."

"We'll remember on the way out," Kaly told him.

"Now, let's get to the Optics Room," Win said, and they quickly continued on. The low parts were easily navigated and the narrow spots they had to get through were no problem. In less than twenty minutes they were in a larger cavern that had hundreds of conduits running vertically and horizontally connecting large metal boxes to each other. There were some standard looking high voltage boxes, but Boone had never seen anything like some of the items in the room.

Otai walked quickly across the room and placed his palm on a pad, and an electrical cabinet door opened silently. He turned and smiled at everyone, and they walked up next to him as he hooked a wall monitor to an open port. Immediately, twenty-eight small views appeared of different areas of the cave network, and one by one Otai reduced it to three live views.

One appeared to be an office; it had a desk, a table and chairs, and monitors on a wall. The second one was a long, well-lit, tiled hallway with light grey walls, that had pictures hanging every few feet. The third view was of a caged area where there were some dinosaurs moving around. The view quickly reminded everyone of why they were there and what they might have to face.

Otai told everyone, "I have brought up the three areas I think are most important for the success of our plan." He pointed and said, "This is August's office. There are no locks on the door, so when we go, we can walk right in. As you can see the hallway in front of his office is clear, and that's the way we will want it before we move. At the end there are a series of sharp turns in the hall which will block anyone from accidentally seeing us."

"And those guys?" Vic asked as he pointed at the animals.

"I always want to know where the dinosaurs are," Otai replied. "And, they are where they are supposed to be. There has been no escape; there are no surprises waiting for any of us."

"I always want to know where the dinosaurs are," Cam repeated. "Words to live by. That's my next tattoo."

Win asked, "What are those '*saurs*, Otai?"

Before he could answer, Kaly asked, "Shouldn't we be quiet? Won't someone hear us?"

Otai smiled and replied, "It's okay. Most of the rooms are soundproof. Sometimes the animals can get loud, and besides the noise being distracting, they can elicit a primal fear response. Very uncomfortable." He took a deep breath and continued, "And Win, it looks like three different carnivores in the cages closest to the camera and some smaller duckbills further back."

"They might be useful," Win said excitedly.

"What do we do now?" Vic asked.

"We wait," Win told him. "We know August is here or we wouldn't have stopped at this time. That's his office we're looking at. Just like I showed you with the holograph, it's down a short hallway from here, so hopefully he'll be back soon, and we can get this done before he knows what's happening."

After a few seconds of staring at the screen, Kaly said, "Odd thought. I wonder how many times something like this has happened?"

"What do you mean?" Boone asked.

"I mean, how many times has time travel been discovered. The discovery has led to something terrible, and that particular mode of time travel was destroyed so that no one ever knew it existed. Then, twenty, fifty, a hundred years later, someone else discovered time travel, and the same thing happened. Something terrible occurred, and a different set of people sat, just like us, waiting to stop it again." She paused and looked at Win and added, "You did say time travel might not be allowed to happen, right? So, no one knows about it, and it gets invented again. And...deja vu."

"You'd be saying," Win started slowly, "that time travel was a constant. An inevitable event. But, like an epidemic or plague, when it appears, it is a disease and has to be destroyed."

Kaly shook her head and replied, "I'm not sure I'm saying all that. I'm just wondering if this is a cycle or loop of some sort? I mean, this could be the one and only time that time travel has been invented. I'm just asking, what if it isn't?"

"That's deep," Vic said. "I mean, it's like when you wonder when time began. How do you say there's just always been time? But, wouldn't there always be time? Does that mean there was no start for it? If so, how did that work? What was there before time? Is time actually a concept that we can wrap our heads around in only the most basic way? Or, are we thinking about time all wrong and...and...okay I'm not sure where I can go with this."

"Why drive yourself crazy like that?" Cam asked. "If you want a loop to drive you crazy, come to the track with me and bet on the ponies. Then the only time you wonder about is why yours was the slowest."

A man suddenly walked into the screen by the office and then stopped and turned to talk to someone. As he walked back out of the screen, Vic asked, "Who was that?"

"That was Patre," Otai answered. "One of the members of the board I didn't even know existed until I returned. Win, should we follow him with the cameras?"

"No, I don't want to chase people around and then miss August arriving at his office. He's the only one we care about."

Otai nodded then continued, "I will tell everyone a quick story about Patre. He is the only person I know who fought a dinosaur and lived."

"Tell us more," Sheila said quietly.

"He has been with August longer than anyone. He was the first to arrive in this time to begin laying out roads and building traps to catch animals. But, it was early on, and sometimes things went the way they were supposed to, and sometimes...not so much. Patre was working on a harness his team was using to hoist an animal onto a truck. It suddenly broke free and killed a man and a woman just like we have seen in the recent attacks. Quickly and viciously.

"Patre told me all he was holding was the knife that he had been using on the harness. He knew he was going to die. The animal was a carnivore, about five feet tall and ten feet long, so he knew he didn't have a chance. But he wasn't going to give up without a fight.

"So, he threw himself forward at the animal, but also twisted his lower body away from it. He got clawed across the chest and took a bite to his left shoulder but stuck his knife in the animal's eye. It stepped back and lifted its head, and Patre slashed its throat. He told me to win a fight, sometimes you have to take away the opponent's advantage by surprising them."

No one said anything, and it was a quiet thirty minutes until August Adams walked into his office with Patre, another man and a woman. Otai told everyone, "Gina and Yang are the other people with Patre. Gina is particularly sadistic, but all of them are capable of thinking up terrible ways to use dinosaurs to benefit their plans. Remind me one day to tell you about some of the worse ones that didn't get put into action."

"Worse than attacking the president and killing all those people in other countries?" Kaly asked. "I'm not sure I want to know about them."

"Bring them up at his trial," Boone said.

"If there is one," Vic and Cam said at the same time.

Then Cam added, "I'm just thinking this. We need to keep the team small that takes this psycho down. Win and Otai, I know at least one of you needs to come with us to talk with him if you can. But it has to be quick. The longer we are in his office, the more likely we will be discovered. I understand you'll also need to check for computer programs, electronic safeguards, booby traps, that type of thing, but it will have to be quick. Sheila, Vic and I have to go to stop him cold before he can do anything, if necessary. And I mean stop him however we think we need to. Maybe he'll listen to reason, but he'll have to make up his mind in about two seconds or we'll do what we have to do."

Cam continued as he turned toward Kaly and Boone, "That leaves you two here. I'm not doubting your courage and ability, but the three of us have done this type of thing before."

"I don't mind staying here," Boone told them. "I will help in any way you ask."

"This is more of a military type operation," Kaly replied. "It does fit all of your skill sets better. We'll wait here and open the door as you get close."

"Monitor those 'saurs," Vic said. "Let us know if any of them start heading our way."

"One other thing," Win said. "Otai, when we decide it is time to get August, I want you to open the cages of those 'saurs we saw on the monitor."

Otai laughed as he said, "So, that's what you meant by they might be useful. Yes, I agree. A problem at the other end of the tunnel, far away from us, should draw everyone away who might accidentally see us. Good plan, Win."

Everyone laughed as Win replied, "See, I told you I had a plan."

A few seconds later, August Adams walked into his office and paused as he looked at the monitors on his walls. "Now?" Vic asked.

"Scan the hallway," Win said excitedly.

"It's clear," Otai said.

"Open the cages," Win whispered. They watched as the carnivores sped out of their cages and ran directly toward the duckbills.

"Can they get this far?" Boone asked.

"No," Otai replied as human figures ran into the dinosaur area. "The containment teams are there, and if they get past them, there are other checks."

"Let's go," Cam barked. Otai switched the monitor view back to the office, and in an instant, they were out of the Optics Room. Boone and Kaly stared nervously at the monitor and saw the five of them arrive there in just a few seconds.

As his office door opened, August did a double take as he looked up at Cam, Vic and Sheila entering his office. Then he froze as the gun barrels came up, and Vic ordered, "Don't move."

For a few seconds Win readied himself for gunshots, and when they didn't come, he relaxed and stepped forward and said, "Move away from your desk."

"As you do," Cam added, "put your hands up, don't speak, and now, don't move toward any of your equipment."

Otai moved past them and swept the entire room with something he held in his hand. A pale yellow light came from what he was holding, and as he moved, all the monitors and computer screens went blank, and the overhead lights dimmed slightly. He nodded at Win who said, "Let's get him out of here."

Vic and Cam grabbed August roughly by his arms and dragged him out into the hallway. As he looked around, Vic said, "Everyone is busy." As they raced down the hallway with their captive, Kaly opened the Optics Room door, and in a few seconds, they were back inside. They dropped August on the floor as Sheila cuffed his hands behind his back.

"What did you do?" August snarled at Otai.

"I broke every program you had."

"That's impossible. I -"

Otai laughed and asked, "Because you used an encryption program based on a three-level system? It took just seconds to decrypt your qutrits, destroy all of your codes, and follow all the breadcrumbs to whatever dark recesses they led to. There's not a 0 or 1 left anywhere in any device, cloud, or spiderweb. Everything is erased, gone; your threats are empty now."

"You don't know what you've done," August shouted. "The world is now under control. There is order and -"

"Stop, brother," Win said. "There is no order; the world is living in fear. You have killed thousands of people just to become the king of Earth. And now, you must answer for it."

"I don't have to answer for anything," August said defiantly. "It is you, all of you, who will have to answer."

"He's wasting time," Cam said. "He's stalling, hoping someone will find us. Let's get out of here, now."

"Now," Sheila echoed, and they started back through the tunnel. They roughly dragged August against his will through the sections of the cave where the ceiling was low and paid no attention to his screams of indignation.

As they stepped into the cavern near the start of the tunnel, Kaly laughed as Win warned them, "There might be some slight discomfort." It was still disconcerting to Boone, but at least he expected it this time.

As they moved into the shorter tunnel that led to the mouth of the cave, August pleaded, "Please, don't do this. Listen, all of you, I can make you rich. I can give you anything you want, and you can live anywhere you want. Just let me go. You'll be part of my team."

"We've seen what you do to members of your team," Kaly told him.

He looked closely at her and said, "You're the Secret Service agent that saved your president. You're talking about Russell." August laughed, "He was part of my team, and I might add, never a part of yours. He stopped being a member of my team as soon as he became complacent and more of a liability than an asset. You, though -"

"Shut up," Kaly snapped. "In a few minutes you'll be gone from our lives and world forever."

"Will I?" August asked. "Or will the truly intelligent demand that I be returned when everything that has stopped returns? Or, when everything that has started, such as global collaboration, ends? There are those who see what I offer, a better world. Don't any of you want your children to grow up in a world free of fear where everything is possible?"

Boone turned suddenly and said, "The only world you offer *is* one of fear. Everyone, children, mothers, and fathers fearing they might somehow offend you and the only possibility offered is a horrible death. You are an evil, twisted person who I hope one day will experience the fear that all of us have."

"And I'm sure you want to be there when that happens," August said sarcastically.

"Actually, I never want to see you again," Boone told him.

As they entered the cavern, Cam looked out the entrance and said, "Wait." As everyone paused, he continued, "Something is wrong."

"What?" Win asked.

"That," Kaly told them as she pointed at the cave entrance. "Look, it's changed. There's a forest outside now."

They continued forward slowly until they were looking out on a world they did not recognize. The flat plains and short grass that had been all around them had been replaced by a thick tangle of ferns, tall grass, and a wide variety of trees including several with long broad leaves. Most of the vegetation was short and tangled, but some of the trees towered high above the unrecognizable land. It was hot and humid and with a wetness they could feel on their faces. As if to emphasize the change in landscape, a long neck stretched upward from the forest and an animal began tearing leaves from some of the taller trees. As a shadow passed over them, they looked up quickly to see several bat-like animals flying west.

From behind them there was a groan, and Sheila called out, "There's someone over by that wall." The daylight coming in the cave entrance had shut off their orange lenses, so Cam turned on a flashlight and Sheila gasped, "It's the president."

"What?" Kaly shouted. She was by him in a few seconds helping him to his feet and to the middle of the cave. "Sir...Dennis, how do you feel? What happened?"

"I'm not sure," he said as they lowered him to a sitting position on the cave floor. "I vaguely remember watching all of you leave and then...and then -"

"And then I brought you here," Patre laughed as he entered the cave from behind them. He turned to Cam, Vic and Sheila and said, "Everyone, drop your weapons." All of them paused for a moment then the cave lit up, and as people began appearing with weapons aimed at them, they slowly placed their rifles and pistols on the cave floor.

Patre pointed off to the side and laughed again as he said, "Don't forget him."

"Ricky," Boone said and knelt down beside him.

"Is he alive?" Kaly asked.

"Yes," Boone assured her. "He's just out of it too." They sat him down next to the president and then stood up.

"Look at him," Patre told everyone. "Boone, isn't it? Look at him, defiant, ready to fight. I tell you, I know these three," he gestured at Sheila, Cam, and Vic, "by name and their considerable track records. But you, and you too, Agent Winters, out of nowhere rising to a level I would not have thought possible. Impressive, very impressive. I'm sorry to hear you don't like what we are doing; you would have been valuable assets."

"So, now what?" Boone asked.

"Now I have to decide what to do with the six of you," August said.

"You mean seven," Win corrected him. "Otai, come on and -"

Win trailed off as Otai didn't move, and everyone realized he was standing next to August. "Sorry, Win. I'm actually with August. You know, the side that is in control of the world right now. The side that has solved the world's worst problems virtually overnight."

Win stepped back as if someone had pushed him and stuttered, "O...Otai, I...I can't believe you would -"

"Would and did," August pointed out. "I've had him keeping tabs on you and feeding me information for the last two years. He also passed on just enough information to you to make you think you could stop me." He paused and looked at Patre and apologized, "Sorry, Otai let me know the moment Win contacted him. I told no one on the board."

Patre smiled and replied, "You don't have to tell me anything, sir. I'm honored to help in any way I can. And, did they hurt you?"

August smiled and replied, "No, they just roughed me up a little. I think those two," he nodded at Cam and Vic, "really wanted to shoot me, but I was sure they wouldn't. I didn't think my brother would let anyone kill me. And I was right. I actually enjoyed playing the captured villain." He looked at Win and said pointedly, "But, I'm not captured, am I? You are."

Win choked out, "What are you going to do? All of the others are here with me because I talked them into it. Let them go. I'm the one you want. What harm would that do to you?"

"What harm, brother? The first crack in my armor, a weakness that some might try to exploit. 'He let some live' people would say, and then they would think they could start getting away with things again. No, I'm sorry, there has to be a punishment for all of you."

"Then just kill me, and let them live in a different time period. The early 1900s maybe. They couldn't tell anyone anything; no one would believe them."

"First, Win, I don't plan on killing you. I have thought a lot about what I tried to do to you and decided I have to applaud your resourcefulness. And then you try to stop my plan? I didn't know you had it in you. Maybe you picked it up from your travels while you hid from me. Maybe even from Honest Abe himself, if what you say is true. But whatever, no, I am not going to kill you. I feel you have earned that much from me."

"So, you are not going to feed us to your dinosaurs while the world watches?" Kaly asked.

August shook his head and asked, "And turn you into so many martyrs? I don't think so. Especially you, Agent Winters and Boone. You are both admired and respected, and it might cause more problems than it would solve if something happened to you in front of an audience. No, it's better if you just disappear."

"Us too?" Cam asked.

"You're not as well known to the public, I'll admit," August replied. "But you are still heroes many times over. I don't need your stories out there either."

"What about me?" President Powell asked as he struggled to his feet. "I'm a world leader who has defied you."

"True," August admitted. "But I think in your case if you just simply disappear it will seem much more sinister somehow. Besides, why break up the team? You put it together, you get to be a member."

"What about this man here?" President Powell asked as he looked down at Agent Martinez. "He's still out. You could take him back, and he would never even know he had been here. He's done nothing to you."

"But, he will remember all of you when he wakes up. He'll wonder what happened, and he might ask questions and what would be the answers? No, he goes where you go."

"And where will that be?" Boone asked.

"Why here of course," August laughed. "You were all in such a hurry to get here, I'm just going to let you stay."

"So, you *are* feeding us to the dinosaurs?" Boone said.

"I am not," August replied. "You'll have your guns, so I'm sure you can hunt for food…and defend yourselves. I heard there were supplies in your vehicle. It's not here to drive around, so I had the stuff you left behind brought here. I was told there was a tent…so you can all have a nice place to sleep.

"I doubt if you'll want to take a walk though, lots of bad things out there. But if you have to, be sure to take your guns. Fortunately, not many dinosaurs ever come into this cave. Well, not many of the bigger ones, anyway. Of course, one day you'll run out of ammunition, and grenades, and whatever else you brought to kill me with and then of course, you will die. But I will not feed you to anything."

August paused for a second then asked Win, "What did it feel like, the bite from the *Rex*?"

"It hurt," Win answered.

"I know your arm hurt," August sneered. "I want to know how much."

Win touched his chest and told August, "This is where it hurt. My own brother tried to kill me without a second thought. We played together, grew up together, time traveled together. We're family. My heart has hurt more than my arm ever since. And that's something you'll never understand."

"That's quite touching," August replied. "But I remember a brother who turned against me without a second thought. You would never have gone along with my plan and would have let TIM know, so I would have been taken away for rehabilitation, or would it have been for revenge? TIM can be so petty sometimes.

"But, enough talk. I see Agent Martinez is waking up, so you'll need to help him understand what has happened and how you have doomed him to what I'm sure will be a very unpleasant time for all of you." August glanced at Patre and as August smiled, he and his workers along with Otai, disappeared.

Immediately, Win said, "I thought they would never leave."

Everyone looked at him incredulously as they picked up their guns and Kaly asked, "What do you mean? You almost sound happy."

"August didn't kill us, didn't kill any of us. I was afraid in a fit of anger he would do something unpredictable. But he didn't."

"He has killed us," Vic told him. "We're trapped in the past. It doesn't matter how many millions of years ago it is, we don't belong here."

"We can't survive," Cam added. "Not for very long."

"We can, and we will," Win assured him. "I just have to figure out why we are when we are. Why did he pick this time? What is special about it?"

"He picked this time because he wants us dead," Cam shouted. "Don't you understand what has happened? Your brother wants us _"

"Not August," Win replied quietly. "Otai."

"Why would Otai leave us in a special place?" Kaly asked.

"Because I asked him to," Win replied. Then he walked to the cave entrance and repeated, "Because I asked him to."

WE'RE IN A CAVE

"**Wait, wait, wait,**" **Vic shouted.** "**What** do you mean you told Otai to leave us? And, why are you glad they are gone? What else is going on here?"

Win smiled as he replied, "Otai and I have been working together to stop August's plans for years. The dinosaurs suddenly appearing would have happened sooner if Otai hadn't slowed down the process as long as he did."

"Then Otai should have killed him a lot sooner," Cam said. "Look how many people have died because he didn't."

"Remember, Otai wasn't part of the initial planning," Win told him. "By the time he was made aware of Jurassic Sword, August already had set things in motion. And, more importantly, we suspected he had initiated a failsafe program like I have mentioned. Otai has walked a razor's edge trying to slow August down yet at the same time seem to be supporting him. Any misstep and Otai would have been the first casualty. It is tragic so many have died, yet unavoidable to keep the entire world from being overrun by millions of dinosaurs."

"Millions?" Kaly asked.

Win nodded his head as he answered, "Our greatest fear is August opening time portals all over the world. This would allow dinosaurs from the entire Mesozoic Era, the Triassic, Jurassic, and Cretaceous Periods, to walk into the present time."

"I don't understand," Sheila said. "Why did he ship animals around when he could have just opened these portals?"

"He wanted to keep things completely under his control," Win replied. "With animals just wandering around, who would have paid any attention to his threats? Plus, they could have just focused on controlling the portal sites. The way he has done it so far has made everyone think he can control where, and when, the animals appear…even inside completely sealed off areas. More panic and control that way."

"But, Otai stopped his plans and failsafes when he swept the room, right?" Vic asked.

"No," Win sighed. "Hopefully, he got all of the information we need to understand what August is doing, and how. But he couldn't end all of his programs."

"But, with this information -" Vic started.

"Yes, we may begin to understand, which may lead to someone shutting him down."

"I don't like 'may begin', or 'may lead'," Sheila said. "What about *will* do something? Shouldn't your future people be able to figure out what he is doing?"

"Why?" Win asked. "Because they are from the future? August has created something that no one else actually understands. But, maybe," and he looked at Sheila, "-maybe they can. This was just a first step in Plan A. If it doesn't work then we move on to Plan B, then -"

"The minute you can shut down his failsafes, you let me know," Vic growled. "My plan B involves one well-placed bullet."

The silence that followed was broken by Ricky sitting up with a moan and asking, "Where am I?"

"What do you remember?" Kaly asked him.

"I was driving...stopped at a light, I think. There was someone knocking on the window and then...I don't know." He paused then asked, "So, where am I? Where are we?"

"We're in a cave," Kaly started. "Millions, maybe hundreds of millions, of years in the past. We came back to get August Adams, and instead, he got us."

As Ricky tried to say something, Boone stepped up and held out his hand. "Let me help you up, and you can see for yourself."

As Ricky stood up, Sheila took his other arm and said, "Take it easy. Does your head hurt? Did they hit you?"

"No, I don't think I was hit with anything," Ricky told her. "I seem to remember feeling strange, then just being here."

"That's the same as me," President Powell agreed.

"Mr. President," Ricky shouted. "How did they...this is terrible."

"Considering where we are, I think you, actually everyone, should call me Dennis. And, let's face it, if I hadn't been so insistent, all of us wouldn't be here right now. I thought you needed a team."

"And, so did Otai," Win pointed out. "He felt that it might seem strange to August if the attempt to save the world was just him and me grabbing my brother. A small army would seem more believable. And remember, we did not know August would stop time travel. I'm still not sure why. If he knew that Otai was going to return to save me, or us now, he would have left Otai too. I just have to figure it out."

"I appreciate what you've said," Dennis started, "but, I'm not very important to this group. I wasn't a part of your small army. We won't survive because of something I do now, but rather how I can help. Just tell me what to do."

"You're right, to a point," Cam replied. "We may be specialists in firearms and other things, but I know you can shoot a gun. You can warn us about danger. But, you are important, one of the most important men in the world. So, we need to make sure you get back. When this is over, and August has gone down, you'll need to help lead the world back to some type of normalcy."

"Cam's right," Vic agreed. "And to go even further, we're a team right now. It doesn't matter what you think you can or can't do. We all need to be focused on getting back. So, Win, have you figured out yet why Otai left us here?"

"Not yet," Win admitted. "But, while I'm working it out, why don't you, Cam, and Sheila check the equipment they left for us, food, and water. Let's see what we've got to work with."

"That's a good idea," Vic said and the three of them went over to the supplies and began spreading them out.

Kaly put her hand on Boone's shoulder and asked, "How is your back?"

"I honestly don't feel anything," he told her. "I'm too amped up, I guess. How are you doing?"

She shook her head as she answered, "I don't know what to think. I mean, unless Win has some trick up his sleeve, we're actually looking at…well, how long can we survive here? I can't imagine for very long."

"Don't say that," Ricky joined in the conversation. "There has to be a way back, right? There has to be some way of surviving, right?"

"Have you looked outside yet?" Kaly asked him.

Ricky shook his head and walked slowly to the cave entrance. As he looked out at the jungle, the long necked dinosaur raised its head again then it disappeared back into the trees. Above him the huge, bat-like shapes glided across the sky. "What are those?" he asked as he instinctively ducked.

"*Pterodactyl* or *Pteranodon*," Sheila answered. "I don't know which. I don't think they'll bother us."

"*Terror* something or other," Ricky said. He almost continued with, "It might not be too bad," when a small dinosaur ran out of the jungle. It was pursued by three smaller dinosaurs who stood on their back legs. They quickly caught up to the fleeing dinosaur, and in seconds, had it on the ground as they tore at its body with claws and teeth. A few seconds later, they were feeding.

Ricky turned to Win and said, "Tell us you have some trick up your sleeve."

Win reached over to his left arm and with a twist and a pull, his prosthetic slid out of his shirt sleeve. "Actually, I do," he replied.

Kaly would have laughed if they weren't stranded millions of years in the past. Instead, she asked, "Is there something special about your arm? All this time I didn't give it a second thought. I thought it was real."

To answer her, he reached inside of it and pulled out a rectangular, metal object. Everyone crowded around close as one side of it lit up and then began blinking. Win slid his prosthetic back into his sleeve and stared at the object. He frowned and told them, "Okay, we still cannot travel. My guess is August has blocked access from here and probably the surrounding area as well."

He rubbed his left temple then asked, "Then why here? And now?" He moved his hands around the object then he looked up quickly and took a step toward the cave entrance. "There is a monitoring station," he said excitedly.

"That's good, right?" Boone asked.

Win didn't answer as he walked a few feet outside the cave. Then he took a deep breath, and as he walked back inside, he said, "I guess it's the best Otai could do. The station is about three miles north of here. I can't contact it, more of August's work I'm sure, but it's there."

"So, we have to walk through that?" Ricky asked as he pointed at the forest.

"We do," Win said as he turned to Vic and asked, "What do we have?"

"Not as much as I would like, but we can protect ourselves…at least for a while. Whoever packed our equipment thought ten was a good number. There were seven of us to begin with and Otai kept his gear when he disappeared, so we have three left out of most of the issued items.

"That means all of us will have a rifle and a handgun with one of each for a spare. Since grenades and a mini RPG was not in Otai's pack, we'll have two extra of those, and, that includes the smoke grenades." He paused and smiled as he held up a black disc and continued, "But, we have twenty of these."

"Mines," Cam said. "Those may be very useful."

"They just might," Vic agreed. "We'll each have several bottles of water and energy bars. Not a lot; this wasn't supposed to be a long mission. In and out so just enough to cover an extra day. Also, we have the extra things, like a five-person tent, bug spray, and rain gear, that we didn't think we'd need."

"Throw in your special weapons," Win said, "and it sounds like we have enough fire power and food to get us three miles."

"Sounds like?" Dennis asked.

"I may have spent more time in thick, pathless areas than anyone here," Sheila spoke up. "It will be so dense in places that we'll have to force our way through, unless we have some machetes I haven't seen?"

When Vic shook his head, she continued, "That means we'll be making noise, and that means we'll be attracting attention. I study jungle predators: leopards, tigers, mambas, crocs, and dinosaurs as well. I've always found them fascinating, and now all of us have seen them on TV." She smiled and looked at Boone and Kaly and added, "And, up close and personal."

She walked over to the cave entrance and continued, "But in the thick stuff, where we're forced to go slow, we'll be in their home. There will be vines, and roots, and other things to get tangled in and possibly some rock formations to climb up or ravines to climb into or over. They'll go through the leaves, and vines, and around trees like they weren't there. Because they have evolved to survive here and now.

"We'll have limited visibility, but the animals will be used to picking up movements. So, to the best of our ability, we'll have to be quiet. No excess talking, and watch where you step, so you don't disturb rocks and sticks. Besides making noise, we don't need a turned or broken ankle either.

"Depending on when we are, there could be *Rexes*, *Tops*, *Allosaurs*, *Stegosaurs*, different types of raptors, and we've already seen the large *Sauropod* sticking its head up over the treetops. It won't eat us, but I bet it would ruin your day if it stepped on you."

"This cave is starting to look better and better," Ricky said.

Sheila smiled and replied, "There's more. There has to be biting, stinging, blistering bugs of all sorts. Spiders, scorpions, bees, and from the movies we know there are mosquitoes. So, that brings up a different danger. What germs and bacteria and whatever else can get into your blood is just waiting for us to come along? Will our bodies be able to fight off a disease we've never known before? We'll need that bug spray."

Sheila used a shirtsleeve to wipe her forehead as she added, "But, that's not the worst of it."

"Jesus," Cam exclaimed. "What's left? Are the dinosaurs carrying guns and wearing body armor?"

"No," Sheila said. "The most dangerous part will be the heat and humidity. We'll be moving, working, getting hot in an environment that is already like an oven. A body can only sweat so much, and if you're not careful, you won't be able to sweat enough to stop your core temperature from getting too hot. Then the heart works even harder to get the blood to the skin for heat exchange, and it becomes a vicious cycle. If it goes on too long it can result in heat stroke and a whole list of problems like cramping, dizziness, throwing your guts up, and the kidneys shutting down. We've all experienced a minor heat problem at some time or another but probably not heat stroke. If it happens here, where there isn't any possibility of medical assistance, you'll probably die."

"Makes me wish we were closer to an ocean or big lake," Cam said.

"Not really," Sheila told him. "The closer you are to large bodies of water, the worse it can be. The water helps raise the humidity level. Hopefully, all we'll have to worry about is sunburn. We've got water, we'll need to stay hydrated."

"When we get back, you should write travel brochures," Dennis said. "I'm starting to think Ricky is right. Stay here, and Win's people will come for us after they get through with August."

"But, that would have already happened," Win pointed out. "The moment they could rescue us they would come back to now, not later."

No one spoke for several seconds as they all slowly gathered just outside the cave entrance. The sun was behind the butte and casting long shadows to their right. Kaly spoke up, "It's several hours past noon now. Do we have any idea how long the day is now? Is it summer or fall or, I guess it could even be winter. If we leave now, would we have time to travel three miles through that jungle?"

"That's a great question," Win answered. "We could walk a three-mile road in about an hour without any problem. But -"

"But, there's no road and plenty of problems out there," Vic noted. "I think we should at least consider staying here tonight and then having all day to make the trip tomorrow. That way if we have to stop and hide...or fight, we can still make it to the monitoring station before it gets dark. And, speaking of the station, can we get in when we get there?"

"Yes, yes," Win said. "And, as much as I would like to leave right away, I do see the merit in staying here tonight."

"I think it would be best," Sheila agreed, and Cam nodded his head.

Dennis said, "All of you know more than me about walking through hard places. I'm a city boy and before I became president I considered walking from the Capitol Building to the Lincoln Memorial quite a hike. But, I'll keep up," he added quickly.

"Maybe my head won't hurt so much if we wait," Ricky said. "I would like to be as sharp as possible."

"I wonder if there is a road?" Boone said.

"Why?" Kaly asked.

"Well, if they used this whole area for catching dinosaurs, they would have needed roads for their trucks. Maybe they had one on this side of the butte too."

Kaly smiled as she told him, "That's a good thought."

Vic looked at Sheila and Cam and told them, "If there is a road we could leave now. We could definitely be there in an hour, maybe two, and not have to worry about being exposed to who knows what in this cave. Let's take a look."

As Cam turned to get his gear, Sheila hissed, "Look."

A *Tyrannosaurus rex* had just stepped out of the tree line. It paused only for a moment before moving to the spot where the three small dinosaurs had taken down the slower animal. They could hear a rumble coming from the *Rex* as it bent down and chewed at what was left of the kill. Then it snapped its head up and began walking west just outside the thick vegetation. They watched it as it quickly grew smaller and then disappeared back into the trees.

"That thing was huge," Cam whispered.

"But, did you see how it moved?" Vic asked. "Fluid. Like a cat."

"Am I the only one who thinks we should step back into the cave and out of sight of anything else that might want to eat us?" Dennis asked.

They quickly filed back inside, and Vic said, "On second thought, I vote we stay here tonight. Let's give that thing a chance to be several miles away by the time we decide to start."

"I don't think anyone's going to say no to that," Dennis agreed. "But, should we move back into the narrower part of the cave? Block it so nothing can get to us?"

Boone looked around for a few seconds then suggested, "I think we would be okay here. There's no sign that any animal has ever been in here. I don't see or smell anything that indicates anything, big or small, has spent any time here. Maybe August's group had something that kept them out, but I think we'd be safe. Personally, I'd rather stay in this bigger area than be in a smaller cramped one, especially if something attacks."

"Good point," Vic replied. "The cave entrance isn't that large; we can take turns keeping watch."

"I've got an idea," Ricky said. "Didn't I hear someone say there was a five-person tent?"

"The cave floor is pretty clear," Vic pointed out, "but there are still too many rocks in here to set it up."

"That's not where I was going," Ricky replied. "What if we erect part of the tent and then stuff it in the opening? Then we could use some of these rocks inside the tent and on the part that's still flat to weigh it down. Anything trying to get in would be slowed down and make a lot of noise, so we would have more time to react."

Sheila put her arm around his shoulder and said, "Cute and smart."

As Ricky smiled and blushed, Cam said, "That is actually a good idea."

"It is," Vic agreed, and everyone pitched in to get the entrance blocked. Vic nodded when they were finished and announced, "That looks great. It won't actually stop anything determined to get at us, but it will slow them down. I feel like I can relax a little."

"What about the other direction?" Kaly asked.

Boone started walking as he said, "Piling and wedging rocks in the lowest part should take care of that." In a few minutes, Boone, Vic, Cam and Dennis were back, and Boone told the rest of the group, "If they are small enough to fit in that low tunnel I don't think they'll be strong enough to move all the rocks we blocked it with. I think we're as safe as we can be."

The group set up a couple of flashlights to reflect light off one of the walls and the ceiling. Cam dug through his pack, and as he pulled out a protein bar, he said, "We should eat and drink to keep our energy up. Tomorrow will be a hard day, perhaps the hardest any of us have ever had. I just can't think that we will walk three miles without running into something that wants to get up close and personal."

"I agree," Vic said. "Sheila, what are your thoughts?"

She paused for a second then started, "Animals could be a concern, but there are far more herbivores than carnivores. We just saw an apex predator; they are territorial. Hopefully that was the one for this area, and it was heading away from us because it has a lot of territory to protect."

She paused then continued, "Actually, I'm more concerned with the smaller pack animals, the wild dogs so to speak, of this time. But, there won't be a thousand of them. So, if we see smaller raptors like *Utahraptor*, *Bambiraptor*, or *Dakotaraptor* heading toward us, we have enough firepower to take them out...if we see them quick enough."

"What is smaller to you?" Dennis asked.

"Not quite as tall as we are but ten or so feet long when you add in the tails," Sheila answered. "And they probably have feathers, so they'll look like giant birds attacking us."

"How will we know which ones they are?" Ricky asked.

"Their interest in us," Sheila told him. "If they are like modern animals the herbivores will watch us, maybe even face us, but they probably won't track us. Carnivores though, they will seem *very* interested in us. Also, we might just see flashes of shadows in the trees that stay with us as the animals keep out of sight."

"Okay," Kaly started, "I understand *Utahraptor* and *Dakotaraptor*, dinosaurs get named after they are found and other things. But, *Bambiraptor*?"

Sheila smiled and replied, "There are a couple of stories on how *Bambiraptor* got its name, and yes, one of them connects it to the movie. The animal was less than three feet from the head of its feathery, five-pound body to the end of its tail. You know, cute and cuddly. But, it had the *Velociraptor*-type slashing claw on its hind feet, so it could rip apart bigger animals. Fortunately, *Bambiraptor*, and for that matter *Utahraptor*, are extinct by this time. But, there are always niches to fill. What replaced an extinct, small, pack-hunting carnivore?"

"What?" Ricky asked.

"Another small, pack-hunting carnivore," Sheila answered. "Right now there aren't any fossils that indicate such an animal existed. But, it's estimated that only about twenty-five to thirty percent of dinosaurs have been found. Think of the new dinosaurs that are discovered every month. There's more to find."

"So, *Dakotaraptor* is a raptor like in the movies?"

"You're thinking *Velociraptor*, and yeah, something like that."

"How do you know the others are extinct now?" Kaly asked.

"The *Rex,* we saw," Sheila replied. "We're near the end of the Cretaceous. The *Utahraptor* and *Bambiraptor* are extinct by this time."

As they continued eating, Boone said, "I know it's going to be hot, hot and humid. But I'd rather it be hot than cold."

"Why's that?" Kaly asked.

"If you're outside when it's cold there's no place to go to get warmer. Every place is just cold, and if the wind blows, it's just that much colder. There's no escape.

"But, when it's hot out, there's always a shady spot somewhere to get just a little cooler, under a tree or next to a building, or even if it gets cloudy. When there's a breeze, you feel better; it helps you forget the heat. And, if it should rain, sometimes it feels chilly, and you have to put on a long sleeve shirt or a jacket. I don't want heat stroke, but if I can't ask for it to just be warm, then I'll take the hotter weather."

"You can get cooler in water too," Kaly added.

"I guess I'll have to start thinking about summer a little differently," Dennis said.

"Just remember, any water around here will have something in it, so you may not want to stick your hands in it to cool off," Sheila advised.

"Why can't we see the *Rex's* teeth?" Ricky asked.

"What do you mean?" Cam asked. "Every time one has opened its mouth I've seen all kinds of teeth."

"I get that," Ricky acknowledged. "But, in the movies you can see the teeth even when the *Rex's* mouth is closed. You know, they stick out along the side of its mouth."

"Like a croc, right?"

"Yeah, that's right," Ricky agreed.

Cam smiled and replied, "It might seem funny now, but when I was younger I thought about becoming a dentist. So, odd as it might sound, I still find the subject interesting, and I read articles about teeth. Recently, I read several articles about dinosaur teeth. Now, they were like any other teeth, covered with enamel. If you don't keep the enamel moist then the teeth will rot. No teeth, no food, no *Rex.*"

"So, being in water keeps the croc's teeth moist," Ricky said.

"Now you know," Cam said. "*Rex* and the other dinosaurs the movies make look badder by showing their teeth, actually had lips."

"What about that odd rumbling noise the *Rex* made? Why didn't it roar? Is that movie stuff too?" Kaly asked.

"Yeah," Sheila answered. "*Rex*, and probably most other dinosaurs, didn't have a syrinx, or the same type of larynx as birds and even crocs. It's thought they could hiss, grunt, and make a sub-audible rumble that, if the animal was large enough, produced incredible, spine rattling vibrations. Apparently scary movies use the same type of vibrating tones to set the audience on edge. So, tomorrow, if you feel a shiver running down your spine, speak up because there might be a *Rex* close by."

"Dinosaurs are still evolving," Boone said.

"What do you mean?" Kaly asked.

"When their fossils were first found, the animals were called dinosaurs, 'terrible lizards'," Boone replied. "The leg bones were arranged so their bodies were at odd squatting angles, and the tails drooped down so they would have dragged on the ground behind them. And though they started rearranging the bones and got the legs to look better, it wasn't until fairly recently that their tails were straightened out. I've always wondered if the tail on the ground and the head high in the air skeleton was built to make the dinosaur look scarier.

"Then, we found out they are most closely related to birds and some, if not all, actually had feathers. Or, well, protofeathers. Now they have lips, so their teeth don't show, and they can't scare you with a loud roar. It's some sort of sound an audiophile would get out of their woofer, or subwoofer, or a tweeter, or...I don't know. They're not as tall, look like a chicken, have toothless smiles, and purr like a giant cat. If I hadn't actually seen one, I would think a dinosaur might actually make a great pet."

"Great," Vic laughed. "As I'm being chewed on by some 'saur tomorrow, I'll be sure to notice their fluffy feathers, how nice their lips would look with a little gloss, and wonder why they're purring."

"Don't even joke about that," Dennis said. "I don't want any of you to get killed or even hurt. I okayed this mission, and it failed to the point that none of us may get back. I've been so caught up in what we are doing right now that I hadn't even thought about why we are here. I shouldn't have given the go ahead. I should have gotten more information."

Win shook his head and told Dennis, "You're wrong. We had the best intelligence, straight from Otai, an inside source. Everything worked the way it was supposed to, except for -"

"Except for being stranded here," Dennis finished.

"That's true," Win replied. "And though I admit I don't know why, I'm sure Otai picked this exact day because he felt it would help us."

"Will you be able to use the monitoring station's time travel...uh, machine?" Ricky asked.

"Yes, but not yet," Win replied. "I'll want to get a clearer picture of everything that is happening once we get there."

"Getting there," Dennis said slowly. He nodded at Cam, Sheila, and Vic and continued, "You three are used to team movements. The rest of us aren't. How will you get us there?"

Vic asked Win, "Your arm will tell us the direction we need to go to reach the station?" As Win nodded his head, Vic continued, "Then we try to stay on as straight a line as possible. We can scout around a little, and there's always the possibility there'll be a road or animal trail to follow. They may be watched by predators though, so we may be off-road the entire time.

"If we have to force our way through dense vegetation, watch your footing. There might be snakes, but I'm more concerned with someone stepping on something loose and injuring themselves. But, no matter what direction we might be forced to go, we get back on the line Win wants to follow as soon as possible.

"Either Cam, Sheila, or myself will always take the lead. Basic hand signs like pointing at someone, waving you to come forward, go back, get down, those you should already understand. I will add that if anyone motions for us to get down that we should also move to concealment. A raised fist means to stop, and we already know to not make too much noise.

"Everyone who is not leading must keep a continual watch that covers 360 degrees. Look left, right, back, ahead, up, and down. I don't know what's out there, but I'm guessing a threat could come from any direction. I take that back. I don't want you to guess there *might be* a threat, I want you to think that a threat *is* coming from any direction, at any time. It's their world, and I know they can be invisible, but we need time to react to any attack.

"Which means, rifles are always in both hands, safety off, ready to fire immediately." He held up his rifle and showed everyone his finger was on the trigger as he told them, "This is hot." He took his finger off the trigger and moved it up above the trigger guard and laid it flat against the rifle as he continued, "This is not. Keep your finger on the lower receiver just like this until you're ready to fire. Cam, what do you want to add?"

"When you point a weapon at someone it's called muzzling. If your finger is on the trigger, and you trip and fall, or say, when a dinosaur jumps out at you, your hand and fingers may instinctively pull back toward you. That's the grasping reflex, and if your finger is on the trigger you will accidentally fire your weapon. If you are muzzling someone then you just shot them. That would be especially bad with your handgun since they carry explosive rounds. Let's keep that to a zero.

"The first firearm rule of safety is always treat your weapon as if it is loaded. We're past that; your weapons *are* loaded, and we'll make sure of that before we try and get some sleep. Next, don't point your weapon at anything you aren't ready and willing to destroy. Such as me. Don't muzzle me, or anyone else.

"Keep your finger off of the trigger until you are ready to fire. Remember, this is hot; this is not, just like Vic just showed you. You don't want to accidentally shoot one of us. I would say especially me but more to the point, especially Win. He's the only one who can get us out of here.

"And finally, know your background and foreground. In this forest we're getting ready to walk through what's behind that *'saur* you're shooting at may not be that important, unless we get spread out and one of us is behind the animal. But, in the confusion of the moment, one of us could get between you and a *'saur* and you may have to hold your shot.

"But, I'll tell you right now, in the heat of the moment, when tunnel vision sets in as you're focused on the threat, you might not see anything else around you except teeth and claws. We focus on threats and the bite, and the ripping and tearing possibilities are going to have all of your attention.

"So, your muzzle will be everywhere. You won't be able to aim. You'll probably jerk the trigger, and you'd be lucky to hit the side of a barn even if you were standing inside it. But, if you keep the rifle pointed at the 'saur, try and control your trigger, and all of us are shooting, hopefully we'll stop the attack, and none of us will get hurt."

The cave was silent for several seconds before Ricky asked, "Is there any happy news?"

Sheila smiled and replied, "Well, there are far more herbivores than carnivores. So, unless there is something unexpected, it is possible that we can make the walk to the station without any problems."

"What I'm hearing then," Ricky started slowly, "is that tomorrow we'll be taking a leisurely, sun drenched walk, through a forest of interesting plants, amazing animals and insects, to have a delicious lunch at the local monitoring station with people from the future who will help us get back to our own lovely, time period."

As everyone responded with, "Uh, yeah, sure, of course, you're right, no problem," Ricky laughed and asked, "I'm going to lose a leg tomorrow, aren't I? Maybe most of my body? Go ahead, tell me, I can take it."

"Think about it," Sheila said. "Not only are you protecting yourself, but you have to take the bite for the President too."

"I hadn't even thought about - hey, Kaly too."

Vic shook his head and told Ricky, "No, she's already proven she's indestructible. You got knocked out and kidnapped while you were driving to get something to eat. You're toast."

"Am I in your insurance policy?" Kaly asked.

"That doesn't matter," Boone answered. "Kaly, you're part of the federal government. You can just have his policy changed, right?"

"Easy peasy," Kaly agreed.

Dennis put his hand on Ricky's shoulder and said, "Don't worry, son, I'll name a bridge after you."

Ricky burst out laughing as he said, "Thanks, guys, for keeping it real. I mean it.'

Sheila hugged him and said, "Stay by me, and I'll get you home. It's been a while since I had a date. How about you?"

"Uh, well…"

As Ricky blushed, Sheila told him, "Let's get out of here tomorrow and take care of that, okay?"

"Okay," Ricky said, then blushed again.

Vic stood up and told the group, "I think it's time we tried to get some sleep. Before we do though, I want everyone to check your rifle and handgun to make sure they are loaded. Remember, keep your finger off the trigger and no muzzling. Check that your pack has everything in it and then practice picking it up as you stand up. You want to know exactly where it is. If possible, sleep with your helmet on and practice turning the night vision on. I want you to see what you're shooting at before you start pulling the trigger.

"Finally, find a comfortable way to sleep with your rifle slung on your back or side. If something comes into the cave tonight, we need to get on target as quickly as possible. I would like to point out though that we are in a cave, you will hit a rock wall if you miss, and there will be ricochets. They hurt too." As Vic turned to check his guns and gear he added, "If you think you hear something wake everyone up. No one will get mad."

After checking their gear Boone and Kaly sat next to each other, and Kaly said, "This is not the way our next date was supposed to go."

"Really?" Boone answered. "So far it's exactly the way I thought it would be."

She put her head on his shoulder and asked, "Are you ready?"

He paused for a moment then said, "Actually, I am. I'm not completely calm, but I have a lot of faith in everyone. Win will get us there, and if there's trouble, we'll take care of it."

Kaly kissed him, and as she closed her eyes, she said, "I believe you."

A few seconds later a tremor ran through the cave, and some dust drifted down from the ceiling. "What was that?" Dennis asked.

"Let me think," Win answered. "Maybe the Rocky Mountains are having growing pains."

"Great," Ricky said.

Sheila sat down next to Ricky and told everyone, "Don't worry. This cave and the entrance are here millions of years from now. It's going to be okay."

Slowly, everyone dropped off to sleep. And, though the sleep was fitful for all of them, they were all sound asleep when the first massive tremor hit.

THE BRIDGE

The shock picked everyone up and threw them several feet in different directions. As they landed, the vibrations continued as they frantically turned on their night vision. Packs had been thrown, and in some cases had burst open, and their valuable contents lay strewn across the cave floor. Small rocks were falling from the cave ceiling along with an occasional boulder that hit with a dull thud.

"Out, out, out," Vic shouted. "Earthquake. Get what you can and get out, now." He turned and began tearing at the tent but was unable to move it until Dennis, Sheila, and Ricky came up. Slowly, an opening began to appear to the right of the tent, and a few seconds later, Vic shouted, "It's large enough. Out and down the slope. Watch out for loose rocks."

Just as quickly as it had started, the vibrations stopped, and in the silence that followed, everyone could be heard breathing hard as they forced their way past the tent. Outside, treetops were still swaying as they started slowly down from the cave entrance. They could not go fast because the rocks gave way with every step they took until they were half sliding on their feet and backs. A minute later, they were all at the bottom when another tremor knocked them off their feet.

"Stay down," Vic and Boone yelled. As rocks began rolling down from the cave, they followed Cam as he crawled toward the tree line. He stopped about a hundred feet from the cave and they hugged the ground until the shaking stopped.

Kaly sat up and asked, "Is anyone hurt?" Everyone reported bumps, bruises, aches and pains but no bad injuries. As everyone else slowly sat up, Kaly asked, "Will there be more?"

When no one answered, Win asked, "I don't know anything about earthquakes. Does anyone else?" He waited a few seconds then continued, "I don't know if that was two separate quakes, or a quake with aftershocks, or what. But, I think after a quake there are smaller ones for a while. I don't know how long of a time aftershocks can happen or what magnitudes to expect."

Ricky got to his knees and asked Win, "More growing pains?"

"I'd say, yeah," Win replied. "The Rockies aren't as tall as they are going to be yet. But, it may not be the Rockies. I think there is one, and possibly two, fault lines in or near North Dakota. Or, maybe all of North America just shakes every once in a while."

"I should have known this could happen," Vic said.

"Why?" Kaly asked.

"There were large rocks on the cave floor when we arrived yesterday. Smaller ones when we went to sleep. The bigger ones had to come from somewhere."

"But, you couldn't have known it was going to happen now," Kaly pointed out.

"The sun is coming up," Dennis said. "Whatever it was that woke us up decided when we were going to start walking."

Everyone else realized at the same time that it was light...too light. They all felt that every animal around them was staring at them, and some might be ready for breakfast. They moved rapidly to a group of ferns that were about three feet tall and covered about half an acre.

As they knelt down, Cam said, "Vic and Sheila, stay down, but get your guns up. Everyone else, stay down and check your packs and your guns. If you think everything is okay, get your gun up."

Dennis immediately held his rifle up, showing the oddly bent barrel. "Yeah," Cam said, "that ain't going to work anymore. Grab one of the extra ones. Oh, keep the mags out of the damaged rifle and put them in your packs or pockets."

Vic stayed low and walked over to hand him one of the extra rifles but stopped. He shook his head as he said, "You're not going to be carrying a rifle for a while."

"Why not?"

Vic touched his left shoulder and asked, "Does this hurt?"

Dennis flinched away from the touch and said through his gritted teeth, "Yes, that did hurt. What's wrong?"

"My guess is you have a dislocated shoulder. The good news is, I can fix that. Oh, and there's more good news. You get to lay on your back and relax for a few moments." As Dennis sat down then stretched out on his back, Vic continued, "Relax a little more, a little more as I move your arm up a little, over a little, and there. It's back in."

"I heard the pop," Dennis told him. "I thought there would be some pain."

"No, if it goes in easily, it just takes the pain away. How does that feel?"

Dennis moved his arm and shoulder slowly and told Vic, "It does feel a lot better."

"Good," Vic said as he picked up Dennis' backpack and lengthened the straps. "I want you to wear this on the front of your body and put your arm across the top of it. We don't have anything we can use for a sling."

"Thanks," Dennis said.

"Don't thank me yet," Vic told him. "We can't strap it down which means it's going to move. We can't med you to feel no pain because then you wouldn't be much of a lookout. You're going to have to be tough today." Dennis just nodded.

"My pack was torn apart," Ricky said.

"Mine too," Vic added. "A boulder landed on it instead of me. So we know we're down some food and water. Now then, Cam, Sheila, and I are going to take a few seconds to check ourselves for injuries. I know Kaly asked if we were hurt before, but when you had an adrenaline dump like we did you may not feel pain for a while. Believe me, when it starts wearing off, like Dennis, we'll all be in for some aches and pains that will talk to us for quite a while."

No bad injuries were found, but Sheila and Kaly both had small cuts on their arms from falling rocks inside the cave. Cam told them, "Rinse the wounds then bandage them tight. We don't want anything to catch the scent of fresh blood." They knew exactly what Cam meant and made sure the wounds were wrapped tightly.

Boone started to kid Kaly, "Can't have you drawing dinos after you before -"

Suddenly, Sheila whispered, "Get down, now. What am I seeing over there?"

About 100 yards to the east of them, the group saw a dark mound in some higher ferns start moving and then a long tail whipping around. Something was trying to stand up, but it kept falling back down for a few more seconds. Then it fought its way to its two large legs and shook its head. It stood facing away from them as it swayed from side to side. The animal was about ten feet tall and twenty feet long. It was splotched with dark and light brown areas with traces of red running from its neck to its tail. On its shoulders and partially down its back were patches of lighter brown protofeathers.

"Is that a *Rex*?" Sheila asked nervously.

"Maybe," Kaly said. "Maybe a young one. But...but it doesn't exactly look like one. What's wrong with it?"

"Same as us," Boone whispered. "It probably got knocked down by the quake and slammed its head on the ground."

The animal shook its head again and then slowly turned and began walking west in the space between the group and the forest. Kaly was the closest to the tree line and was ducked down so she was looking at Boone. He slowly started to bring his gun up when Kaly shook her head 'no' with small movements and smiled. Even when the animal paused thirty feet from her, she just gave Boone a wink. Then with an exhaled whuff the animal continued west and veered into the trees.

Vic let out a long breath as he said, "Man, I'm glad that thing didn't know we were here. It was way too close to us. I think it would have made a mess before we brought it down. So, take your RPGs out of your packs and sling them so they don't get tangled with your rifle."

"Weren't you scared?" Dennis asked Kaly. "And why did you smile?"

"I was scared," Kaly admitted. "If that thing saw us I was pretty sure I'd be the first to know. But, it reminded me of my brothers when we go camping. They get a little drunk, and the next morning they wander around for a few minutes before they get their act together."

Cam shook his head as he said, "Let's hope all the *'saurs* fell down this morning. But in case some of them are getting their act together, let's get out of the open and into the forest. If they want us, make them work for it anyway."

Vic stood up and led the way toward the tree line. As Ricky walked past Kaly, he said, "I want to be just like you when I grow up." Everyone else began falling in line with Sheila as the rear guard. She paused to check behind them and then they were all in the shadows.

It was loud. There were sounds that were probably made by insects and others by animals. But they couldn't recognize any of the chirps, barks, coughs, and calls that sounded far away and at times alarmingly close. Small animals, barely twelve inches tall, could be seen running through the smaller ferns and every once in a while a taller shadow back in the vegetation. Everyone was watching everywhere, but nothing seemed interested in them. Yet.

They had only been walking a few minutes when Vic turned and waved everyone up. As they gathered around he told them, "There is a road here. Not much of one, just two tire ruts, but it will help us make good time. But, there are also animal tracks on it because it makes it easier for them too."

"How dense is it on either side of the road?" Sheila asked.

"Not too bad. Maybe twenty to thirty yards of visibility. It looks like the area beside the road was cleared at some point and then slowly allowed to grow back."

"I'd chance it," Sheila said. "We can move quicker, and every step gets us closer to safety. But, thirty yards of visibility doesn't give us much of a chance of stopping something from getting us."

"Why not?" Dennis asked.

"Well," she started, "a lion can run a hundred yards in about five seconds. A cheetah, under four. That means if they were already charging they would cover thirty yards in under two seconds or so. You have to remember the four steps of reaction, PEDA. You have to perceive the animal and what it is doing. Then, after you are over being startled by the sudden appearance of a dinosaur, you have to evaluate its actions. If they are running at you, I'm sure you'll decide they have bad intentions.

"Next is the decision. What do you do? You're probably thinking, start pulling the trigger, and that's a great response. But, the decision phase is what slows most people down. If it's not in your toolkit from hours of practice, then you have to find it. For some, that is hard to do under stress. A good example is the kids that are playing in a driveway when a car pulls in. Most of them immediately run out of the way, but there is usually one who freezes, legs moving, but going nowhere until they get it figured out and then they go.

"Now I have trained with Vic and Cam, and I know their skills. We all watched Kaly and Boone jump into action, so I have to think they are ready to go too. But, Dennis, Win, and even you Ricky, I can only hope you can move quickly through the decision phase and then act. Pull the trigger, throw the grenade, whatever it is you have to do."

"If we don't," Ricky said, "we're dead."

"Maybe we're all dead," Dennis added.

Ricky smiled at Sheila as he said, "Shoot the dinosaur that pulls into the driveway. Got it."

Vic walked out onto the road and said over his shoulder, "I'm looking forward, and my gun is ready to be brought up so I'm covering everything in front of us. Whoever is behind me looks right, the person behind them, left. Do that all the way down the line and rearguard watches our six. Sweep your eyes and your lowered rifle back and forth together, and don't forget to look up. And practice for a few seconds bringing your barrel up so it's pointing at what you would be looking at. Let's keep it quiet for a few minutes and watch out for these ruts. Nobody break an ankle."

They started forward and saw or heard nothing that caused any concern for about fifteen minutes when there was loud crashing to their right as something large made its way past them from front to back. They never saw the animal, but everyone started moving slower and sweeping their rifles a little quicker back and forth.

Vic signaled for everyone to pause just before they reached an open space and called them up to him. "Okay," he started, "I'm going to rotate to rearguard. Sheila to point, and Cam you move to the center. Whenever we're in the open, like we're getting ready to be, keep checking above you just like when we're in the trees. I don't want one of those *Terror*-whatevers to drop down on us unexpectedly. Take a drink, then let's go."

Another fifteen minutes passed as they moved slower than before. As Cam moved up to replace Sheila, he said, "Let's start moving a little quicker. We haven't even gone a mile yet. We'll take another break when we switch again. Stay focused."

Five minutes later he began motioning everyone to move off of the road to the right and to get down. When they were in position he held up his rifle and began shaking his head 'no.' They felt it first, then they understood. The head was lower than they expected, just barely skimming the tops of the trees. Then, out of nowhere, it just appeared. The tiny head seemed out of place sitting on a thirty foot long neck, followed by a gigantic body, and then the seventy foot long whipping tail.

A few seconds after it disappeared, Cam said, "That was like watching an apartment building walk past. Let's go." After another fifteen minutes, he motioned for everyone to follow him to the right of the trail again and motioned for them to circle up. Vic and Sheila faced away from Cam while everyone else listened as he said, "We're doing great. I'm guessing we've gone a mile, and we heard but didn't see one 'saur, and definitely saw another. Let's take ten and eat something, and it's mandatory you drink some water."

"Can we take our helmets off?" Dennis asked.

Cam paused for a second then shook his head, "Sorry. I'm going to have to say no. I'd rather wear and not need it than wish I had it on while something was chewing on my head. I don't know for sure what's out here, and no one else does either. You can take it off right now if you want to, but they go back on when we start."

Dennis nodded as he took his helmet off and took a big breath. "That feels better," he told everyone. "I'll be glad when we get to the station."

"How are you holding up?" Kaly asked Boone.

"Most of me is doing okay. My back is talking to me because of all the sweat getting in the wound."

"Anything I can do?" Kaly asked.

"Piggyback ride?" he asked, and they both smiled.

As Sheila gazed around, she said, "I knew there were flowers in this time, but I wasn't expecting bees and butterflies. It makes sense, but when I think about this time period, I just think about the dinosaurs.

"And the plants, lots of palm looking trees and shrubs, lots of thick leaved bushes, but fruit too. I mean, I wouldn't eat any of it, but again, not what I think about. And, some of the trees look like pine trees. I guess a lot of things have been around longer than a lot of us probably think about."

Then there was a skittering noise in the trees above them, and Dennis put his helmet on quickly, and everyone else started scanning the trees. "Let's start moving," Vic told them. "Same as before. We're doing great, but don't relax. Stay sharp. It's not the butterflies and bees I'm worried about."

They had moved down the trail for just a couple of minutes when they started up a small hill. As they approached the top they heard odd cries and bellows mixed in with grunts, vibrating sounds, and high pitched calls. Vic held up his fist and continued slowly up the road, and when he reached the top, he lay down on the ground. It was a minute before he faced back toward them. He looked stunned, and as he shook his head, he waved them all up.

As they dropped down beside him, Cam uttered, "What kind of hell is this?"

Below them they saw a lake about twice the size of a football field. It was surrounded almost entirely with mud, though in a few places trees and shrubs ran down to the water. At any other time the reflection of the blue sky and white clouds in the water would have made them think of the lake as a peaceful, idyllic place. But in the mud around the lake was a horror they had never dreamed of.

Over twenty animals were stuck inside the mud. Some, just most of their legs, others almost their entire body had been swallowed up. There were large, heavily plated animals, a *Triceratops*, several duckbills, small herbivores and carnivores that walked on their back legs, and a smaller version of the long necked animal that had walked past them.

All of the animals were bellowing or calling as they struggled to free themselves from the mud that trapped them. Their struggles were useless though and their cries were only accomplishing one thing; drawing carnivores who were moving across the mud without any problem. They were coming in from the forest alone and in packs and attacking the helpless, trapped animals. Some of the animals were already dead and the others bleeding badly and drooping slowly toward the mud. But, all were being fiercely fought over, and fed upon.

"What is this?" Vic asked. "If it's quicksand, how can some of the animals walk on it and others can't?"

"That's because it's not quicksand," Boone replied. "At least not anymore."

"What do you mean?" Dennis asked.

"Liquefaction," Boone answered.

Kaly nodded her head and said, "Of course, liquefaction."

"What is liquefaction?" Sheila asked.

"It is something you worry about when you're building near water," Boone replied. "You see, there are a lot of things an architect needs information about before they even think about starting construction on any type of building. One is, what is the building being built on? The ground, obviously, but is it loosely packed material, or water logged? Architects check liquefaction hazard information to determine how vulnerable a site is.

"One of the risk factors taken into consideration is seismicity. Earthquakes. When the ground starts shaking poorly packed, water logged dirt that seems solid suddenly takes on the properties of a liquid. When that happens, buildings, houses, roads, whatever, just start sinking. It can cause a lot of problems.

"In this case, these animals were in the wrong place at the wrong time. When the earthquake started this morning, they were on the waterlogged mud when it turned into soup. They sunk into it and when the vibrations stopped the ground regained its normal hardness, trapping the animals. Even without all of the carnivores appearing, these animals were going to die."

"My grandfather told me about a car that had sunk halfway into the ground," Kaly said. "Also, I saw a documentary on liquefaction where it happened to some mammoths, or mastodons."

"I'm just glad we weren't walking by the water when it happened," Vic said. "That would have been us down there."

Everyone grew quiet as they thought about that until Cam said, "Look, we couldn't hear these animals until we were almost to the top of this hill. But, the wind is blowing toward us, and the smell of blood and death is going to start drawing animals from this direction. Let's get back on the road and get around this mess. We still have a couple of miles to go."

Win spoke up with, "I know no one wants to hear this, but things may get slower now. The road veers west along the lake and keeps going. That is not the direction we want to go. We need to go a little more northeast so we need to go right, around the lake, and then see if there is another road over there.

"Then let's stay below the top of the hill and start moving east. When we can start north out of sight of the animals, we will see how we stand." He paused then continued earnestly, "Listen, there's not going to be enough room down there for everything that wants a free meal. Some animals will be driven off; others will just decide to look for something that isn't already being chewed on. There are eight of us, and that may give some animals pause, but not all of them. Stay sharp just like before." He looked at Dennis and asked, "How are you holding up?"

"It's hurting," he admitted. "But I can make it. We all can. Just two more miles." Vic nodded and led them into the forest.

As they walked, Ricky asked Sheila, "I guess this would be an example of an unknown circumstance?"

She nodded her head and advised, "Yeah, just what we didn't need."

For a few minutes it wasn't too bad, but slowly the vegetation grew denser. As they pushed and pulled at the intertwined leaves and vines, Ricky asked, "Can we just blow some of this stuff up with a mine? Make a hole?"

"That would be a good idea," Cam agreed, "if we knew how big of a hole the mine would make. You blow up what's in front of you, and it might be just as thick behind it."

"Plus, the noise," Sheila pointed out, "might draw a crowd."

A few minutes later, an opening appeared that led them to an area of more spaced out trees and small ferns. They paused for a drink of water, and Win said, "Let's start north." Vic nodded and they made good time for about ten minutes before they ran into another wall of highly packed bush.

Behind them, Sheila said calmly, "We have company."

As they turned they could see four animals following their trail. They were about four-feet tall, completely covered in light brown and gray feathers, walked on their rear legs, and had straight stiff tails. The animals stopped about thirty yards away and spread out and hesitated when they saw the humans. Then the larger animal in the group stepped forward and began bobbing its head up and down and side to side.

"It's going to charge," Vic stated. "And, if it does, so will the others. Keep your eyes open, control your triggers, and stop shooting when they go down."

As everyone raised their guns, the lead animal paused, lowered its head and, with a loud chirp, burst forward. The others didn't hesitate and followed their leader in the attack. In five seconds the shooting was done, and the animals lay still, their bodies partially hidden under a group of ferns. They were less than twenty feet away.

Cam was to the far right of the group, and he commanded, "I'm going to put in a fresh magazine right now. As soon as I'm back up with my weapon, the next person does the same and on down the line." Though it took Dennis a few extra seconds to put in a new pistol magazine, in a few seconds everyone was finished.

"They were fast," Ricky said. "I've never seen anything that fast."

"But, we won," Kaly said.

"I don't know if I actually hit anything," Boone said. "I hope I did."

Vic smiled as he replied, "I guarantee if we check those 'saurs they each have multiple holes in them. We all hit them; we all did what we needed to do." Then he turned to Ricky and said, "I've just had a great idea."

"What is it?" Ricky asked.

"I'm thinking this brush is only dense in small areas, and, since we just made a lot of noise, I thought I'd see if I could blow a hole in some of it."

Ricky smiled and said, "Only a genius would have thought of that."

Everyone smiled then spread out in a half circle to protect Vic who placed the mine about five feet from the thick brush. He looked around for a moment then motioned for everyone to follow him. He walked fifty feet to a slight incline and told everyone, "Lay down here with no part of your body above the top of this little ridge. Now, this is a directional mine which means the full blast will go directly into that thick stuff. With any luck, and you guys can see how much luck we're having, it will tear out a hole we can go through.

"When the mine goes off it will throw lethal projectiles away from us, but of course, some of them may ricochet in different directions." He took a quick look over the embankment and continued, "Reach up under your helmet to cover your ears. I'll speak loud enough so you can hear me count down and then don't move until I do." He quickly did a 3-2-1 countdown, and just a few seconds after the explosion he was saying, "We're good. Let's take a look."

The blast had taken out a huge chunk of brush, and though not quite all of it, they were able to push through to another open tree area. "It looks fairly clear for a couple of hundred yards anyway," Vic said. "Cam, you're on lead. Keep your guns up, call out if you see anything, and let's get going."

The group moved forward quickly and kept their quicker pace up. "This feels good," Ricky said. "We're making good time now."

"If we have enough mines we may not have to stop for very long at all," Dennis added. "How far have we gone, Win?"

"About a mile and a half, maybe a little more," Win answered.

A little further, and they started down a long slope that ran toward a small stream. They picked up speed, and it took a few seconds for them to stop when Cam suddenly held up his fist. They dropped down and looked at Cam who was staring intently ahead.

Sheila joined him and whispered, "What is it?"

"Right now, just a feeling," he replied. "Follow my thoughts for a second. There's a stream ahead of us. It's too wide to jump over, and we don't know how deep it is or what might be in it. Directly in front of us are three or four trees that have fallen over the stream and formed a natural bridge. If you look closely you can see a trail leading to it on both sides of the water. But, that bridge butts right up against a lot of trees and ferns and other vegetation. It may be nothing, but I thought I saw something moving in the shadows."

No one spoke or moved. Around them there were animal and insect sounds that they had grown accustomed to but nothing else. There were shafts of light coming through the trees which made the bridge, and the brush, seem even darker…and ominous. Vic said, "This is where we wish we had binoculars." Then he asked Cam, "What do you think?"

Cam turned to the group and started, "Okay, we can just walk on down to the bridge and go across. I'm sure I saw *something*, but that doesn't mean it's waiting for us. We can check the stream in either direction; maybe a tree has fallen across it someplace else. I'm also open for suggestions."

"Light it up?" Dennis suggested. "We walk down there, and when we get close, each of us puts five rounds into those trees. That would scare anything out, and we'd probably hit anything that might be hiding."

"I like the idea," Cam agreed, "but I don't think we should use up the ammo. The trees are too short to hide a *Rex,* but that doesn't mean we won't run into one later. Then we would need the ammo. The same with any of the exploding ammo, we need to save it."

"Throw rocks instead," Ricky said. "Get enough of them bouncing around in there and it might scare something. Hopefully, into running away from us."

Cam looked at Win and asked, "Going across the bridge and up the hill on the far side keeps us heading straight for the station, right?"

'It does," Win agreed. "But, I don't think any of us would mind walking a little further if the way was safer. We trust you, Vic, and Sheila. It's whatever you say."

Sheila spoke up, "I've been watching the shadows, and I haven't seen anything else. But, that doesn't mean there isn't something waiting there. It's a perfect ambush spot. But, you're on point, so we'll follow your lead."

Cam nodded his head and then looked up. "You know, it's past noon already. This day is going slower than we hoped and not going over that bridge will make it worse. Bring some rocks, limbs, I don't care what, and when we get close, we'll throw them into the trees and see if something comes out to play. Then I'm going across, and if I make it, the rest of you can follow. Guns ready, cowboys and cowgirls. This could be interesting."

A few seconds later they started down the hill much slower than they had been moving. With each step they anticipated something;

a shadow moving or some type of noise. But nothing moved or made a sound.

Ten yards away from the bridge, Cam instructed, "Throw half of what you brought with you. Ready? Throw." The crashing noise lasted for only a few seconds, and five small, green animals ran out and away from them. "Again," Cam said, but this time nothing came out. He took a deep breath, and as he started across the fallen trees, he said, "Okay, let's go…but be ready. Wait until I'm on the other side so I can cover –"

One second the space at the end of the bridge was empty, the next there were two dinosaurs standing in front of Cam. They didn't wait. One immediately jumped on the bridge just as Cam got off two shots. The second animal had followed the first and ran into the now collapsing body of the first. As the two dinosaurs became entangled, their momentum carried them into Cam who ducked down, put his arms around both animals, turned to his left, and dove into the stream.

Vic ran onto the bridge as he moved his gun back and forth from where the dinosaurs appeared, to where Cam went in the water. When he finally decided no more dinosaurs would appear, he focused on the water, shouting, "Cam, Cam." A long tail whipped up out of the water and then disappeared with a splash. The water swirled and eddied in different shades of brown and tan as somewhere below the surface a violent struggle was taking place.

Boone and Kaly moved along the bank hoping to help Cam if he was able to break free and surface. Over a minute had passed, and still the water moved in ever slowing circles and waves. Then they disappeared, and it grew quiet. Still, no one moved, no one took their eyes off of the water. Two minutes passed, and as it grew closer to three, Vic walked on across the bridge and motioned for everyone to follow.

He took a deep breath but seemed at a loss for words. Just as he started to speak there was a splash and splutter behind them, and they turned to see Cam crawling out of the water. They rushed to his side and saw that his head was bleeding, and he couldn't stand on his right foot. "What were you thinking?" Ricky asked.

"I had a sailboat tied up to a berth in Hawaii a few years ago," Cam started. "Wasn't able to get to it for almost six months. The day I finally made it back I found some guy living on it. I told him to get off, that he was trespassing, and he just laughed at me. I called the police and the guy spits out a good story; he sounded really convincing.

"He tells them that since my boat has been left unattended for a continuous period of over thirty days I had abandoned it. Since he had lived there for over thirty days he had established residency there or something, and couldn't be removed.

"You know, the officers were on my side, but because the guy sounded like he knew what he was talking about, they started wondering if they needed to check with some government agency or something. Okay. I knew the guy was blowing smoke; I could wait a few hours. Then he walked right up to me, nose to nose, told me what I could do with myself, laughed, and walked away. So, I followed him real slow, put my arms around him, and dove into the water. I kept him down for about a minute. Just long enough he wasn't moving much, but I didn't want to kill him. Then I brought him up.

"The officers pulled him up onto the dock, and I piled all of his stuff around him. Then I knelt down real close to him and said, 'The next time you're standing next to water, and you get in someone's face, make sure they're not a master diver'."

Everyone laughed as Cam continued, "I looked up at the officers, and the older one says, 'Sir, I can tell you're the type of person who wouldn't want a lot of publicity for saving this man from drowning. So, I think we'll escort this gentleman to a nice park where he can rest and then we're going to lunch.' The younger officer smiled, and as they took the guy away, I called the older officer back and told them to drop by anytime I was around. They did too. Good guys."

As Kaly and Ricky checked Cam's head and leg, Sheila slapped him on the arm and said, "You are crazy. Don't ever worry us like that again."

Cam laughed and said, "Ow. That hurt worse than the 'saurs."

"How does he look?" Vic asked.

"Nasty laceration to the head, but we got the bleeding stopped. But, between the claw that did it and the dirty water, we need to get him to the station for some antibiotics."

Ricky stood up and told Vic, "The cut on the ankle goes all the way to the bone. Looks like it might be broken too."

"But, you're still alive," Vic told Cam. "If that second one had crawled over the one you shot you'd probably be in worse shape than you are now. Guess you did what you had to."

"Seemed right at the time," Cam agreed.

"Okay," Vic said. "Sheila and I will switch point and rearguard. To start with I want Win under one shoulder and Dennis under the other to keep Cam steady. Boone is left side, and Kaly right. When Sheila and I switch, Boone and Kaly take the shoulders. Then we just keep switching."

He looked up as he had before and said, "It's getting late. We need to move quicker. That makes us more vulnerable, but we have to take the chance. Let's go."

They moved faster than they had been, but it was still slow going. Twice they had to stop and hide as something walked unseen. They also had to use another mine to get through another dense section of vegetation. As Vic moved to the point he told everyone, "You're doing great." Then he asked Win, "How far have we come?"

"It's a mile away," Win said excitedly. "Just a mile."

Then Kaly said, "I've got some shadows on this side."

There was a moment of silence that Sheila broke with, "We have   company.   Lots   of   it."

LAST MILE

"Talk to me," Vic said quickly.

"I've got at least six behind us," Sheila said. "I caught a quick glimpse when Kaly said there were shadows on her side; four more there at least. They're on two sides for sure, so maybe there's a few waiting all around us."

"The animals that filled the niche you were talking about," Cam said.

"Yeah, I'm afraid so," Sheila replied. "They have stopped, like they're making plans or something."

"Then we have to make our plans first," Vic said. "First, we can't mix it up with them in the woods, and there's nothing to put our backs against to make them attack from one place. So, we're staying right here in the open to try and confuse them. Maybe they'll leave. If that doesn't work then we'll try and funnel them the best we can."

"Again, I wish we had some binoculars."

Boone reached into a pocket and said, "I just realized we have the next best thing."

He pulled out his phone and Kaly asked, "How will that help?"

"I'm going to take some photos, and we can enlarge them on the screen. But, I'm not sure it will help you see an animal behind any of the trees and brush."

"A head looks like a head," Vic told him.

"What do you mean by that?" Dennis asked.

"It means, you know a head when you see one. No matter what a person hides behind, if you can see their head, you know where they are. If you want to make it harder to be seen, you wear a hat that changes the silhouette of your head. These 'saurs have distinctive shaped heads too, and they aren't wearing hats."

Vic started nodding his head as he looked at Boone's photos and said, "Okay, little guys, maybe three feet tall. They're on the right, and behind us."

"Well, three feet tall isn't too bad," Dennis replied as he sat down.

"I imagine someone throwing a medicine ball made out of razors at me," Boone told him. "Not a fan."

"Do you think they're the same ones from before?" Cam asked. "The ones that ran away from the bridge?"

Vic looked at the photos again and replied, "I think they might be. They didn't get to pick through the scraps of the bigger ones, so now they might be thinking about taking down one of us on their own. I'm going to see what they think about something other than rocks being thrown at them."

He brought his experimental rifle up and said, "If those 'saurs are still in the same place, this will be an unpleasant surprise. Everyone get ready; I'll say hi to the ones behind us first, and I don't know if they will charge or run again." As he pulled the trigger there was a quiet *phht*, and a second later a small tree exploded. An animal stumbled from the brush and fell to the ground as running sounds could be heard. Vic fired a second round at the group to their side, and though they did not see any bodies, they heard at least one animal cry out and saw shadows streaking back toward the bridge area.

Ricky put his hand on Vic's shoulder and said, "That was awesome. I can't be-"

He was cut off by Boone who asked, "What is that?"

Out of the trees behind them an animal stood watching them intently. It was about four feet tall and twenty feet long. There were sharp claws on the two feet it stood on, including one that arched up higher than the others. Its scaly skin was mostly black and green, but it had a yellow and orange head. As Vic brought up his rifle it turned and disappeared slowly back into the brush. It disappeared into the darkness along with two other silhouettes.

"It was afraid of us," Ricky said.

"Was it?" Boone asked. "I got the feeling it knew what Vic was about to do, so it moved out of sight."

"So, you're saying it's still watching us?"

"Just a feeling."

Kaly told everyone, "We all have the five senses: sight, touch, hearing, smell, and taste. But we have another one that we don't think about. That inner voice that tells us when we are in danger.

When you *just feel* something is wrong. Boone has a feeling. I think we should pay attention."

"We think alike," Vic said. "That '*saur* wasn't just looking at us, it was sizing us up. I think it liked what it saw."

"Then let's get moving," Cam said. "Stay sharp. Let's go."

There was an urgency to Cam's voice that got everyone moving quickly. The ground was fairly clear which meant the hot sun shone directly on them. The long sloping hill slowed them down, and they had to stop for a few moments at the top of it. When they did, Sheila pointed down to their left and said, "Now that's what I've always imagined."

Below them was a smaller lake than the first one. Around it there were no dead and dying animals being attacked by multiple carnivores. Instead, a herd of duckbills intermingled peacefully with some *Triceratops* and other animals that walked on all fours. The young of all darted around with playful honks and grunts on the land and in the water.

"I haven't really had time to think about things since we were so rudely awakened this morning. But this…this is like a postcard from some dinosaur vacation spot. I know *T-rex* and every other carnivore will eventually show up, but right now it's the nicest thing we've seen so far."

"I see something nicer," Win said with a smile as he pointed. "Look."

They followed his gaze, and Cam asked, "What is that? A dome? Is that the station?"

"It is," Win replied excitedly. "Less than a half mile. We're almost there."

Ricky started, "Let's get -" But Dennis sat down hard beside him and fell onto his back. "Sir, sir," Ricky shouted as he sat Dennis up.

He was extremely pale and gasping for breath as he struggled to get out, "S-S-Sorry. I'm going to need a minute."

"You're going to need more than that," Kaly told him as she took off his helmet and emptied a water bottle on him. She nodded off to their right and added, "Let's get him into the shade of those trees." They quickly moved Dennis, and everyone took turns slowly pouring water on his head.

"We need more water," Kaly said. "His color is coming back, but we need to cool him down some more."

"I don't think there is any more," Boone said.

"There is down there," Sheila said with a nod toward the lake. "Put the caps back on the bottles, and I'll go fill them up."

It was silent for several seconds, and Boone said, "No. I'll go get the water." As Kaly started to protest, he continued, "All of you need to stay here and protect Dennis and Win. All of you have been trained to shoot in case we are attacked." He smiled and continued, "Through my years of working construction, I've been trained to go get things."

He nodded toward the lake and continued, "One person, walking slowly down to the water is not going to excite those animals. They've never seen a human, so I probably won't set off any alarms. They're just having a picnic by the lake. Besides, I'm smaller than they are, and they're all herbivores, right? Piece of cake."

As he stood up, Kaly stood up with him and grabbed his arm and said, "Keep your gun ready and don't let anything get close to you."

He put a hand on her shoulder and said, "I'll be right back."

As he started toward the lake, Vic commanded, "I want one gun watching his left, another the right, and everyone else turn around and watch out for those three that are behind us. I'm like Boone; I can feel them watching us."

Boone took his time and watched where he was stepping; he didn't want to trip or slide and draw attention to himself. He found that he was actually calm; he didn't want to harm any of the animals, and they seemed to be ignoring him. A few of the animals looked up at him then simply went back to feeding or drinking from the lake.

There were several animals though that interested Boone. They weren't very big, two feet long from head to tail, and looked like every other dinosaur that stood on two feet. But their front claws were longer and more curved. And, they acted like prairie dogs. They ran in and out of holes in the ground. Some were obviously lookouts, and others were digging new tunnels. A niche to be filled by mammals, Boone thought to himself.

As he dropped down beside the water, he suddenly thought about crocodiles, a nature special or something that he had seen. But again, when he looked up, none of the other animals seemed troubled by anything in or around the lake. The water was light brown and had some type of algae in it, but at least it was wet. Dennis wasn't going to drink it; they were just going to pour it on him.

As he started filling the bottles, he was startled by a head that poked above the water. Then he laughed; it was only a turtle. As it crawled onto land though he was surprised to see the sharp spikes sticking up from its shell. It was made to live side by side with dinosaurs.

He finished filling the last water bottle and was stuffing it, and the other bottles, in various pockets when he heard a honking sound across the lake. A whole herd of duckbills walked out of the trees and headed for the water. He had seen pictures of the animals with various crescents on their heads, but never like these. They started just above the animal's nose and swept back, so they almost looked like antlers.

Another herd of *Triceratops* walked out of the trees and filled in the space between Boone and the hill. He turned around and glanced up and wondered for a few moments what Kaly was thinking. He had just decided how he was going to walk around the herd when two of the animals walked toward him and then split up so they were on either side of him. Boone could vaguely remember how large the *Triceratops* was that he and Kaly had run past. But standing next to them was something completely different.

They were huge. No, they were gigantic. The top of his head was about even with the animal's eyes, but the top of their long arched backs towered at least another four feet above him. They were thirty feet long and their barrel-shaped bodies made it seem as if they were right on top of him. It felt like he was standing in an alley between two buildings. They paid no attention to him as they began drinking water.

As Boone instinctively swatted at a bug that had landed on him the animal on his right swung his head toward him as if it just realized he was there. Boone felt like he could reach out and touch the long horns and knew if the animal started moving there would be no place for him to run. But, after a few seconds, the *Triceratops* turned away and began drinking again.

Boone felt he had stayed long enough and slowly began walking away. He knew he shouldn't do it, but he slowly reached out and ran a hand along the flanks of both of the animals. Their muscles shivered like they were keeping an insect away, but neither of the animals paid him any attention. He kept moving and though a few of the others looked up, and one moved a few feet away from him, everything remained calm.

He was almost ready to start breathing again when a very young *Triceratops* almost ran into him as it scampered about. As several of the adults turned their heads toward him, he froze until the juvenile ran off. When the heads dropped again, he continued slowly up the hill and didn't stop until Kaly hugged him.

"Why did you pet those animals?" she asked. "They could have killed you."

Boone smiled as he replied, "It was just a spur of the moment thing. I felt like I had to."

He handed the water bottles to Sheila who asked, "What was it like? I want to go down there."

"It was amazing," Boone told her. "Exhilarating, scary, exciting, unbelievable. You should go."

"Not yet," Dennis said. "I think I heard you say the station was close?"

"Yes, it's close," Win replied.

"There are fewer spots in my eyes now, and I'm feeling better," Dennis told everyone. "Let's get to the station, and you can visit any dinosaur you want to after that. But, I have to get someplace to rest."

"I'm sorry, Dennis," Sheila told him. "I got carried away. Yeah, it's time to get inside someplace cooler."

"I couldn't agree more," Vic said. "We need to get Dennis and Cam there as soon as we can. Let's help each other and get this done. One last push."

"One last push," everyone repeated, and they started toward the dome they could easily see shining above the treetops. The sight of it gave them renewed energy, and they moved quicker than they had all day, until Vic stopped and took a knee. They thought the heat might have affected him also until he turned around and told them, "They're back."

Ricky looked around and asked, "The little ones or…?"

Sheila was shading her eyes and said, "No, it's the bigger ones. And, this is wild dog pack size."

"What do you mean?" Boone asked.

"Ten, maybe a dozen adults, and five to ten smaller ones who are being taught how to hunt."

"What's the plan?" Cam asked.

Vic smiled and replied, "The one that sounds bad from the start, and you know can't work, but you figure it's the best you're going to come up with."

"Sounds great so far," Sheila said.

"They're all on the south side of us," Vic pointed out. "If they're like dogs they probably are going to burst out here in a minute and figure we'll run for our lives. They catch up to all of us one by one and take us down, just like they do with larger prey. But, we won't be running, so hopefully that surprises them.

"I'm going to guess their approach and lay down the seven mines we have left in front of us. Then we're going to try and make all of them come out at once. I'm going to snipe as many of them as I can while they think they're hiding in the trees. At the same time, Boone and Sheila you're going to fire RPGs into each side of where we think they're hiding.

"Hopefully, that starts them running away, but I don't think so with these guys. They will come for us. So, Cam sets off the mines when they get to them and hopefully it takes out the majority of them.

"As they break past the mines we fire our rifles on full auto. Make sure to aim low. If you are going to miss you want to miss low where it's possible a round will still hit a leg, or ricochet and then hit one of them. A high miss just sails past them and into the trees without doing any damage.

"The few, we hope, that make it to us, we'll have to handle with the handgun special ammo. That means exploding 'saur parts. Everyone needs to know we're going to get bloody. We're all going to need stitched up after this. Accept it, get your mind right and then do the best you can. Start taking deep breaths, think about where your rifle will be pointing, picture them falling, and be ready for pain and close quarter combat with your worst nightmare."

Sheila explained to Boone how to load and use the RPG and made sure that everyone knew not to stand behind them when they were fired. "As soon as you fire it," Sheila told Boone, "drop it and get ready with your rifle." They then walked to the outside of the group and stood by.

"One last suggestion," Cam said. "Let's take a few seconds to move our packs to the front. If they get through they may come in feet first. The packs will give us some protection, until they start biting us." Everyone quickly moved their packs and then waited.

Vic nodded, and as he started forward, Dennis and Cam braced themselves against some trees. They knew they had to help. Boone and Kaly stood next to each other, and as he looked at her, she winked just as she had earlier. Sheila took Ricky's hand for a moment, and he said, "We're all going to make it."

Win said nothing but thought about how he had always hoped to save his brother. Now he knew that couldn't be done, no…shouldn't be done. They were all here, facing a terrible death all because of him. There was only one way to stop August's mad plans. He thought about all of the times he could have done it before but didn't out of some misguided hope things would end differently. He wondered if he would be alive to see August stopped.

Then Vic was back, saying, "Don't move your rifle in a wide movement from one side to the other. Just spray the area right in front of you from side to side. Change magazines if you get a chance, but when you're empty, or they're too close, work your pistol." He paused, then said quietly, "Good luck."

At that moment, one of the animals stepped out into the open and chirped loudly. It was the last sound it ever made. Vic nodded at Boone and Sheila who fired their RPGs and transitioned to their rifles. Vic fired the remaining bolts into the forest as fast as he could, threw down the weapon and unslung his rifle.

Through the dust of the explosions, and past falling animals, they were coming.

In less than a second Cam set off the mines. Boone was surprised the explosions weren't very loud. Then he remembered that during stressful situations a person might develop auditory exclusion. Then the thought was gone.

Wounded and unwounded animals broke through the flying debris and dust at a dead run.

Animals fell everywhere in front of them, collapsing in writhing heaps or sliding limply forward as they died. There was a brief moment of no gunshots as it seemed everyone dropped their rifles at the same time and started drawing their handguns. But, it was too late. Three of the animals crashed into the group as two others, badly wounded, struggled forward.

Boone and Kaly rushed toward Cam and shot an animal that had just taken him down. There were two muffled explosions and they both fell in a splash of crimson.

As Sheila started toward Dennis, she was knocked down by an animal's tail, and it spun quickly and landed on her legs. A second later, Sheila fired her gun as she lay on the ground and Ricky stuck his arm toward the animal's head and also fired. The explosion knocked Ricky backward as the dinosaur's body collapsed onto Sheila.

There were still two badly wounded animals coming for them when Dennis stepped forward with a rifle and shot them until they fell. Then he collapsed to one knee and took in a long breath as it grew quiet. Then he asked, "Is anyone still alive?"

Instead of an answering voice, there was a rumble of thunder and a light rain began falling. There was a groan close by and Dennis found Kaly. None of the blood on her, and there was a lot, seemed to be hers. But, she did have a large bump on her forehead and said, "My back is killing me." Then she immediately asked, "Where's Boone?"

"Right here," he said as he sat up. "Now I remember why I didn't play college football."

"Are you injured?" she asked worriedly.

"I'll get back to you about that as soon as I can feel my body again. What about you?"

"My head and back hurt, and then I'm like you. When we start to move we'll know more." She paused, then asked, "Dennis, how are you?"

"Nothing even got to me," he told her. "I shot until I ran out of ammo and thought with my shoulder out, I was done for. Then I remembered the ammo I had from my broken gun. I reloaded in time to shoot some animals off Vic, Sheila, and Ricky. Hope I wasn't too late."

"Check on them while I look at Cam," Kaly said.

A second later, Dennis called out, "Vic's here, and he's bad. Looks like a bite on his shoulder, and he's bleeding from his right side."

"Fortunately, I'm still alive," Vic said. "At least I think I am. Check on Cam, Sheila, and Ricky."

"Cam's out, and he looks like he has a bite on the shoulder too. His ankle is now a compound fracture and his chest is bleeding again," Kaly said.

Sheila was sitting up and as Dennis approached she told him, "My legs got sliced and diced good. I may not be able to walk anymore today." She paused then called out, "Ricky, how are you doing?" When Ricky didn't answer she tried to turn around but couldn't and called out, "Ricky...Ricky, talk to me."

He suddenly sat down beside her and she asked, "Are you okay? When you didn't answer, I..." She trailed off as she looked down at his right arm and saw his hand was missing. "Oh, no -" she started, but Ricky cut her off.

"It's okay. We're still alive. We're all still alive." Sheila hugged him but didn't say anything.

Suddenly, Boone asked, "Where's Win?" A movement by one of the animals out in the open area startled all of them, but they relaxed as they realized it was Win. "How did you get out there?" Boone asked.

As Win stood up they saw his prosthetic arm had been torn to shreds, and he said, "I was lucky. It grabbed me by my fake arm and started dragging me away. I almost dropped my gun but was able to shoot its foot off and then its head. Other than losing *another* ten years off my life due to a dinosaur biting my left arm, I think I'm okay."

"Alright," Vic said. "First, before anything else shows up, do we have any ammo left?"

"I have a magazine left," Dennis said. "Part of what you had me save from my broken gun."

"You should have seen President Powell shooting those last dinosaurs," Ricky said with admiration. "Thank you, sir."

"You're welcome," Dennis replied embarrassedly.

"Dennis, you're on rifle," Vic said. "That leaves us with our regular grenades and the smoke grenades. Not much to defend ourselves with, but hopefully we won't need to."

He paused then continued, "So, now, injuries. Win, other than that arm, you're ok?"

"Yes."

"Dennis, the dislocated shoulder only?"

"That's right.

"Kaly, bumps and bruises only?"

"Yes."

"Boone?"

"Blood on my back, from my previous injury, I think. A few minor scrapes on my face."

"Ricky, I am sorry you lost your hand."

"I'm alive; that's what matters at this moment. We're all alive."

"Okay. Let's get the bleeding stopped on Sheila's legs, my shoulder and body, and take care of Cam."

Ricky spoke up, "I have a suggestion."

"Throw it out there," Vic said. "Your ideas have all been good so far."

"Let's run some sticks or limbs through our pack straps and make sleds to carry Sheila, Cam, and you. The rest of us can pull you to the station. It's not that far now."

Vic nodded as he said, "You know, I'd like to say I can walk it, but I can't. But first, get your wrist wrapped tight, so it doesn't start bleeding. Use what's left in the first aid kits, your shirts, whatever. Tie us up tight, and then let's get going. This day is getting close to ending, and I want to be inside when it does."

They got ready as quickly as they could, and it helped when Cam woke up enough to climb onto his sled. "I guess we won," was all he said before becoming unconscious again.

Kaly and Ricky pulled Sheila, Dennis pulled Vic, and Boone had Cam. As Boone looked over at the fallen dinosaurs, he said, "I want to personally thank whoever it was that added the mines and RPGs. Without them, we wouldn't have made it."

"And I want to thank Dennis," Win added. "I didn't think I needed any help. I would have been here with only Otai for help. Without Vic, Sheila, and Cam, and all of the equipment that came with them, I would have eventually left the cave, alone." He paused for a second then continued, "And now, the three of you are injured, badly. And, you too, Ricky. I'll find a way to make it up to all of you. TIM will see to it."

Through a break in the trees they could see the station dome was now just a few hundred yards away. They began walking faster; their ordeal was almost over. But, they all stopped as a *T-rex* stepped out of the forest from their right, fifty yards in front of them. Dennis raised his rifle, but it didn't stop. It continued across the opening in front of them and disappeared on their left.

"This is unbelievable," Dennis said. "How can we keep running into things that want to eat us?"

"It doesn't make sense," Sheila agreed in a low voice. "Too many carnivores. Plus, our luck just can't be this bad."

"What do we do?" Kaly asked. "Stay still? Hide in the trees until we think it's gone?"

"I'm going up to take a look," Boone volunteered. "If it is far enough away, we can go past it as fast as we can. Surely there's nothing…"

Boone trailed off as a second *Rex* walked out from the same area as the first one. It started to cross in front but stopped and stared at them. Dennis raised the rifle again, but it just snorted and raised its nose higher. It sniffed loudly, then it just kept going and disappeared.

Cam was awake, and he asked, "Why are we just standing here?"

"Because we don't understand what just happened," Win told him.

"Well, the last I remember I was being chewed on by one 'saur and then I just now woke up lying on my back looking up at a different one. A lot bigger, different one. So, I'll ask again, why are we just standing here?"

Kaly looked at Boone and said, "Go and take a look. This can't be a *Rex* parade. Make sure they're gone, and we'll head straight for the station. If not, we'll go around."

Boone started forward, and Dennis handed him the rifle as he passed. Boone nodded and then started sprinting toward the area where the two animals had crossed. He laughed at himself; before they saw the first *Rex,* he was sore and tired from dragging the sled. Now he was full of energy. He thought about the attack on the president and Kaly, and wondered when the surprise animal was going to appear. And, then it did; a third *Rex* following the others.

Boone slid to a stop which drew the attention of the *Rex.* It pivoted toward him and unlike the other two took a giant step toward him. He could sense the rumbling sliding up and down his spine and had to focus to stop himself from running away. He started up with the rifle then reached into his pack instead. He decided to throw his two smoke grenades to see if they would confuse the *Rex* and chase the animal away. As they exploded and the smoke swirled around the animal's feet it rumbled even louder and stepped through the smoke. It didn't look confused.

Suddenly six small lights appeared around its head and began circling as it snapped at them. As the lights closed in around the *Rex,* its rumble changed and then it turned and followed the other *Rexes.* The lights stayed behind the animal and followed it out of sight.

Boone turned toward Kaly and the others and lifted up his hands and shook his head. As he walked back toward them, he asked, "What was that?" But they weren't paying any attention to him as they stared over his shoulder. He turned around, afraid another *Rex* had appeared, but instead it was a white vehicle speeding toward them. Boone turned back and said, "Okay, new question. What is this?"

The vehicle, which looked like a long, white, plastic, windowless tube, stopped in front of them, and three people got out. One was very irate as she asked, "What are you doing here?" Then she stopped as she saw Sheila, Cam and Vic on the sleds and said, "Okay, we'll figure that out later. Can you get them inside the carry all? How badly are you hurt?"

Boone quickly described their injuries as everyone got into the vehicle. As he stepped inside, the door slid silently closed behind him, and he felt cool air envelop him. Instead of turning around, the vehicle started moving backward the same way that it appeared. The woman who had spoken to them was speaking to a monitor in front of her, "There are multiple injuries from superficial to possibly critical. Have the Med Unit meet us at dock 3 to take over."

A few seconds later, the door slid open without a sound, and four members of the Med Unit came in to quickly examine them. They were wearing dark blue uniforms and after a few seconds Ricky was instructed to sit beside Vic, Cam, and Sheila. Then the entire section they were on gently lifted out of the vehicle, and one of the Med Team guided it through some doors at the end of a hallway.

Another Med Team member instructed Kaly, Boone, Win, and Dennis to follow him. The woman who had been irate followed, noting, "All of you are injured also, but not as badly as the others."

"Will they be okay?" Kaly asked.

"Yes, they will. But, though we'll talk later, I have to ask, why are you here, Mr. Adams?"

Win stopped and pointed at Dennis as he told her, "This is a 21st century United States president, Dennis Powell." He placed his hand on Kaly's shoulder and said, "This is Secret Service Agent Kaly Winters," and with a nod continued, "and this is Boone Christopher. The others are members of military special forces unique to their time period. We are here because time has been broken in the 21st century on an unprecedented scale. We're trying to stop the damage."

The woman started to speak and then stopped. Then she nodded and advised Win, "Sir, I'll do whatever I can to help."

"Thank you," Win said.

The Med Team member led them to a room with four beds and many pieces of equipment they did not recognize. "My name is Trace," he said, "and I must apologize. There are only five Meds here, and the ones with the highest levels are examining your friends since they need a more focused medical assistance approach."

"No need to apologize," Kaly told him. "If you need to leave, go ahead. We're just in a little pain; our friends are in bad shape."

"True, but they arrived in time for us to take care of them. As for the four of you…extreme fatigue, dehydration, epidermal solar damage, mild functional neurological disorder, abrasions, there's a slight concussion, a few vertebrae out of alignment, a few broken ribs, a dislocated shoulder, and one destroyed, uh…experimental arm. Sorry, Mr. Adams, our replacement will not be as good.

"Now, Superintendent Gating has authorized me to use the same medical procedures on all of you that will be used on Mr. Adams. That means you will heal quicker than in your time, but not instantly. In a couple of hours you will be amazed that you feel better, and ask how we did it. Sorry, I can't tell you. So, sit back and relax."

Boone fell asleep as he watched Trace, and when he woke up, there were eight beds in the room. Two of the beds still had equipment next to them, and Vic, Ricky, Sheila, and Cam were heavily bandaged, but everyone was sitting up. As he sat up, Kaly got up and walked over and sat on his bed. "Better?" she asked.

"Yes," Boone answered. "Whatever they do here that we can't ask about, even took care of the pain from our first dinosaur fight."

Kaly smiled and said, "I feel great too. In fact, we all feel better than before."

Superintendent Gating walked in at that moment and said, "And that's something I need to speak with all of you about. Getting straight to the point, if any of you go back to your timeframe and discuss how your splintered legs, shredded arteries and veins, various punctured internal organs, or a missing hand, were completely healed, the timeline will be broken again."

"How so?" Dennis asked.

"Since time travel is now known to you, everyone would be demanding that doctors from the future heal those in the past. What Win has explained to me in detail is horrible enough. It can't be allowed to go even further. So, please downplay your injuries in all of the books you'll write. Just tell everyone how you escaped all of the dinosaurs."

"That brings up a point," Sheila said. "Why did we run into so many dinosaurs, especially the three big boys at the end?"

"The feed boxes," the superintendent replied. As everyone stared at her, she advised, "This is Science Station 7. We study the habits of dinosaurs. The feed boxes draw in all types of dinosaurs that we then tag and track so we know what dinosaurs do, instead of just guessing. You were near the meat boxes."

"Lucky us," Boone said.

"If we go out again, where are the fruit boxes?" Sheila laughed.

"Go out again? You don't know how lucky you are that you got here when you did," Superintendent Gating said.

"We know it was bad for us," Win said. "Sheila had lost a lot of blood, and even had she survived, would have suffered irreversible tissue and nerve damage. Vic would never have recovered from his open wounds and the damage to his liver and kidneys. And Cam, from what you told me, his body now has more fabricated pieces than a puzzle.

"Boone and Kaly could run marathons now, and Dennis had no idea he had a hereditary disease hidden away in his DNA. Ricky will be getting a new hand and me, I feel like I..." he trailed off then said, "I can tell by the way you're looking at me I'm missing something. What is it?"

"If you walk around Station 7 you will see how empty it is. We were supposed to have a full complement of visiting scientists here all month. But we've been unable to contact anyone or time travel for five weeks. Now we know why the most important event in human history will be watched by only a handful of people.

"But, more to the point, tomorrow isn't going to wait on anyone."

"I'm still in the dark, Superintendent. Why can't we go outside tomorrow?" Boone asked.

She folded her hands together and replied, "Because tomorrow morning, an asteroid is going to crash into the Yucatán Peninsula, ending the age of dinosaurs, allowing humans to evolve."

THE END OF THE WORLD

"What?" Sheila asked. "Tomorrow is *the* day?"

"Yes, I'm afraid it is," Superintendent Gating replied. "Why does that upset you so much?"

"I...I, it's stupid I know, but I wanted to see more animals. I wanted to go back to the paradise spot again and touch a *Triceratops* like Boone did." She closed her eyes for a few seconds then continued, "I wanted something peaceful, to forget a lot of things. It looked like...like -"

"Like home," Vic said softly. When Sheila looked at him, he smiled and said, "You've told us a hundred times about the pond behind your house when you were a little girl. The animals that visited it and how you would sit near the pond, and they were all around you. We all have that place, Sheila."

"But I'm supposed to be -"

"Human," Kaly filled in. "You're human and you have feelings. You're not a machine. Think of what has happened to our world and then what has happened in this one. The abnormal seems to be the normal now, but it isn't. And you, all of us actually, know that. We'll each have to deal with it in our own way, and I'm sure we'll all get it figured out. It will just take some time."

"Which you now have, Sheila," Superintendent Gating said. "We've repaired the damage to your legs, but you still have to heal. All of you have healing, physically and mentally. For some of you, it may not start immediately; there are still some things that need to be repaired. But, we will help all of you with the next part of your healing process whenever that time comes."

"Thank you," everyone told her, and she smiled and left the room.

As everyone drifted back toward their beds, Sheila smiled at Ricky, and as he stopped beside her, she said, "You haven't said anything."

"I didn't know if I should," he started. "I mean, you're close to Vic and Cam, and I'm just a guy you met...literally, yesterday, I guess. We don't really know each other. You're confident and take charge, and I'm just some bonehead who tries to say funny things. Stupid things, really. I mean, I'm here for you if you need me, but I don't want to get in the way of your healing."

Sheila shook her head as she took his hand and said, "I don't mean say something nice about *me*. What are *you* feeling? I want you to start healing too. I want you to know I'm here if you need anything. You're smart. Think of all the great ideas you had. You saved my life and lost your hand, but you haven't complained once. You're just glad we all made it. I think…I think we should help each other heal. I do need you." She paused and then continued, "And, I hope you need me." Ricky smiled and took her hand in his. Then he pulled a chair up next to her bed, and they began talking.

Kaly and Boone were sitting on the edge of her bed as Win and Dennis stopped to talk. "I feel so bad for everyone," Dennis told them. "I know people get hurt on missions, but I've never been part of one…or sent anyone after dinosaurs. Everyone could have been killed today. Vic, Cam, Sheila, and Ricky could easily be dead right now. How can we get back, and what are we going to do?"

"I've been thinking about that," Win said. "August will think there is no one that can stop him now. That will help us, I'm sure."

"But how?" Kaly asked. "We're stuck here. Apparently this world is getting ready to be destroyed, and if I remember correctly, nothing grows here for a long time. What kind of food supplies do they have here? When this world ends, how long will we survive? Right now, none of us can stop your brother for 66 million years."

"You're right," Win agreed. "But that is right now. We don't know what the future holds, and I'm planning on taking advantage of anything that happens that will help us get back to your time period. I think there is a way, I just don't know yet if it will be there."

"But you're hopeful?" Boone asked. As Win nodded his head, Boone smiled and added, "Then, I am too."

The door to their room opened and Trace walked in. As he checked each of them he said, "I'm glad everyone is feeling better, but it is getting late and you need more rest. Oh, and if you are interested in watching everything tomorrow, I was told there is plenty of room for you in the dome. We were supposed to have about two hundred scientists and students here for the event, but there has been a problem with traveling. Only a dozen or so came in early enough to avoid being left out."

"Will all of us be able to go to the dome?" Cam asked.

"Yes," Trace answered. "Each of you will be able to move better tomorrow, and if there are any problems, we can easily move your beds. Get some sleep, and I'll see you in the morning."

As he walked out, the lights started dimming in the room and everyone said 'goodnight'. As Boone and Kaly hugged, Boone said, "We're one day closer."

"You think Win can figure something out?" Kaly asked.

Boone smiled and replied, "I think he already has."

The next morning the lights came on as Trace walked into the room. Boone woke up and smiled as he saw Ricky still sitting next to Sheila with his head resting on her bed. She was asleep, and her hand was on his head.

Vic stirred, and as he stretched, he said, "There's hardly any pain now when I move. Trace, you're a medical magician."

"It wasn't me," Trace replied. "I'm just a junior surgeon. The senior surgeons worked on you, Cam, Sheila, and Ricky. Mostly routine, but there were a few interesting things they had to deal with."

"Well, I feel great," Cam joined in. "I feel like I could get up and walk around."

"You can," Trace advised.

"What about me?" Sheila asked as she rubbed Ricky's hair to wake him up.

"You can get up too," Trace told her. "You will be walking slower, your legs will feel heavy and like they aren't in sync, but you can get up. You'll get tired quickly, and you'll need to rest frequently, but we'll take care of you."

"You'll take care of me, too?" Sheila asked Ricky as he woke up and saw everyone was looking at him.

He smiled and turned red as he realized he'd been asked a question but didn't know what it was. When he said, "Yes?" he turned even redder as everyone laughed.

Superintendent Gating walked into the room and smiled as she said, "Well, I wasn't sure how everyone would be this morning, but I'm guessing you're all doing fine?"

Everyone looked at Ricky then laughed again as he said, "Yes?"

"We're doing great," Vic told her. "But, I could use something to eat."

"Breakfast is on the way," Superintendent Gating assured him. "Then, whoever is interested can come to the dome and listen to my lecture as one era ends and another begins. You can wear your patient clothing. Everyone else has been told you were the last to come through before travel stopped, and there was a problem. Besides, everyone else is here for either scientific or academic purposes. They aren't really concerned with everybody else."

She smiled as she continued, "My talk may be boring, but I assure you that what you will see will not be. I'm sure all of you have an idea of what happened, but seeing it will be the most extraordinary event you will ever witness. And that includes everything that has happened to you so far. Is everyone going?"

They all replied they would be, and as breakfast was brought in, Superintendent Gating and Trace left. As they ate, Win moved closer to Kaly and Boone and said quietly, "In a little while you will see someone you recognize. Don't act surprised, or do anything that will make him suspicious."

"Who is it?" Kaly asked.

"The driver of the truck that pulled the trailer damaged by the *Triceratops*. He was not in the cave when August caught us, and remember, no one knows that we were there and saw them."

Boone smiled as he said, "He's our way back, isn't he?"

Win nodded and replied, "He's part of the plan. A couple of things have to happen first, but I think they will. Then, we'll have to move fast."

Thirty minutes later they were all in the dome. No one said anything as they gazed around at the unbelievable structure. The base of the dome was 200 feet wide, and it arced another 200 feet high above them. It was made of some type of clear material that allowed them to see 360 degrees around Science Station 7 and up at the few scattered clouds in the bright blue sky.

They felt tiny as they sat in a small section of about two hundred seats. About forty other people were scattered about so any noise echoed across the floor. "I'm a little disappointed," Boone told Kaly.

She looked around for a moment and said, "I know. Just one more thing August caused a problem for."

"No, not that. Look at their clothes."

"What about them? They look okay."

Boone shook his head as he replied, "But, they look like clothes we would be wearing if we went to a movie. I expected something different from the future. Holographic clothing, long flowing robes, or everyone just walking around naked."

Kaly shook her head and laughed, "We definitely have different thoughts about the future."

"What are yours?"

"Underwear models." As Boone raised his eyebrows, she continued, "All guys will look like underwear models."

"What will the women look like?" Boone asked.

"They'll look like whatever they want to."

"I better start working out," Boone said.

Then they both laughed as Kaly took his arm and said, "Boone, you'll do…for now."

As they continued talking, Boone heard footsteps and saw the man who had driven the *Triceratops* truck walking toward them. He was watching them closely as he approached and smiled to himself when they didn't appear to know him. Boone looked back at Kaly, and as they looked at some animals flying above the dome, the man stopped by Win and said, "Mr. Adams, what a great pleasure to meet one of the founding members of TIM. I'm Dr. Chapel."

"I'm pleased to meet you, Dr. Chapel, and please call me Win. I'm glad a few scientists made it here before travel stopped. Have you had an interesting few days getting ready for the big event?"

"I have, but it looks like you may have had much more of an adventure."

"More of a misadventure," Win replied. "My colleagues and I left the TIM transport site a couple of days ago just before everything stopped. It must have shut down as we traveled because our transport vehicle was affected. We went right into some trees a few hundred yards from here. The four of us on the left side were hardly injured but unfortunately, well you can see. Nothing that can't be mended by the excellent Med Staff here though, and we're all still anxious to see everything."

"Well, I'll let you be then, and again, nice to meet you."

"We're all in a Med Room," Win told him. "After the presentation, please come and see us."

Dr. Chapel smiled and said as he walked away, "I'll do that."

Boone and Kaly made a point of not looking at Dr. Chapel as he left, and Kaly said, "Look at all the animals." Around the dome, in a large open space between the building and the surrounding forest, were herds of duckbills, *Triceratops*, and several other animals she didn't recognize. Over 100 dinosaurs grazed contendently on various shrubs and ferns, and Kaly wondered if they had been planted there so the animals could be studied. On one of the screens were several *Rexes*, and she told Boone, "They must be at that feeding pit."

Superintendent Gating stepped behind a podium in front of the seats and started, "Welcome, distinguished guests. In just a short while you will watch as the Cretaceous Period ends in a cataclysmic event. Dinosaurs, which have ruled the world for approximately 165 million years, will disappear not only in the blink of the evolutionary eye, but, as you'll see, actually in just minutes."

A dark square with a glowing circle in the center appeared in the dome above them, and the superintendent explained, "We all know what is about to happen; the asteroid. *The asteroid.* We have had satellites in place for several months now monitoring it, and you are watching an enhanced video of the last few weeks condensed into a few seconds."

As the glowing circle got larger and brighter other screens began to appear. "As you can see, we have many video units recording as much of this event as possible. We have a satellite directly above us that will monitor exactly what happens here, in

North Dakota. There is another unit above the Yucatán Peninsula which will record the asteroid strike and everything associated with that area. Other units are above other Science Units in Western Europe, the Mediterranean, and Africa.

"There are recording units at ground level in strategic parts of Mexico, the southern United States, Yucatán, and of course, here. They will not survive what is about to happen, but we hope they will provide us with valuable video of the seconds and minutes after the impact."

As all the screens disappeared except for the glowing circle, Superintendent Gating continued, "It is not quite seven miles wide, and weighs approximately 2 trillion metric tons. As it begins to experience atmospheric friction, it will burn at 20,000 degrees celsius and create a 1,000 mile per hour blast wave. We will instantly see the flash of the burn here in North Dakota. If you were outside, and looking to the southeast, the brightness would cause you to turn away. It is hypothesized by some that the shadows of the dinosaurs who were within 500 miles of the flash were burned into the ground, just like at the sites of the 20th century atomic bomb sites.

"We will obtain accurate event statistics, but until then I can provide you with what has been theorized will happen. The asteroid will take just four minutes to cross the Atlantic Ocean as it approaches from the northeast, at a 60 degree angle trajectory, toward the Yucatán Peninsula. It will then punch through 60 miles of atmosphere in three to five seconds as it increases velocity from 27,000 to 45,000 miles per hour.

"When it slams into Earth it will generate a force of 100 trillion metric tons or, one septillion, three hundred sextillion kilojoules of energy. The impact will ripple through Earth as seismic waves that some believe reached a magnitude of 13. That means it would have felt like a magnitude 9 earthquake on the opposite side of the planet. Here, in North Dakota, it may still generate a 10 or 11 magnitude quake. Many people who have studied this event believe Earth rang like a bell.

"Yucatán will be destroyed, and the asteroid will disintegrate in a giant ball of fire as it liquefies the Earth and drives eighteen miles into the planet, almost to the Earth's mantle. This will create a ninety mile wide crater as it throws out 25 trillion metric tons of debris. Additionally, it will create another overpowering flash of light as well as a second blast wave.

"Most of the debris will be turned into ash and dust particles which will circle Earth, blocking the sun for years. In fact, some of the debris will reach exit velocity for our atmosphere and actually travel to the moon and beyond.

"Another event we will witness will be a seiche wave. These waves occur when seismic waves create a rocking motion in lakes and rivers until their waters burst out of their banks in waves up to thirty feet high.

"Aside from the seismic activity, because of the asteroid's high trajectory, the molten material from the crater will be thrown out at over 99,000 miles an hour. Some of it will escape our planet's gravity and end up on the moon, and possibly beyond. The high trajectory of the asteroid will also allow burning rock to be spread around the world easily. This debris is hotter than the sun, and we will witness its effects here, in North Dakota. This molten rock will result in wide-spread forest fires within 1,500 miles of the strike, and eventually, seventy percent of Earth's forests will burn.

"As the asteroid impact creates the crater, a tsunami will form moving away from it, then another tsunami will form as water floods back into the crater, filling it with debris and water. Giant tsunamis, 150 feet high, will crash into Mexico and South America and lower wave heights will batter the southern United States. Tsunamis will also reach the coasts of Europe and Africa, and sweep through the Mediterranean Sea.

"But, it doesn't end there. The debris that didn't quite make it into space, from pea-size to as big as an SUV, starts falling as red hot rock and glass pellets. Tektites. They heat the atmosphere like an oven to over 300 degrees as they fall at 100 to 200 miles an hour. The tektites will riddle dinosaurs like they are being shot by a cosmic machine gun.

"Don't worry, I'm almost finished. The two blast waves arrive a few minutes apart and are so loud that any animals still alive will have their eardrums ruptured. The winds they create sweep across America from east to west with hurricane force, then suddenly change direction producing tornadoes.

"And finally, within an hour, the oil deposits that burned in the initial impact explosion and shot into the sky condense and begin to coat the upper atmosphere above the cloud layer with a black soot. It reduces sunlight by ninety percent worldwide, resulting in a two to three year global freeze."

Superintendent Gating stepped from behind the podium and put her hands together. She paused, then said, "Distinguished guests, this dome was built for you, for this momentous occasion. Rest assured, it will protect you from the flashes of light, the sound and fury of the blast waves, the unknown magnitude quakes, the seiche waves, and the tektites."

She smiled as she continued, "But, the creators of this beautiful dome thought it would make the experience more interesting if you could at least feel some of the seismic vibrations, see some of the flashes, and hear some of the outside noises. So you will feel like you are part of things."

She looked around and continued, "We thought there would be many more of you. Scientists seeking to peer into the unknown, students anxious to add to their knowledge in an exciting environment. Fate has decided otherwise. But, as I have told each of you, this day will not wait. It is here and about to start."

She walked over to Win and asked everyone, "What do you think so far?"

Vic was looking at the image of North America and said, "I have a question. I thought the Inland Sea cut North America in half. Where is it?"

"You're right," she answered. "The Western Inland Sea did cut North America in half at one time. But, it has now receded to an area to the east of us. For a long time this portion of the sea was not known to exist, but very shortly it will be the source of the seichi waves that will roll past us."

"How much time is left?" Boone asked.

"Only about ten minutes," the superintendent answered. "I'm going to speak briefly with everyone else who is here and then begin narrating again. I'll talk with you afterwards."

As she walked away, Sheila said, "I don't know if I want to see this." She took a deep breath and continued, "But, I'd probably always wish that I had, so, I guess I'll watch."

"A day you'll never forget," Vic told her.

Sheila laughed and replied, "I had one of those yesterday."

"What about you?" Kaly asked Boone. "Ready for this?"

"I am," he told her. "But I wish I could take a look at the specs for this dome. It can withstand forces that would destroy the buildings in our time. I wonder what it's made of and how it's put together."

"And here I thought you were going to say this was going to be the bossest thing ever."

"It will be…but still…"

"Does work always come first?"

Boone smiled as he took her hand and said, "I may have to rearrange my priorities."

Superintendent Gating reappeared at the podium and began, "You are facing toward the impact area of Chicxulub. The screen with the asteroid will switch in a moment to a side view. I will do my best to narrate what is happening, but there will be many things occurring at once, and things will move quickly. At the end I will show some portions of the video in slow motion, so you can see things you may have missed."

Her voice changed pitch as a bright flash spread across the sky followed by a steady glare of light. Everyone knew it wasn't as bright as outside, but it still caused them to blink. "There! The asteroid has just begun encountering our atmosphere, and the air in front of it is igniting. If you take a moment to look at the screens with dinosaurs from Mexico and South America you will see some of them stumbling and others actually falling. They were looking in the direction of the flash which disoriented, and blinded those who were closer."

A screen from above the Atlantic Ocean continued to track the asteroid as fire burned in front of it and a vapor cloud trailed behind it. "You can see the northern coast of South America just coming into view as it continues to track from the northwest. Any second now it will -" She stopped as the asteroid suddenly surged ahead and then disappeared for a second.

An instant later every screen surrounding the Yucatán Peninsula showed the same massive fireball. The sky in front of the dome flashed again, even brighter than before. "There," the superintendent shouted as a geyser of material shot straight into the sky while what appeared to be sparks arced outward like a giant fireworks display. "Look at the ocean," was all she had time to say as screens from lower angles blacked out as tsunami waves crashed into them at supersonic speed.

Suddenly the dome started rumbling and the superintendent shouted, "The seismic waves are arriving." Everyone watched in disbelief as all the animals they could see were tossed into the air like they were rag dolls. Not once or twice, but repeatedly as the ground rose and fell over and over again in never-ending ripples. At first the animals fought to regain control of their bodies, but soon their flailing stopped, and they all became limp.

Ten minutes later, the ripples began to lessen. When they stopped, Vic asked, "Are they all dead?"

Dennis answered, "No, look at the *Triceratops*." It was slowly rolling side to side as it fought to regain its feet. When it finally did, it was obvious that one leg was broken as well as one of its brow horns. An *Ankylosaurus* lay on its back, its leg feebly clawing at the air until it went still. Several duckbills and a *Packycephalasaurus* stumbled around but seemed to be regaining their senses. Other animals, large and small, limped feebly in circles with their heads hanging low.

The large *Rexes* were all down, dead or unconscious. Scattered around the dome were an additional thirty animals, all lying inert on the ground.

"Look at the trees," Ricky said, and everyone saw they were still waving back and forth, some of them falling to join others already on the ground.

"That was intense," Cam said. "How many animals do you think are dead?"

As if to answer the question several screens came on as video from drones that were sent out after the earthquake hovered over the downed dinosaurs. Their deformed bodies, twisted and crushed into macabre positions, left no doubt that most were dead. A few were still breathing but were obviously paralyzed and would die shortly.

"Some are still alive," Kaly said. "It almost seems impossible after the earthquake, but there they are. Some are still walking and trying to just get back to what they were doing."

"Just living," Dennis said. Then he added, "What is that?"

A few hundred yards in front of them, trees could be seen swaying and then disappearing as a thirty foot tall wall of water crashed through them. "This is the seiche wave," the superintendent announced as the three story wave slammed into the dome, swirled around it and kept going. Trees, ripped up vegetation, rocks, mud, fish, dinosaur bodies, and live dinosaurs were rolled along in tangled clumps of horror. The bumping noises the watchers heard, and the cries of the animals, made them understand just how hard the debris was hitting the outside of the dome and the fear the animals felt.

The flow of the water slowed as it peaked near forty feet and then started to recede. It flowed back toward the unseen lake much slower, so all of the debris that it carried was left behind. Mounds of vegetation, mud, and animal bodies lay strewn all around the dome. Live animals fought to stand up in the sticky mud and fell over and over.

As everyone thought that threat was finished, a surprised Superintendent Gating said, "Here comes a second seiche wave." The water leveled off at only twenty feet for the second wave as it hurled more debris at the dome. The second wave washed the live dinosaurs away and began dropping more bodies and debris.

The water was still about three feet deep when Superintendent Gating interrupted their thoughts with, "If everyone will look up now, you will see the sky has already started to turn orange. It is the harbinger of the fiery rain; the tektites. And they are falling at 200 miles an hour." Above them the blue sky of a few minutes ago was now light orange but deepening in color with every passing second.

As the sky turned a pale red, Vic groaned, "This can't be good."

Several people ducked down as if they were trying to escape the sky as it deepened to a dark red and visibly started as the superintendent said, "The friction of the superheated rock falling back to Earth is raising the outside temperature by hundreds of degrees. The animals who survived the earthquake are now being baked and would not have very much time left. But they actually don't have any."

The dark red sky suddenly turned incandescent red and then the tektites began hitting the dome. Even though the sound had been dampened, it still sounded like a never-ending barrage of gunfire. The tektites did not damage the dome, but dinosaurs, living and dead, were riddled. Bodies were torn apart, and every live animal fell to the ground mortally wounded. And the tektites kept falling.

As the water finally receded, the ground was covered with tiny, pea-sized, glowing rocks. Ricky said, "The forest is on fire." And everywhere, all at once it seemed, smoke billowed from every tree around the dome as they exploded into flames. A few animals, miraculously still able to crawl as they tried to escape the falling death, burst into flames. Ricky shook his head, saying, "It's Dante's Inferno on steroids."

"It's Hell on Earth," Sheila added. "It's worse than I imagined anything could be."

For fifteen minutes the deadly rocks fell until everyone wondered if it would ever end. As the deadly spheres began to stop falling, everyone relaxed, thinking the worst was over.

A boom startled everyone, and Superintendent Gating said, "That is the arrival of the first blast wave which was traveling much slower at the speed of sound." The burning trees circling the dome were blasted to the ground by an unseen hurricane force wind, and the flames leapt higher as they were fanned by the rapid air. A few minutes later the second blast wave followed, creating competing wind gusts that began swirling into small tornadoes. In the distance, a large tornado could be seen moving slowly away from the dome.

A shadow passed over them, and everyone looked up to see the sky was no longer red but beginning to darken. "It is not evening yet," the superintendent informed them. "Black soot, and dust particles are circling the globe. The sun is being blocked, and soon only about ten percent of light from the sun will reach Earth's surface."

She paused then said, "There has always been the question; how could a rock falling from space cause so much destruction? How could it have ended the reign of the dinosaurs? And the truth is, it might not have. Had the asteroid hit at a different angle, in a deeper body of water, the global destruction might not have occurred at the level it did. Today was the worst case scenario for an asteroid impact. Everything about the strike added up to maximum damage.

"It is officially now the Cenozoic Period, and it is starting off poorly. Seventy-five percent of all animals will soon be dead. Ninety percent of all mammals will die. The oceans will become more acidic, and most of Earth's forests will be burnt. Still to come are acidic rain and a three year global freeze. Plants and plankton will die, disrupting the natural food chain.

"Out of this catastrophe only two four-legged animals that weigh more than fifty-five pounds will survive; turtles and crocodiles. They will join snakes, lizards, some birds that nested on the ground, and burrowing mammals as inheritors of this new world."

Superintendent Gating spread her arms and said, "Look outside," and to everyone's amazement they saw the land as it had been before. There were tall trees, lush vegetation with beautiful flowers, walking dinosaurs, and a clear blue sky. Then the image slowly faded away and was replaced with the new reality. The forest was gone, and they could now see for miles in every direction. Trees and vegetation, animals, and parts of animals lay in grotesque shapes in large pools of muddy water left behind by the seiche. Fire and smoke dotted the landscape. But, not a single living animal moved anywhere.

"From this, a completely devastated, nightmarish world," she continued, "one thing we know for sure will happen, another is only a possibility. We know the way is now open for the diversification of mammals. They will thrive and in 66 million years we humans will reach a pinnacle of evolution that no other animal ever has. We will even develop the means to go back in time to watch the moment we inherited the world.

"What we don't know is this; the asteroid impact threw Earth microbes into space. We know some reached the moon, and it is highly likely they went further. Did the impact, which ended the world the dinosaurs knew and paved the way for us, also introduce seeds of evolution on the planets of our solar system? And, are they still part of some cosmic dust that might eventually settle on a planet we have never even heard of?"

Superintendent Gating paused, and one large screen appeared in front of the audience. She put her hands together and said, "As I explained earlier, we watched the event unfold in real time. So, I was unable to call attention to some details because they were only brief glimpses of the much larger event. They were important though, so please bear with me for just a few more moments as I go through a few details in slow motion."

The asteroid streaking across the Atlantic Ocean appeared, and she started, "The asteroid itself is not on fire. Because it is moving so fast, it has compressed air in front of it and the gasses are what is burning. The asteroid is unharmed.

"As it gets closer, watch the screen that shows a herd of animals walking along the Gulf of Mexico shore. They are only a few hundred miles from the impact zone, and as you watch, you might be astounded to see them just disappear. The animals are still there, the light is so bright, it is actually shining through them."

The scene switched to a view of an ocean, and Superintendent Gating continued, "We are looking at the water directly below the oncoming asteroid. You must watch closely because, even though it is in the slowest frame time we have, it still happens almost faster than we can see.

"Notice the water is starting to spread out from an invisible force. It is caused by the compressed air below the falling asteroid pushing down into the ocean. The heat from the asteroid is also boiling some of the water away even though the asteroid itself has not touched the surface. All the water down to the seabed has evaporated, so the giant rock crashes into a rocky surface with so much pressure that everything becomes a liquid. That is why molten rock is thrown out of the crater."

"Faster than the video can track, the asteroid strikes and a giant ball of flame erupts from the sea. Watch the tsunami wave start out from the crater as massive amounts of water and underwater rocks are displaced. You can't see it through the flame, but the sea bed is now rising up from the bottom creating a temporary mountain as tall as Mt. Everest. Then, within seconds the rock and water are all rushing into the void, and the rock will be pushed out into two rings which will define the ninety mile diameter crater which is all that is left to tell us of the violence of the impact."

Another set of animals in a jungle filled the screen as the superintendent told the audience, "This herd is only about two hundred miles from the blast. In seconds the heat of the blast will boil all the water out of their bodies and they will simply burst into flames." Some in the crowd gasped as the scene unfolded exactly as she said it would.

"And finally, watch as the tsunami waves crash into the Mexican and Texas shorelines. The water will carry across the land for hundreds of miles. And as we go back into space for one final look at today, notice the tsunami wave lines heading toward Europe and the African coasts. There is more death yet to come on the worst of all days."

An overhead view of the dome appeared above them. It was surrounded by lush forests, there was a large lake a few miles away, animal herds could be seen slowly walking along well trodden paths. As before though, the view slowly changed, and all that was left were fires, mud, and small, dark hills of unknown material.

"Thank you for being here today," Superintendent Gating said. "I know that for some of you this was hard to watch. But, please remember, without this terrible day 66 million years ago, we probably would not be sitting here today. I will get with each of you later today, and I look forward to all of the research that follows. Thank you." She smiled at the applause as she stepped from the podium and walked from the dome.

Vic was shaking his head as he stood up. "That was literally unbelievable," he said. "I'd always thought the asteroid hit, and it killed some dinosaurs immediately, but some lived for a few thousand years. You know, it took a thousand years or so for the nuclear winter and volcanoes and that type of thing to get all of them.

"But, if the rest of the planet is getting the same things we did, well, I'm surprised anything survived for more than just a few years. Molten rock falling from the sky. Tsunamis. Everywhere, there was death."

"Only small animals survived and a few birds," Cam added. "What if it happened today, I mean, what if it happened in our time? Makes you think."

"Paradise is gone," Sheila said sadly. "All those animals, even the two you touched, Boone, all gone. Win, I'll tell you right now, if we save the world, and there's some sort of reward, I want to go back to that little lake. Just for a few minutes when there are no carnivores around, nothing we have to shoot. I want to walk around and be at peace." She took Ricky's hand and said, "And you're coming with me."

He smiled and replied, "You bet I will."

Dennis put his hands on their shoulders and asked, "Why don't we all go?"

"If they don't shut down travel, we will," Win said. "Even if they decide to, I'll make it happen."

"Let's just make sure it's not your brother that sends us back again," Boone said.

"I think it's great," Kaly agreed. "But first, we have to get back, then we have to take care of August before anything can happen."

"That's true," Win agreed. "And I said there were two things that had to happen...here's the first." He waved his hand and shouted, "Dr. Chapel, we're headed back to Medical. Would you like to join us?"

He walked quickly to them and said, "I certainly would, and please, call me Lon."

"What are you a doctor of?" Kaly asked.

"History. I love studying the way things were."

"That sounds interesting," Kaly said, "Do you have a favorite area?"

As Lon answered, she caught a glimpse of Win and realized he was staring at her. At first she thought he didn't want her talking to Lon and then she realized there was a meaning behind his look.

She immediately remembered a time in the woods with her father when she was nine years old. Her dad had been talking while she picked some berries, and she realized he had stopped. She looked up, and it was the same look, a look telling her to pay attention. Her father had smiled, brought his hands up, and then just stood still, even when she heard the noise by her feet that told her something was moving past her. A few seconds later he had motioned for her to come to him and then told her about the two rattlesnakes she had almost stepped on. He was surprised when she wasn't scared and had actually wanted to look for the snakes.

But Win wasn't smiling, and instead of just bringing his hands up, he made a fist with one of them. She gave him a wink, and there was just the hint of a smile on his face as he turned away. Kaly was back in the present just in time to hear Lon say, "And that's why I'm here. These animals just fascinate me. Win, what brought all of you here today?"

Win opened the door to their room and said, "Step in and I'll tell you all about it." As the door closed behind them, Win simply said, "Do it now."

Kaly kneed Lon in the side of his right thigh, and as his leg flexed and he dropped, she punched him in the side of the neck. Boone was surprised but reacted quickly enough to catch Lon and lay him on the floor. Everyone stared first at Kaly and then Win who simply said, "Oh, that was the second thing that had to happen."

NO PLAN PLANS

"First," Vic **started, "that was a** great knockout. Second, why did Kaly just knock the doctor out?"

Win didn't answer for a few seconds as he used the tech from his prosthetic arm to sweep Dr. Chapel. He reached into a shirt pocket and pulled out a small object that none of them recognized as he answered, "Because I didn't want him using this."

"What is it?" Ricky asked. "Some cool future tech?"

"No, just a video camera."

"Why is it so important then?"

Kaly answered, "Because he's a spy and was going to let August Adams know we were still alive."

As everyone looked surprised, Win added, "Kaly, Boone, and I recognized him from a previous encounter. I didn't tell any of you because I wanted to make sure no one acted differently around him. He had no clue, so he came down here to talk with us."

"What good would a video do? He's stuck here just like the rest of us," Cam pointed out.

"We're not stuck anymore," Win replied. "That was the first thing that had to happen. The impact destroyed my brother's block of time travel, and other things that went with it. So, the good doctor would have live streamed us back to August, showing we still lived. I'm sure a good-sized number of his workers would have arrived shortly to ensure the job was completed."

There was a moment of silence, then Vic asked, "How do you know time travel is working again?"

"Because, my arm is fully functional again. Certain things worked, like knowing this station was present and what direction to go. But, if time travel had not been blocked, I could have used it to get us back to the present, that is, where we are supposed to be."

Ricky smiled and asked, "So, you can get us out of here right now?"

"Let's go," Vic said.

"Not so fast," Win said. "There's a few things we need to do first."

"Is one of them getting rid of this clown?" Sheila asked. Then she patted Ricky on the arm and continued, "Not that I've ever done such a thing."

"No, nothing that drastic," Win replied. "Superintendent Gating has agreed to lock him in a very secure area until TIM comes for him."

"What needs to be done then?" Kaly asked.

"I need to make a very poor quality video with a lot of interference and send it to August. It has to ensure we are dead, but not be so good that he can tell anything else about it. When I send the transmission to my brother, it should give us a read on where he is. Then, we have to figure out how to get close to August and finally -"

"And finally, stop him," Vic cut in.

"Actually," Win replied, "if we catch him, I know exactly what to do."

Before Vic could reply, the door opened and Trace came in with a cart and started, "Here is your lunch, I hope..." and then he trailed off as he saw Dr. Chapel lying on the floor. "Uh...I'm not sure what -"

Superintendent Gating pushed past Trace and said, "Win, I see you have taken care of your problem." Then she turned to Trace and said, "Please unload your cart, so we can place Dr. Chapel on it. Use the food covers to hide him and then take him to Room 101. Be sure to lock the door on the way out."

"Should I -"

"No."

"What about -"

"No."

"And I should keep -"

"Yes, you should. Be sure to join me in my office after you have finished."

The lunch cart was quickly unloaded, and Dr. Chapel was put on it by Boone, Kaly, and Dennis. Trace smiled as he wheeled the cart away, and the superintendent laughed as she left.

As Cam started eating, he asked, "So, who is starring in this low quality video?"

"Just Dr. Chapel's voice," Win replied. "Please go ahead with lunch, and I'll be back in just a few minutes."

After he left, Sheila said, "You know, I was pretty down after watching everything that happened after the impact. But watching Kaly's knockout brought me back to reality. I'm ready to get back to our time and take care of business."

"Agreed," Vic added. "I'm feeling better, and it's time to get going."

"It's not going to be easy," Kaly pointed out. "I'm sure we can locate him, but he can move through time any second he wants to. Remember how everyone just disappeared from the cave? We have to stop his time travel."

"Win will know how to do that," Cam said. "Also, he seemed to have an idea about what to do with him, so yeah, let's get it done."

They ate in silence until Win came back into the room and said, "Watch this." A holograph view that showed the decimated area around the dome appeared in the center of the room. Static and sudden jumps in the picture kept interrupting the video and Dr. Chapel's voice. The few words they could understand were, "successful," "earthquake," "fire," "rushing water," "everything has been," "no sign of," and "obviously dead."

"I tried to hide as much as I could yet still get the point across that everything was dead," Win started. "I used lots of static because I don't know if Dr. Chapel was supposed to use any key words to ensure a transmission was actually from him. I sent the video to August, so something could happen at any moment. We have to be ready to leave immediately if necessary."

As Vic and Cam stood up, Win continued, "Not all of us are leaving."

"What? Why not?" Sheila asked.

"Because you, Vic, Cam, and Ricky still need intensive medical care."

"But I feel great," Cam told him. "We all do."

"Yes," Win agreed, "you all feel great. And you are getting better. But, you only feel great because of certain medications.

You are still healing from some very horrific wounds. You have to get better first."

"But, we could all stay here," Sheila pointed out. "Then we all go back to a few minutes after we left and take care of things."

"We could have, if August wasn't fluctuating time travel. I believe something will open for Dr. Chapel but then will close quickly. I think August is trying to keep TIM from moving against him. So, August might be the one who stops all time travel. He wouldn't want anyone going back and stopping him before he began his time line break. So, when the time comes for Dr. Chapel to go, we'll go. We'll take care of my brother, while you take care of you."

"I could go back," Ricky said. "I'm just waiting for a new hand."

Win smiled as he replied, "You are waiting to heal also. And, as soon as someone saw your hand was missing, there would probably be some questions. That leads to news and then August finds out we're back."

"How are you going to get past all of his people?" Vic asked.

"Well, hopefully, most of his people are back catching dinosaurs," Win replied. "To August, it's still business as usual. Patre, Gina, and Yang may be around somewhere, but surprise should be on our side."

"To a point," Vic said. "But they will react quicker than what you think. They've probably trained for it. They will have weapons; you'll have to get some. They won't play by the rules. I know you will want to...but you can't. You will have to be ruthless. Can you be? Can you walk into a room and just shoot everyone? If you can't, they will just disappear, and they will be even more terrible than they have been. I'm talking about your families, your friends, maybe even your past, will be targeted. Can you do that, Boone?"

"I don't know," Boone admitted. "If you're right, we're talking about the fate of ourselves and everyone we know. I guess we'll see."

"One thing to think about," Win added. "All the others have traveled and obviously have access to whatever it is that allows that. But, I don't think any of them actually carry something on them at all times. Otai certainly did not. I think they all disappeared from the cave at the same time because of something August did. If we can take out the others without alerting August, we'll have our chance."

"Won't Dr. Chapel have some type of tracker on him? Something that lets August Adams know when he has returned?" Ricky asked.

Win smiled as he replied, "Ricky, you are very smart, and correct. Remember, you asked about cool future tech a minute ago? The doctor did have some, and I have it now. We can travel from here to someplace close to Washington, and they'll think it is the doctor returning. Then, we go from there."

"Well, since our elaborate plan didn't work, how can 'go from there' possibly fail?" Vic asked. "Won't he suspect something when Dr. Chapel doesn't make it back?"

"I'm hoping that the compromised video convinces August that time travel problems are understandable, and maybe even expected. I actually plan to have our time travel appear to go wrong. After all, there are still problems with the atmosphere and acidic rain in this time period." He glanced at his arm and added, "We have to go, now."

As Win, Kaly, Boone, and Dennis walked from the room, Vic called out, "Be careful and remember what Otai said about Patre. He's dangerous. Expect him to react immediately."

It only took them a minute to get to the travel emitter, and they found Superintendent Gating waiting for them. "Win, are you sure you don't want me to guide your stop from here?"

"No. Any odd site initiated energy signature will draw suspicion. I have to do it from inside the travel conduit."

"That sounds dangerous. Be extremely careful," the superintendent said. "I hope that -"

"Wait," Boone interrupted. "Do you have any weapons here?"

"Why, yes. I could…" and then they were gone.

They were still sitting inside the travel unit, but now it was surrounded by a bluish mist. "Thought of that a little too late, didn't I?" Boone said.

"We will think of things as we go," Win told everyone. "I am confident we will be successful."

"Superintendent Gating seemed concerned you would be guiding us from the inside," Dennis said.

"And I am too," Win admitted. "The time on the screen is a countdown to when we arrive at the D.C. site. I'm going to stop us about one thousandth of a second before we're supposed to arrive."

"Why? And can you do that?" Dennis asked.

"I want to land where we'll just be travelers on the road, and hopefully D.C. is on the map. From my time in the city I can get our bearings, so we can make a better second time travel. And, I'm not going to stop us; my arm is. Its chronometer will be much more accurate than my reflexes."

"How will we know -" Kaly started and then they were in a grove of trees. As they stepped out of the travel unit, it disappeared and Kaly finished with, "Never mind."

"I was wondering if I would ever see another tree," Dennis said. "Where, and when, do you think we are?"

"Wait right here, and I'll be back in a minute," Win replied and walked through the trees and disappeared.

"At least we're not 66 million years ago," Kaly said. "I feel better already, even though I don't know what to expect, and it feels like it's ninety degrees."

Win was back in less than a minute and told them, "This is actually not too bad. We're north of Washington, and I can see Fort Stevens not too far from here. Now we'll walk that way, and when we get there, you let me do all of the talking, okay?"

They followed him to a dry, dusty, wagon rutted road and started walking. It only took seconds, and they were covered in dust and sweating profusely. "We're in Washington right now, aren't we?" Kaly asked. "The fort is just a few miles north of the White House, isn't it?"

"Well, we are in Washington, I mean the original grid of the city, but there's only farmhouses out here now. A lot of the houses here, and at other places around Washington, were torn down so forts could be built. We're about five long, hot miles from the White House. Remember, there are canals by the city which draw mosquitoes, and the sewage system is almost non-existent. The only thing you will recognize for sure are the White House, the Capitol, and part of the Washington monument."

Suddenly three Union soldiers burst out of the trees to their right, and one asked sternly, "What you be doin' here on the turnpike? State your business."

"Dang it, Smitty," Win drawled. "Don't you recognize me? I was with you'n at Fort Massachusetts fer six months."

Smitty stepped closer and smiled as he said, "Yeah, I rec'nize yuh, Win. But, what yuh doin out here? There's a Reb army right behind ya."

Win paused for a second then said, "Last I heerd they's was at Rockville. They attackin' the fort?"

"Yessir, they swung this away, and they's headin' straight fer us. Spect' their calvary pretty soon. So, what are you a doin' walkin' out here? An where's yer uniform?"

"I've been on a mission an I'm takin' these folks to see Gen'ral Augur. They got some information fer him. An' we was in a waggin but when a wheel came off the plugs broke free and took off. Prob'ly still a runnin'."

"Well, come on with me," Smitty said. As he walked away, he turned to the other soldiers and said, "Fire a few shots at them Johnnys when they's get close then skedaddle on back to the fort. Ya hear?"

They walked briskly and Win said. "Cain't hardly breathe 'cause of all the dust."

"Ain't rained here in over a month," Smitty replied. "We can see the Rebs kicking up dust as they head this away."

Win asked, "Can the Massachusetts hold?"

"We'll hold, but it ain't the Massachusetts no more," Smitty told him. "They's named it Fort Stevens at the end of '63."

"You know I 'memeber hearing somethin' about that," Win replied. "An say, you think we can git a square meal when we git to the fort?"

"Not likely. I tell you, the Rebs is close. A bunch of the VI corps boys jus' got here. I can help you git a buckboard since yer goin' to a gen'ral and all, but if they see you, they might make you stay. It's gonna be hot here in just a while."

"Smitty, I 'preciate any help you can git us. I do."

Twenty minutes later they were in a wagon slowly moving through a crowd of soldiers beside Fort Stevens. As they gazed up at the men standing on the tall mounds of earth, they suddenly hit a rut and Dennis said, "Well, I guess it's better than walking."

Behind them was a loud explosion and Kaly asked, "What was that?"

"Siege gun," Win advised. "Early's boys must be getting in range."

Kaly said, "I've known where Fort Stevens was, but not about its history. I thought it had to do with the Revolutionary War or even the War of 1812. It was interesting seeing all of those soldiers; it looked like they meant business."

"They do mean business," Win told her. "Fort Stevens is about to come under attack by General Early. They're trying to pull the Union Army from Petersburg and Richmond, the Reb capitol. If they can do that, they can keep the war going. But Grant, General Grant, isn't about to send his army up here, so Fort Stevens will have to hold. If they don't, Early will march into Washington. Fortunately, his men are tired from long, hot marches, and he can't take the fort. He has to turn around and head south.

"We actually stopped at a pretty interesting moment in history. I was in Washington a lot during this time, so I knew where we were. I'm just glad we got here before Early's men. It might have gotten hot for us and then...well, would you believe it? Look."

Dennis started, "Look at wha..." then he trailed off and just stared.

Boone stood up and said, "I don't believe it."

A carriage coming toward them stopped and a tall man stepped out and said, "Win, it's been a while."

Win leaned over and shook his hand and replied, "It has Abe, but I'll see you soon after this fuss is all over."

"I met VI Corps at the docks and watched 'em march up this way and thought I'd join 'em," Abe told him. "Can we hold 'em, Win?"

"Early's boys is tired, Abe. Too much July marchin'. They'll poke some but won't git nowheres. They got the siege guns going already and the Parrotts from Fort Reno, up on the high ground, will worry the Rebs some too. They won't be here long."

"Well I guess I best be getting to the fort before the show is over," Abe said.

Dennis quickly asked, "Sir, would you mind if I shook your hand?"

Abe smiled and reached over, shook his and Boone's hands, then bowed to Kaly. As soon as he stepped back into his carriage it started moving and he called out, "Come by soon, Win." Then he laughed and continued, "You're the only one that gets me away from all those people."

As Win started the buckboard moving again, Dennis said, "You know, I have to admit I wasn't a hundred percent sure about your Lincoln stories. I'm sorry."

Win laughed and replied, "I don't blame you. There's lots of other stories I could tell you that you might not believe either."

"Are you ever washing your hand?" Kaly asked Boone.

"Not until I have it bronzed," he told her.

Win cracked a whip at the sound of a lot of guns being fired behind them as he said, "Let's get a little more distance between us and the fort."

Thirty minutes later Win stopped the buckboard and told them, "We are near 1st and 13th, Franklin Park in your time. We can travel to the park then start gathering information."

"Why not go over to the Mall? Take Constitution Avenue to a larger area?" Dennis asked. "I know that area a lot better from walking around during my Senate years."

"Constitution Avenue doesn't exist yet," Win told him. "There's a canal there now that's used for sewage. Doesn't smell very good that way."

"Not that it smells good here," Kaly pointed out.

"That's because of the outdoor facilities," Boone said. "Outhouses, open trash pits, garbage, and whatever else hasn't been written down in the history books."

"I've been around an outhouse," Kaly said. "Just not a thousand of them all at the same time."

"But, it's 1864 modern," Win said as they climbed out of the buckboard. "Next, I suppose you'll be wanting something to drink besides well water."

"Actually," Boone said, "next, I hope we're leaving."

Win motioned for everyone to stand beside him and colors began moving around them as if they were caught in an autumn leaf swirling wind. A few seconds later they were standing on a sidewalk next to Franklin Park. It was dark, and Kaly said, "There's something wrong here."

"I hope you don't see a dinosaur," Boone said.

"No, the problem is I don't see anything I should see. There's no traffic, no lights in the buildings, just the street lights."

"We need information," Dennis said. "Let's get to the White House -"

"And announce we're back?" Win asked. "No, we have to stay out of sight until we're ready for August."

"Well, this is when we were going to come up with a plan," Kaly said. "How do we get to him?"

"I think," Win replied and then paused before beginning again, "I think someone will come to us. Remember, we're traveling as Dr. Chapel. We didn't arrive where we were supposed to, and I'm sure his tech I took off him is sounding out a signal right now. Let's go over to that garden area and see what happens."

A few minutes later a car stopped near them, and as the driver got out, Win said, "That's Gina. I'm going to drop down facing away from her. When she comes over to me, grab her...and don't be nice about it."

Gina used her cell phone light to check the area and immediately spotted Win lying in the grass. "Dr. Chapel, can you hear me?" she asked as she got closer, and Win moaned. "That event must have really affected your -" She tried to back away, but Boone and Dennis were on her too quickly. As she was pulled backward she reached for her watch, and Dennis was having a hard time keeping her hand from slowly getting closer to it. Kaly stepped in and brought a palm heel strike down on the top of her nose, and Gina collapsed in a heap.

Boone laughed and said, "You know, people would pay to watch you fight."

"Who'd fight her?" Win asked as he looked around. Then he added, "Let's get her back in the car."

"It's nice when there's no one around while you're kidnapping someone," Dennis pointed out when they were all in the car. "Now what?"

Kaly held the phone up to Gina's face, and as the phone lit up he said, "Let's drive to where she came from."

A message from AA suddenly appeared asking, "Dd u fd hm?" Kaly typed in "Y" and immediately received "K?" Kaly thought for a second, she doubted August really cared that much about the doctor so she typed, "He'l lv." August responded, "Yr plc til am, i'l dl w hm thn." The screen went blank, and Kaly told everyone, "I think I pulled it off. Now what?"

"We go to her place," Boone said. "If there's a trace on the doctor, there's probably one on her. Plus, I'm hoping there's something to eat there."

"And a shower," Dennis added.

As Boone drove, they found Gina's driver's license and were glad to see her address was a small apartment building just a few miles away. As they took her inside, Boone said, "That was the strangest drive, no traffic. None. Let's get some news on."

"And, let's find out the date," Dennis added as he turned on the television. "We don't know how long in real time we've been gone."

They set Gina in a large chair, and Win found some rope in her kitchen and asked, "I wonder if this is for the doctor?" They bound and gagged her then sat down and ate. "She's like my brothers," Kaly pointed out. "She doesn't eat leftovers. She has all these partial orders of food and some of them are going bad."

"Since I'm feeling much better," Boone said, "I'm thinking that's not such a bad character trait. Especially compared to all of the things she's probably done."

Dennis spoke up, "Look at this." He turned the sound up, and they heard the voice-over say, "August Adams addressed the mandatory combined congressional meeting earlier today, and his stunning announcement and new threats have the entire world on edge. Even those who briefly argued in favor of his tactics realize now they were mistaken."

The picture cut to August standing behind a podium as he said, "I am very disappointed in what has occurred, with what should never have happened. Your president has been missing for three days, and I will tell you now that President Powell, and a team of mercenaries, including agents from the Secret Service and the innocent civilian they duped, Boone Christopher, tried to kill me.

"You might wonder what happened to them, but you already know. They died 66 million years ago in the event that wiped out the dinosaurs. But they didn't have to. All they had to do, the same as all of you, was listen to me. I am providing you with a way to a better life. All you have to do is follow my path, and there will be no more hunger, crime, or petty politics.

"So, to ensure you listen, and do exactly what you need to do, I am taking several steps I did not want to. First, nations as you know them now, no longer exist. There is no America, Russia, Australia, China, England…no Europe or South America or whatever such things used to be called. We are all simply planet Earth. You will answer to my laws and -" he paused and shook his head. "I did not want any more killing," he told them.

The screen switched to multiple views of people in different places running from dinosaurs and being savagely killed. August came back on and explained, "As soon as I said you will follow my laws, leaders in many countries decided they were going to use force against me. They are dead. The innocent people you saw running, now have nothing more to fear; my dinosaurs have been called off.

"But, everyone needs to listen closely. Though there are no more governments, there are still laws. Crime will not be tolerated. Hunger, lack of medical assistance for everyone, racism, and other petty things such as hating your neighbor, are a thing of the past. Your governments couldn't, or wouldn't do it, so I will. Planet Earth laws will be presented tomorrow. To defy them will not get you a few years in a prison, a few days in a jail, home detention, or a slap on the wrist. I do not want to kill anyone else, but I will."

"My God," Dennis said sadly as he turned the television off. "My wife thinks I'm dead." Then he looked up and added, "And all of your families too."

"Then they'll be extremely happy to find out we're not, after everything is finished," Kaly said. "We can't let anyone know yet."

Gina began stirring, and they were all sitting in front of her as she woke up and realized she was in her own apartment. They could tell she was angry as she tried to yell at them, so Kaly said, "You have a gag in your mouth. You just look stupid trying to tell us off, so listen. We want to know where to find August Adams. When this is finished, whoever helps us will receive consideration. It can be you." As Gina shook her head no, Kaly continued, "Or someone else. And you know, someone will talk. All we have to do is motivate them."

Gina snorted and looked to the side, and Kaly leaned in close and told her, "I know what you're thinking; we have to play by the rules. We just can't hurt anyone, mutilate or kill them the way August Adams, and you, have done. But, there are no rules anymore. August Adams said there's no America. There's probably no Secret Service anymore either. New laws will be out tomorrow. That means I can do anything I want…to *anyone* I want to do it to." Kaly smiled and asked, "Who do you think will be first?"

Gina looked at Dennis and began trying to talk, and he just smiled and told her, "I'm not the president anymore. I'm just an ex-president who once gave the okay for the waterboarding of a suspected terrorist who *might* have been responsible for a bombing. So, if she stabs you in the temple with a pencil and then uses a blowtorch to cut you into little pieces, what would I care? Unless, you'd like to help us?"

As she glared at him and tried to yell at them again, Dennis said, "Get me a large pan of water and a small towel from the kitchen." Then he stood up and walked out of the room for a couple of minutes. When he came back Kaly and Boone had two pots of water and a towel ready. Dennis said, "I'm going to put the towel over her face. Win, you pull the gag out of her mouth, and I'm going to pour this glass of water into her mouth, and we'll begin."

As they gathered around, Gina began pulling and squirming as hard as she could but couldn't get loose. She was trying to say something, but Dennis didn't pay attention to her as he asked Win, "Are you ready?" When he nodded his head, Dennis told Boone, "Tilt the chair back as fast as you can…now." As she went backward, Win pulled out the gag, but instead of shouting, Gina was startled and took in a deep, open mouth breath instead. At that moment Dennis poured the glass of water down her throat and stuffed the kitchen towel back in her mouth as a gag.

Gina was furious as Boone sat her back up and fought even harder against her restraints. Kaly asked, "You didn't poison her, did you?"

"No," Dennis replied. "I just put a lot of pills from bottles with sleep medication in them. Just like her refrigerator, there were a lot of bottles that weren't all used."

"Too many might kill her," Boone said.

Dennis shrugged his shoulders and replied, "I can live with that."

"Where did you learn about waterboarding?" Kaly asked. "You sounded pretty convincing."

Dennis laughed as he replied, "Saw it in a movie. If we just stood around her I thought she would just get ready to shout for help. A neighbor might call the police. But, I figured if Boone pulled her back the surprise would give me the second or two I needed." he paused then asked Win, "Now what?"

As he looked at Gina who was blinking her eyes, Win suggested, "Take a shower and get some sleep? Someone, maybe even August, will be here in the morning for Dr. Chapel."

"Works for me," Boone said, and he dragged two mattresses into the living room. "We'll all wake up if she starts to get loose."

"We just need Kaly to wake up," Win said with a yawn.

"I want to wake up," Dennis said, "so I can see Kaly hit her again. You know, I'll bet those brothers you talk about were always nice to you, weren't they?"

Kaly laughed and said, "Well, now that you mention it." She lay down on the mattress with Boone and continued, "I feel like I'm someplace else, watching us do all of this stuff. Like it's not real. And, even though I don't want to watch it, I have to."

Before he went to sleep, Boone said, "If you figure things out, especially how it's going to end, let me know."

She kissed him and said, "I just hope it ends the way we want it to."

The sun was just coming up as first Boone and then Kaly woke up. They were trying to be quiet as they moved around when Gina's telephone buzzed. Win and Dennis woke up, and for a brief second they all wondered if they should answer the call. But it stopped, and when Win checked the phone he smiled and said, "It's a message. 'Be there in about five,' from Yang."

"Let's get ready," Dennis said. "How should we handle him?"

"I have an idea," Boone said. "First, I guess we should check to see if Gina is still alive." After Kaly said she was, he continued, "There's some sort of red sauce in a container in her fridge. Pour it on her head, so it looks like she is bleeding. When Yang comes in, make sure he sees it. She didn't want to talk, but maybe he will."

Gina's hair and face were soon covered, and Kaly said, "That looks good. I didn't realize we could be so cruel."

"Let's hope Yang thinks we were," Win said from a window. "He's here, and he's carrying a briefcase. And, I found some duct tape."

"Okay," Kaly said. "I'll stay behind the door as I open it and step to the side. Boone, as soon as he steps in, pull him inside and Win and Dennis grab his arms. We can't let him set off any alarm. Oh, and don't be too gentle with him."

As footsteps got closer to the door, Boone whispered, "When do you knock him out?"

There was a tap on the door, and as Kaly opened it and Yang stepped inside, he was immediately grabbed and slammed to the floor. Kaly pulled his watch off as he was sat up, and Win duct taped his mouth. Boone and Dennis tied him up then jerked him to his feet. As he was dragged past Gina, Kaly could see Yang's eyes get wide. He was set down in a kitchen chair, and he didn't fight against the rope like Gina did; he just stared nervously around.

Kaly sat down in front of him and said, "Good morning, Yang. Well, I hope it continues to be a good morning for you. As I explained to your friend, Gina, all we want to know is where August is."

As Yang stayed silent, Dennis opened the briefcase he had carried in and asked, "Well, what do we have here?" He pulled out a syringe filled with an amber liquid and asked, "Just how were you supposed to *deal* with Dr. Chapel?"

"You know," Kaly said softly, "now we don't really need you, do we? When I talk again with Dr. Chapel, who is also...uh, recovering, I bet he'll be quite upset to see what your plans were for him. I bet he'll be more than happy to talk. And, Yang, just in case you don't know, the first to talk gets the most consideration after we visit August. So, do I talk to the doctor, or to you?"

At that moment there was a clatter behind Yang, and as he twisted his head around, Win said, "Sorry, I didn't mean to drop the knife."

Yang faced Kaly and tried to talk, and she held up a hand and motioned for Win to bring her the knife. Yang tried to pull away, but Boone held his head still as Kaly said, "I'm not going to hurt you; I just want to hear you."

She made a small slit in the duct tape and Yang asked, "How did you escape? How are you still alive? Does TIM know? Are they closing in on us?"

"Of course they know," Win said. "They rescued us, and they're getting ready to take August into custody. Did you think we were stupid?"

Yang dropped his head as he said, "I wasn't sure about any of this. They talked about killing people, but I didn't know it was going to be so many."

"It sounds like you're sorry for some of the things you did," Kaly told him. "Just tell us where he is right now, and we'll pass on that you were cooperative."

Yang sighed and said, "He's at the White House. He's getting ready for a large news conference. He's going to talk about how the world will be different."

Dennis knelt down in front of him and said, "Good, I know the White House." Then he asked, "Who else is there with him?"

"Patre."

"No one else is there?" Kaly asked suspiciously. "No guards? No dinosaurs?"

Yang shook his head and told her, "Just Patre. Everyone else was sent back in case more dinosaurs were needed. We told him they wouldn't be needed; the world is afraid."

Kaly nodded and told Win, "Tape him back up, all the way around his head." Then she said, "Wait. Is he expecting you?"

"No," Yang replied. "This was supposed to take a while. I...I want to tell you more. There will be a lot of media there today but no Secret Service Police. No one will be checking anyone as they come in. Also ..."

He trailed off and Kaly said, "You're doing great so far; don't hold anything back."

He took a deep breath and continued, "The real reason I joined was because of the money."

"The money?"

"Yeah, all the taxes will be brought in and then redistributed, but...well, we were supposed to get a large cut of it. I know it sounds terrible, August and all his talk about changing the world, and he is doing that, but, yeah, the money. It would look legitimate under the section heading of World Financial Redistribution of Taxes. Who would know?"

Kaly leaned in and said "Thank you," as Win completed duct taping Yang. Then she knocked him out.

"There it is," Boone said.

Kaly smiled as she said, "Okay, let's tie them up in separate rooms, so they can't see, can't hear, and can't move. Grab their phones in case we need to answer a text, and then we'll get a plan ready."

When they all gathered back in the kitchen, Kaly asked Dennis, "What's the plan?"

"Well, I'm not the -" Dennis started.

"It's your house," Kaly told him. "I doubt he cares about the media crews because he knows he has won. Everyone is afraid of him. We're going to show him how wrong he is. What gets us in the White House quickest, and with the least likelihood of being accidentally seen?"

"One of the wings will give us access to the main building. We can decide which wing when we get there."

"Another no plan, plan," Win said. "They've worked so far."

"Let's eat some breakfast," Boone suggested. "Then go ruin August's day."

WHITE HOUSES

They took the keys to Yang's SUV, and as they got in, Dennis said, "This is a White House Transportation vehicle."

"That's actually good, "Kaly noted. "It has darkened windows, so no one can see us, and it looks like it belongs around the White House. We won't draw any unnecessary attention."

Boone was driving, and he suggested, "Let's poke around for a few minutes, see what's going on."

"At least there is some traffic this morning," Win said. "Some people are trying to keep things normal."

"Your brother did say he wanted things to keep going as usual," Dennis said. "The traffic's not as bad as every other day, so everyone isn't buying into it, but we can blend into what's out here."

Boone drove around for several minutes and parked in different places, so they could assess the area. They noticed the number of media vehicles that were driving through the White House traffic gates, and that there was no one stopping the vehicles to check them.

"I have an idea," Boone told them. "Let me check for the closest store and...got one." A half hour later they were driving through the east entrance gate and parking on the White House lawn because of the number of media vehicles already there. Each of them was wearing a blue baseball hat and blue vest. They each had a black carry bag, and Dennis was also carrying a video camera. As they got out of the SUV, Boone said, "Remind me to thank Yang for buying all of this stuff for us."

"We should go in a different door," Dennis told them as they approached the south entrance. "Once we're inside we'll stand out if we try to break away to get to the weapon storage room."

"I don't think we have a choice," Kaly said. "Everyone is going through these doors, so we probably couldn't get anywhere else from here anyway. Let's just go with the flow and see what happens."

"Remember," Win advised, "we don't have to do anything right now. We can check things out just like we did outside and wait for an opportunity to present itself. But when we go, we can't miss. We have to get August, and stop this madness. If he gets away, the entire world will pay for our mistake."

"And I don't want to think about how we will personally pay," Kaly said.

As they entered, White House staff members waved them toward the East Room, where Boone and Kaly received their awards. The room was packed with media crews and their equipment, so they slowly made their way to the back of the room. No one paid them any attention, they were too busy preparing for the press conference to care about another crew coming in.

The lights brightened, and August Adams walked out from behind a curtain. For the first time Boone noticed there were at least twenty bare flag poles. On both sides of a podium that was set up in front of the media crews were piles of American flags. Discarded, since there was no longer an American government. Boone clenched his fists but did nothing. He wondered how everyone else in the room felt.

As August walked toward the podium, the room lit up as media camera lights were turned on. August smiled; he was the center of attention, just as he always wanted. In a few short minutes the world, and everything in it, would be his. He didn't care that it was hard to see the audience due to the blinding lights. He could feel the tension and fear in the room.

Behind him, Patre and Otai appeared, and between them they wheeled a cage containing a five-foot tall dinosaur. It moved quickly back and forth, and every few seconds it made a rumbling sound. Boone whispered, "There had to be a dinosaur."

The room grew completely still as August surveyed the men and women in front of him, then smiled. "Good morning," he started. "Because it is a good morning. I welcome all of you who are here, and all of you around the world.

"It is the first day of a new world, a new order. It is the day that future generations will look back on as the end of archaic rules, laws, and principles, and the start of a better life for everyone. And, I mean everyone. No one will be left out because of a clinging attachment to an outdated way of life. You will all benefit from my new guidelines…even those who don't want to.

"And it is fitting that this takes place here in the *White House*, where so many bad things have been done all in the name of progress. Perhaps it should have kept one of its first two names: President's Palace, or Executive Mansion. But then there would have been no way of fooling the American public into believing they weren't being governed by out of touch aristocrats." He laughed, "The White House, it should have been called the White Lies House."

He paused as a world map appeared on a screen beside him, then continued, "Here is the old world with its restrictive borders and wide diversity of laws and punishments." As the lines on the map marking country borders disappeared, larger areas marked Region 1 through Region 20 replaced them.

August smiled and said, "This is the new world. You will live in a Region. But you can work, or travel in any Region you want, anytime you want. The laws and punishments in all Regions will be the same. They were created by a committee of government leaders tasked with completing the job within twenty-four hours. These rules are just, as are the punishments. And, there was little bickering or infighting. So you see, world leaders can get things done when properly motivated."

August paused for a moment. He expected some applause, but when there was none, he quickly moved on. After all, they were still sheep who needed to be led. "There will be taxes. Fair taxes based on the *exact* income of a person or family. No one can hide behind a curtain of tax breaks for the rich while the poor pay for everything. There will be no hunger, no poverty, and free healthcare for all. That means there will be no reason for crime, drug use, or people dying over petty arguments about nothing."

Again, he paused, but still, just silence. Stupid people, he thought. Then a small, nervous voice asked, "Sir, how will we pay our taxes?"

"The same as always. Through your paycheck, through your normal purchases of goods and services. But, *all money collected* will go to pay for essential items and programs to provide everyone with a better life. *You* will see where the money goes. *You* will see how the money is spent. *You* will benefit from the programs it funds. There will be no black hole the money disappears into, no kickbacks, or under the table deals."

Another voice asked, "Sir, are you the king of the world now?"

August shook his head as he said, "No, I am no one's ruler. I am the creator of a new world, nothing more. When you start living the life you deserve I will fade into the background, and you will hear nothing more about me. Each Region will have a Guide, and they will ensure you receive everything that is due to you. Equal pay, equal opportunities, equal right to live as you wish, wherever you wish."

Another voice called out, "Why do you have a dinosaur with you?"

"That is a fair question," August answered. "I have my friend, by the way, it's a young *Tyrannosaurus Rex*, to emphasize what waits in the shadows if the world gets out of control again. Remember, law enforcement will still handle problems in the new world, but sometimes...well, sometimes there will be those who need the occasional reminder. Defiance of the new rules will be dealt with by the strongest measures. The Jurassic Sword will not disappear, until it is no longer needed."

He motioned for Patre and Otai to step up beside him and introduced them. "Otai has been with me the longest, an intelligent man who guided me through the myriad of problems that Jurassic Sword had to overcome. Patre joined later but immediately became a valuable asset by taking care of business swiftly and reliably." August paused then continued, "But, to my great sorrow, I have found out that one of these men has actually been undermining me the entire time. Backstabbing me, if you will."

As August walked to the *T-rex* cage, Win said, "I don't like the way this is going. He's found out about Otai, and we all know what that means."

"What do we do?" Dennis asked.

It was Kaly who answered, "Dennis, go up the right side and just step out in front of everyone. That should cause a riot of some sort. Start shouting about the World Financial Redistribution of Taxes. Win, get behind your brother and take him down. Boone and I will focus on Patre; he'll be the real problem. I don't doubt he's armed. Remember what Vic said, we're about to get bloody, so get ready for it."

As they moved forward, Dennis said, "And, don't let that *Rex* get out."

August turned from the cage and shouted, "Patre, bring Otai here."

Otai threw his arms up as he shouted, "August, you're wrong. I have always been loyal to you. Always."

"Then explain -"

"No!" Dennis shouted as he suddenly appeared in front of everyone. Cameras turned toward him as shouts of "Mr. President," rang out. He walked purposefully toward August and asked loudly, "When were you going to tell them about the World Financial Redistribution of Taxes? Tell them where their money was actually going? *You* explain."

"Patre," August shouted again, and this time Patre drew a gun. As he brought it up, Otai lunged forward and grabbed for him from behind. But Patre was too fast, and he spun around and fired a shot just as Otai knocked the gun from his hand.

Dennis pulled a bare flagstaff from its base and held it across his body in both hands. He stepped forward and told Patre, "Step away from him." Just as quickly he remembered what Vic had said about Patre as they left Station 7, that he would react immediately. He couldn't remember doing it, but the point of the flagstaff was suddenly in front of him and a second later Patre had impaled himself on it as he lunged forward.

Patre looked down in surprise and then grabbed the staff as if he was going to pull it out. Dennis didn't give him the chance to try. He started running forward as fast as he could, and when Patre hit the podium, he stopped, but the flagstaff kept going. Patre hung there for a few seconds, fighting to get free, and then his hands dropped to his sides, and he was still.

August had turned toward Dennis and was completely surprised when Win tackled him from behind. Boone and Kaly couldn't get past August, so they paused for a moment to help Win. They thought he was under control when Boone saw August reach for his watch. "Look out, he's -"

Dennis looked just in time to see August, Win, Boone, Kaly, and the dinosaur disappear. He paused for just a few seconds and then as he turned a huge cheer went up from everyone in the room. He bent down to Otai and asked, "How bad are you hurt?"

"I don't know," he replied. "Upper right leg, I think." As Dennis nodded and started to stand up, Otai grabbed him and said, "Don't worry, they will get August."

Dennis moved to the podium and motioned for the cheering to stop. When it did he said, "I need a doctor for this man and the Secret Service back on post." Then he nodded at Patre and said, "And get this out of the White House."

A Secret Service agent who had been part of the media throng stepped forward and began giving orders to the White House staff. Doctors appeared from nowhere it seemed, and within a few minutes, Dennis was facing the cameras instead of August.

"My friends, I believe Agent Winters, Boone and Win will be back in a few moments. I believe they will defeat the madman, August Adams. Then, there will be much to discuss. But right now, I would like the leaders of all the countries around the world to take control again. Tomorrow, I will speak to everyone."

There were more cheers and then a noise behind Dennis, and the room grew quiet.

The swirling motion lasted several seconds and then suddenly stopped. As soon as it did August struggled to free himself from Win who was still holding onto his legs. The cage the *T-rex* was in had toppled over, but the cage stayed locked and the animal appeared to have been knocked unconscious. Boone and Kaly jumped on August, and helped to hold him down. It was only when August stopped moving that they realized it was getting dark. They could hear the wind blowing, and they were beside a wall.

"Where...what...I mean, when are we?" Boone asked.

"I'm not sure," Win replied. "But, it seems muddy, or sticky, here. There's something all over my sleeves and hands."

Kaly brought up Gina's phone, and the dull light showed an odd grayish material that stuck to everything it touched. She looked up and said, "If we're still in the White House, something has happened. Some of the floor is gone and there's not even a roof above us."

Win held some of the grayish material under the phone's light and told them, "It's wet ash."

"Did we burn down the White House?" Boone asked.

August shook his head and asked Win contemptuously, "How can you want to be around such stupid people?"

"Because they aren't trying to kill me," Win told him. Then he told Boone, "We didn't burn down the White House. But, now I know that *when* is some time after the White House was set on fire by the British in 1814. They burned the White House, the Capitol Building, and a lot of other buildings. The rain put out all the fires and helped to keep them from spreading. Hopefully, it's not the very next day because if I remember right -"

A bright flash of lightning crossed the sky above them and then it began raining hard as the wind picked up. "What do you remember?" Kaly asked over the loud wind and rain.

Boone leaned in to listen to Win's answer, "That this storm is actually a tornado."

"You're kidding," Boone shouted. "How close is it?"

"It sets down in the middle of Washington and heads straight toward the British Army."

"You mean...?"

"Yes," Win answered. "We need to get out of here."

As if to emphasize the point, there was another flash of lightning and Win pointed and shouted, "August is trying to get away."

The lightning flashed like a strobe light and made it appear that August was moving jerkily along the White House wall. He went through a burned out window, and Boone quickly followed him and took him to the ground. As Kaly and Win joined them the wind began to shriek, and it became dark as night.

Men ran toward them carrying torches and lanterns which illuminated the red coats they were wearing. In just a few seconds there were four soldiers in front of them, three were pointing rifles at them. The one man who was not pointing a rifle asked, "Who are you, and what are you doing?" When no one spoke, he added, "Stand up, quick now, or we'll have to shoot you."

"We's a gettin' out o the storm," Win said as they stood up. "Thought there might still be a roof here to hide under. It's gonna be a bad'un. It's gonna be bad here dreckly."

"A little wind and rain never hurt anyone," the man laughed.

"This ain't gonna be no little wind," Win continued. "It's gonna be a hurricane. Din't ya see those clouds?"

"We have summer storms in England," the man assured him. "I'm sure we'll be fine."

"What should we do with them, Major?" one of the soldiers asked.

Before the major could answer, there was a sudden stiff wind that blew them all back several steps. As it became even darker, Win shouted, "We's need to git to cover. Right now." The major opened his mouth, but before he could say anything, they heard a loud noise behind them and watched as a roof was torn from a nearby house. The soldiers began running back in the direction they had come from, and after a moment, the major followed them.

As the wind blew even harder Win pulled August down, and Boone and Kaly followed them. They continued to lay on the ground as red coated British troops ran around just a few hundred yards away from them. As a man rode among the troops, he and his horse were suddenly slammed to the ground by a strong gust of wind. Immediately, the rest of the British troops threw themselves to the ground as the wind became louder and even stronger. Nearby houses were lifted off the ground, and roofs were pulled from several homes. As an object illuminated by lightning flew by Boone, he shouted, "Was that a cannon?"

Trees were blown over and some ripped out by their roots. The air was filled with debris, and soldiers began crawling toward anything that looked like it could stop the wind blown objects from hitting them. Some had just entered a home when the whole structure collapsed. It was over an hour before the wind let up enough for just a few moments, so Boone and Kaly could drag August back inside what was left of the White House.

They stopped by the still unconscious *T-rex,* and August told them, "If you had let me go, I would have probably been killed by the storm. Your troubles would be over."

"That's not what I want," Win told him.

As the world blurred and began to swirl around them, August said menacingly, "You're too weak." Then he grabbed Win.

The stop was abrupt and painful as everyone dropped from eight to fifteen feet and landed hard on dirt. August was the first to realize he was okay, and he pulled something out of his pocket. He stared at it then shook it and turned it over and over in his hands. As Kaly started moving, he crawled toward some type of opening and disappeared.

Kaly sat up and wondered why they were in a huge basement with towering walls, scaffolding, dump trucks, and a bulldozer. She glanced over and saw the *T-rex* was still in the cage, unconscious. She looked for Boone and found him a few feet away lying near the top of a mound of dirt. When she said his name, he sat up and asked, "What happened?"

"I don't know," Kaly replied. "I guess we're still in the White House, but I don't understand what I'm seeing."

"It's the White House reconstruction," Boone told her. "It was part of one of my college classes."

A groan from behind them caused them to turn, and they saw Win lying next to a pile of rocks. He had blood on his forehead and was struggling to sit up. They helped him to a sitting position, and he looked around and asked, "Where's August?"

Boone jumped up and said, "He's gotten away. We need to find him before he travels."

Win rubbed his head as he replied, "Don't worry about him. He can't travel anymore without us."

"Why not?" Kaly asked.

"Remember I said I needed three things to happen? Traveling with me was number three. It allowed my arm tech to interact with his time travel program and disable it. Right now he probably can't figure out what has happened and is busy trying to correct something he can't."

"So, when you tackled him you knew he would travel and then your third thing would be completed," Boone said.

"Yes," Win agreed. "I figured when we stopped I'd take him with me when I traveled. Who knew there would be all of these problems."

"Like this," Kaly said as she looked around. "Boone, you said you know what it is?"

He nodded and started, "Sometime...in the early 50s I think, people started noticing some odd things happening in the White House. Chandeliers swaying, floors creaking, and I think a piano, President Truman's daughter's piano if I remember correctly, fell through the floor...or maybe it just partly fell through the floor.

"Anyway, the White House was inspected, and it was in bad shape. Foundations were sinking, the original wooden framing was old and rotting, the interior walls were bad, a third floor had been added, the pipes were bad, and really, the White House was ready to collapse. Someone at the time said it was just standing out of habit.

"So, here we are. The only things still here are the exterior walls. Everything else, as you can see, has been ripped out. There's going to be a steel framework put in, new floors, interior walls, plumbing, two more basements...which explains why we fell. From this gutted shell of a building, the White House we know will emerge. I mean, there will be other additions later, but here we are at the start of it."

"Just like we were at the end of the first White House," Win noted.

"Let's hope that while we're traveling we don't stop at every major White House event," Kaly said.

"I don't think we will," Win said as he stood up and then immediately sat down with a cry of pain.

"What is it?" Boone asked.

"I'm guessing I broke my ankle," Win advised. "I'm not going to be able to help you find August."

"I don't think that will be too hard," Kaly said. "All of the entrances to this work area are closed, and I'll guess locked. I didn't get the feeling he was the most athletic person I'd ever seen, so I doubt if he was able to climb up and check the windows on the upper floors. I think he's still down here, hiding behind one of the piles of dirt or in one of the vehicles."

"Well, let's start looking," Boone suggested.

"Let's just be real still," Kaly replied. "I bet we can be quieter than he can, and in this space, any sound will be amplified."

Kaly and Boone leaned back to back against each other as Win lay back on the dirt floor. About ten minutes later they heard muffled movement behind them, and Boone whispered, "Is he in one of the trucks?"

Kaly shook her head and pointed at a dark space at the far end of the basement excavation. "I think it came from there."

"Oh, yeah," Boone said, "the tunnels."

"They started building the tunnels here, in the 50s?" Kaly asked.

"Yeah, they went to a bomb shelter, I think. Again, stuff I read in college. Don't you know if they're still here?"

"No, I've never had White House duty," Kaly replied. "I mean, I've heard of tunnels, some secret ones supposedly. So, I wonder if these tunnels are hallways now because of other construction projects."

"Could be," Boone said. "But, let's go check and see if that one has caught something."

They made their way through the piles of dirt and past several trucks and a bulldozer that Boone stopped next to and put his hand on. "Wow, an old Cat."

"Uh, should I feel jealous?" Kaly asked.

"Yes," Boone said. "Yes, you should."

She punched him in the arm, and they stopped outside of the tunnel opening and Kaly called out, "August, could you come on out. If we come in I will knock you out and then we'll just drag you out anyway."

There was silence for a few seconds and then the crunch of approaching footsteps on the dirt. August silently limped out, and Kaly said, "Thank you." Then she asked, "Are you hurt badly?"

"No, not that you care."

They walked back to Win and Boone asked, "Okay, can we go back now?"

"Well, not from here," Win replied. "I mean, we're in the White House, one of the basement areas. But, I have no idea where we are exactly. If we travel from here, we can't reappear if there is a wall, or desk, or anything in the way. We might end up months, or even years, past where we want to be."

Boone looked up and said, "Then we have to get outside to the grounds. Move out away from the White House, and we should be able to travel back to just after we left. Yes?"

"I can crawl up with your help," Win agreed. "But what about the dinosaur? We can't just leave it behind."

"Actually, there are pulley systems all over this building frame," Boone pointed out. "I'll hook up the cage and then we'll all go up and out. We'll pull the cage out, swing out an opening, and set it on the ground. There might be some sleds up there to move it with. I don't think everything went out in these dump trucks."

"Why don't we just use a dump truck?" August asked.

"Because I imagine there are guards up there," Boone answered. "Hopefully in a shack, and hopefully not able to hear us when we start clanking around."

"We can't count on another tornado, or whatever that was," Kaly said.

"What else could it have been?" Boone asked.

"I was wondering if it was a derecho. Did anyone actually see a tornado?"

"It might have been in a rain shroud," Boone said. "You know that -"

"Excuse me," August interrupted. "I'd actually like to be sent back to 1814 so the British soldiers can shoot me. Or, is it possible you can discuss the weather at a different time?"

Kaly and Boone both laughed, and it ended up being easier than Boone thought it would be. There were temporary wooden stairs that led most of the way up to an exterior opening, big enough for the dinosaur cage to fit through. They were able to use a pully the cage up and out onto a pallet loader. Then they slowly pushed and pulled it away from the building on the dirt that was packed hard by the construction traffic.

"Now?" Boone asked. Win smiled, and the now familiar blur began. What also started was a low growl that caused Boone to look at the cage to see wide open yellow eyes staring at him. "Hey," he started, "I think -" Then the dinosaur jumped at him as fast and hard as it could.

Boone remembered it all; the twisting, turning, stop and the slam into the ground that reminded him of jumping out of the bulldozer to escape the first *T-rex*. He was lying on his side staring at the now open cage, wondering where the animal was when its foot stepped right in front of his head. He didn't move, but he expected to be bitten at any moment. He remembered Kaly's wink outside of the cave as the dinosaur walked behind her, and he smiled. Don't move.

He had no idea when he was, but the sounds he heard caught him off guard, cows mooing. The feet disappeared, and Boone could hear the dinosaur running away, so he slowly sat up. Win and Kaly were still on the ground, and it was dark. Back sometime before there were lights, Boone thought, since the only light was coming from the windows of the White House. Well, it wasn't burned down, and it wasn't gutted, so now what year were they in?

Win groaned and sat up and a few seconds later, so did Kaly. Boone helped her up as she asked, "What happened this time?"

"I'm not sure," Boone replied. "The dinosaur jumped, so maybe the cage tipped over and caused us to crash and burn again."

"I'm not sure that was it," Win said. "The cage, and the animal were contained in the travel area, it almost felt like -"

"Like what, dear brother?" August asked as he stepped from the shadows. "Like someone else was in control?" Then he laughed, an odd high-pitched laugh, that made the hair on the back of Boone's neck stand up. "Because I am back in control."

"How?" Win asked.

"After you tackled me, and we ended up in 1814, I realized you had done something. We didn't land in the fail safe time period. I didn't have time to fix things in 1814, but then I tackled you, and we happened to land in that nice big hole with the nice little tunnel. A few alterations to your meddling, and you didn't have a clue I was back in control. So, here we are."

"Where is here?" Kaly asked. "And why is it your fail safe area?"

"Look behind you," August said. "What do you see?"

Kaly took a few seconds. There was only moonlight shining, then replied, "I see the Washington Monument, or rather part of it, and a herd of cows beside it."

The cows suddenly started bellowing loudly as they darted in different directions. There was a loud rumble then it got quiet. "That was our *Rex* friend picking out an animal to eat. But don't worry about your precious time line; there's no one around to hear or see him." He paused, then laughed again as he added, "Yet."

"So, what's your point?" Win asked. "Why is this your fail safe area? What's so special about this time that you have picked it to cause the worst possible damage to the world?"

"It's my fail safe point because of you, dear brother. All those talks you had with Otai gave me so much information about you. I don't mean the lies you two were feeding me; I was on to Otai from the start. I mean the personal information about you that he didn't realize he was giving me.

"You see, it's mid August, 1861. The Union Army has been defeated at Bull Run. The military is hiding here in Washington; the American people have had their illusions about the war dashed. It's not going to be easy, or short.

"Abraham Lincoln is wondering about his generals, further war preparations, what needs to be done. So, late in the evenings, he takes little walks all by himself around the White House. Sometimes, he wanders over to the Washington Monument where the army now keeps a herd of cattle to feed all of the soldiers who are in the city.

"He's about to run into a group of six men who will recognize him and tell him what an honor it is to meet him. He'll smile and tell a few of his stories, and his spirits will be lifted, and he'll have a much better day tomorrow. Well, he would have."

"What do you mean?" Win asked angrily as he tried to stand.

August laughed again and said, "What I mean Win, is that I too have met your friend Abraham Lincoln. Right here, in the White House. I placed a chemical on old Abraham's coat. It's a scent actually, the scent of this *Rex's* favorite food, a duckbill, actually an *Edmontosaurus,* I believe.

"Did you know that the *Rex* had an unbelievable sense of smell? Imagine, it's dining on a cow when suddenly it smells its favorite meal just a few hundred yards away. How fast will the attack come? An attack that kills President Abraham Lincoln at one of the lowest points of the war. What will happen now?

"Will Vice President Hamlin continue to fight? Was Lincoln the only man who could lead America during the Civil War? Will there be a compromise now? Or, will the North lose? There will be no Emancipation Proclamation. There won't be a second inaugural address attempting to heal the wounds of the Civil War. No stirring Gettysburg Address.

"The United States will stumble toward…what? Another Civil War years later? Who will the leader be then? Will America become a world power, or will it remain split in two, a house divided? What will -"

Kaly and Boone moved at the same time, and August was unconscious before he hit the ground. They looked at Win who just said, "Go," and they ran toward the Washington Monument. "We have to be the ones to meet Lincoln," Kaly said. "Turn him around somehow and get him back inside the White House. Then we can figure out what to do with the *Rex*."

Boone suddenly slowed and said, "Watch out; there's a fence here."

"Not here," Kaly replied. "It's being repaired I think. See, some of the posts are just lying around in the grass."

Boone picked one up, and then another. They were steel rods, and he showed the decorative sharp ends to Kaly and said, "These might come in handy."

Kaly found two also, and they continued on for only a few steps when they found themselves on a dirt road or trail. To their right they could see six men walking toward them illuminated by the lanterns they were carrying. Unfortunately, they could also see the silhouette of a tall man wearing a top hat between them and the group of men.

"He's already past us," Kaly said.

"Let's get between that *Rex* and him," Boone shouted as he started running.

It didn't take long. The *Rex* wasn't trying to be quiet, but it did pause in the moonlight as it stared at the seven figures standing together. Boone wondered for a second if it was because there was more than one animal in front of it? Or, it didn't recognize its prey? And then it didn't matter as Boone and Kaly skidded to a stop twenty feet away from the *Rex*.

It jerked its head toward them then quickly turned and took a few steps forward. A low rumble ran up their spines.

"It doesn't jump, right?" Kaly asked.

"I…I don't think so," Boone answered.

"Let's go," Kaly shouted as she started forward. She was staying low, and Boone immediately knew why as he followed. She dove into the center of the *Rex's* body, and Boone stabbed at its eyes. Then all he remembered was flashing teeth, claws, rumbles, pain, and then darkness.

As Boone and Kaly ran after the dinosaur, Win crawled to August and placed his left arm across his chest. In an instant they were gone. In just a few seconds Win was back at the same spot with a team of men and women who ran in the direction Kaly and Boone had gone. They paused while a group of men carrying lanterns passed by, laughing and saying, "He was taller than I thought." Then they were across the road. It only took them a few seconds to find the bodies.

Win bent down beside them and said, "Don't worry, we'll take care of you." He paused and then added, "And, thank you."

Dennis turned toward the noise behind him then he rushed toward Win and the heavily bandaged Kaly and Boone. He spoke with Win for a minute then turned and shouted, "It's over."

The crowd erupted in cheering and shouting as Kaly and Boone moved slowly toward the podium. No one noticed that behind them Win disappeared. As the crowd quieted, Dennis said, "I know we were here, just a day…two days ago? At least to you. To us, especially to Agent Winters and Boone, it seems much longer.

"I said I would address everyone tomorrow, but I think the time is now. The threat is over. No longer will we be captives of a madman and his army of misguided criminals. So, now I hve to ask everyone where do we go from here?

"You see, my friends and I have seen two worlds end. First, was our world. It will never be the same. There are dinosaurs living in our world now. The population of Earth has been reduced by thousands of people and we are faced with many questions and decisions.

"Which brings me to the second world we saw destroyed: Earth sixty-six million years ago. You can argue that there is no way to compare the two; but I say both were changed by forces they could not withstand. Each world changed beyond repair, and forced to be put back together. That gives us the chance to do what the world did last time; repair itself.

Now, I have to ask the leaders of every single country, what are *we* going to do? I hope you noticed I did not ask, what are *you* going to do?

"We were forced to solve the world's problems by August Adams. Our citizens, citizens of the world, endured unspeakable violence, and threats of continued violence. People died, so he could rule the world. In reality, as will come out later, all he wanted was to be rich.

"But, to save ourselves, we did solve many problems. And, we came up with possible solutions for many other problems that have plagued mankind. Should all of our work, even though it was coerced, simply be ignored? What does that say to the people who lost loved ones because of August Adam's insanity?

"I ask, no, I beg, that we not lose what we have started. That all of the coalitions, committees, alliances, partnerships...our friendships, continue forward. That all governments, large and small, put aside petty differences to act on the solutions that were found for so many problems. And, that we continue to work toward solutions for problems we did not solve, and those that will come in the future.

"Our world has changed. We were attacked by dinosaurs. There are dinosaurs still living in this world. But, the menace is gone, which means we face, as we always did, an uncertain future. But, it is a future that I think will bring exciting possibilities, and renewed hope, to everyone. Let us look to our neighbors for friendship and support, and move into a new era of peace, prosperity, and the realizations of all of our dreams. Thank you."

As the room erupted in applause, Dennis turned to Kaly and Boone, and he walked slowly with them to a small White House office. "I know both of you need to rest and recuperate, but I understand I'm not the only president you have saved. If you have a moment, what happened?"

Kaly explained how they caught up to the *Tyrannosaurus* then added. "I knew we couldn't wait. If it started toward President Lincoln, we would never have caught up to it. So, we moved in. I went low and stabbed it as hard as I could. I expected to be bitten right away, but Boone took care of that."

"I stabbed it in the face and eyes," Boone said, "but I don't think those fence posts went in very far. It was fast, and I know I got bitten at least twice. Fortunately, the young *Rex* didn't have the adult's 12,000 pounds of bite force. Still, if it wasn't for Win, both of us would have suffered life changing injuries."

Kaly took Boone's hand and said, "Actually, Boone would have died. My shoulder would never have worked the same, and I would have had permanent disfigurement."

Dennis hugged them both as he said, "Thank you. Now, go get well, so I can give you another award."

They were escorted to a waiting car and a familiar voice asked, "Where to?"

"Ricky," they both said, and Kaly continued, "Back wasting the taxpayers' money I see."

"And lunch was going to be on me," Ricky laughed.

"Where to?" Boone asked.

"The Diner," Ricky said. "They have a new item on the menu."

"What?" Boone exclaimed. "They haven't had anything new there since the 60s. In fact, I think some of the food they serve *is* from the 60s. What is it?"

"Flathead cherry pie."

August Adams slowly woke up and realized he was sitting, propped against a tree, on a beach of white sand. It was warm, and the sun glinted off the waves of a beautiful blue ocean. As he stood up, he saw Win standing by the water and walked over and asked, "Are you here to gloat? Is this my last taste of freedom before TIM locks me away?"

He waved his hands as he continued, "You know I was right. The world was in a mess; I did what was necessary to make it a better place. I will be vindicated, I will be freed. I will be part of a changing world."

Win turned toward him and said, "You just wanted to be rich."

August laughed as he replied, "I wanted to save the world, *and* be rich."

Win shook his head and said sadly, "I had always hoped I could save you from yourself. But I was wrong. I know now I can only save the world from you."

"And just how…" August trailed off as a long neck came out of the ocean a hundred feet away and then disappeared. "What? Where are -" He spun around to see the loud noise behind him was a pack of twenty small, green-feathered dinosaurs, chirping and running along the tree line fifty feet away. "What is this place?" he snarled.

Win sighed and replied, "The place I'm going to leave you, brother."

"Oh, so now you're going to leave me to be eaten by dinosaurs?"

Win shook his head and said, "No, this is where their world, and yours, ends."

"Wh…what do you mean?" August asked.

"Goodbye, August."

As Win disappeared, August shouted, "Come back here, now. I know what you're doing. You're trying to scare me. You want me to confess that I was wrong. Well, I won't do it. I -"

The flash of light startled him, and as he instinctively looked up, he was instantly blinded. The sound of the shockwave deafened him as the first blast drove him into the beautiful white sand of the Yucatán Peninsula. He tried to scream as the water boiled from his body as steam, and then came the explosion that was twice as hot as the sun.

EPILOG

As Dennis walked into the room, Vic shouted, "There he is."

"Sorry I'm late," Dennis said. "I got here as quickly as I could."

"No problem," Cam told him. "How are things going?"

Dennis paused then said, "They are going okay. Some countries are still thinking about things, but most have joined in, and we're making a lot of progress. A few cartels have started up, and there are some gangs doing the same thing. But, governments are stepping in forcefully, and the bad guys are finding it hard to maintain power."

"That's great," Boone said. "It's been a year now, and things still seem better."

"Not just better," Kaly added, "a lot better. The news is different, more positive. Things are happening; the negative is being dealt with. The question is, will it last?"

"That is the question," Dennis agreed. "Can we actually keep making the world better? It's an unknown. There are some cracks appearing, but...but, I really think we'll keep it together."

A large screen on a wall lit up, and Sheila said, "Hey, we made it. How is everybody?"

"Great," Kaly answered. "How about you?"

As Ricky sat down beside her, she answered, "We're doing fantastic." Behind them a *Triceratops* walked past a window, and Sheila laughed as she continued, "I feel like Jane Goodall. Being asked by TIM to help study prehistoric animals has completely changed my life."

"Our lives, you mean," Ricky said. "What an experience living with these animals."

"One of the *Trikes*, Molly, has let us interact with her calf," Sheila said excitedly. "It has been fantastic,"

"All your fences are up, right?" Boone asked.

"Yes, and thanks for your recommendations," Ricky said. "No carnivores can get close to the house."

Otai laughed and asked, "Aren't you supposed to be studying all dinosaurs? What about your *Rex* friends?"

"We use binoculars for those guys," Sheila said. "And that reminds me; Vic, Cam, how are your studies going?"

"Top of the class," Vic replied.

"Who knew chronokinesis would be so easy?" Cam asked.

Vic laughed and added, "I don't think Cam has figured out that we are obviously receiving subliminal information. I'm not ashamed to admit I'm not that smart."

Kaly asked, "But, everyone is setting aside time for the wedding, right?"

As everyone started asking, "Wedding?" "There's a wedding?" "When did this happen?" Boone said, "Guys, she'll knock you out; you know she will."

As everyone laughed, Kaly asked, "Win, you haven't said much. Everything okay? Still okay with what you did?"

Win smiled as he replied, "Yes. I did what had to be done. You know, August said he wanted to be part of a new world. When he was turned into atoms...he actually was."

"Okay, that was unexpected," Cam said.

"But funny," Vic added.

Win continued with, "I do want to add that I am proud of each and every one of you. All of you helped to make the world a better place." He started to say something else but then stopped.

"And?" Boone asked. "There's something else?"

Win smiled and replied, "Well, now that you ask." Another screen flickered on with a picture of mud and grass.

"Is that...is that a footprint?" Vic asked.

"It's a lot of footprints," Cam said. "And something tells me they weren't made by chickens."

"That's right," Win agreed. "This is a path on a farm in Western Iowa. They were made by several small animals. Several small dinosaurs."

"Not sent by August?" Boone asked.

"That's right," Win said. "And, there has been no unauthorized time travel in a year. So, now we think Kaly might have been on to something."

"Okay," Cam started, "this part hasn't been subliminally fed to me. Kaly is smart, but...?"

"How many times has time travel been invented?" Win asked. "TIM has the idea that someone else is doing a few experiments and, unlike August, has brought back a few herbivores as a result. No missing pets or mutilated animals have been reported in the area."

"And?" Boone asked.

"And, TIM would like a team to go and investigate. See what's going on, and stop any problems before they start."

"Do they want all of us?" Sheila asked.

"It should only take a day or so," Win said.

"Do we get any cool weapons, or get to blow anything up?" Ricky asked.

"We actually hope not," Win laughed.

"We're in," Sheila said as she took Ricky's hand.

"Cam and me too," Vic said.

"Though we might bring a few fun things," Cam added.

"Win, you know I'm always ready to help," Otai said.

Boone started, "We'll go but I'll tell you right now, if we're not back in time for our wedding -"

Everyone laughed as Kaly finished with, "I'm going to knock you out."

The End

CHECK OUT OTHER GREAT DINOSAUR BOOKS

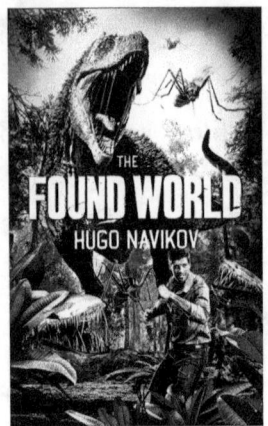

THE FOUND WORLD
by Hugo Navikov

A powerful global cabal wants adventurer Brett Russell to retrieve a superweapon stolen by the scientist who built it. To entice him to travel underneath one of the most dangerous volcanoes on Earth to find the scientist, this shadowy organization will pay him the only thing he cares about: information that will allow him to avenge his family's murder.

But before he can get paid, he and his team must enter an underground hellscape of killer plants, giant insects, terrifying dinosaurs, and an army of other predators never previously seen by man.

At the end of this journey awaits a revelation that could alter the fate of mankind ... if they can make it back from this horrifying found world.

HOUSE OF THE GODS
by Davide Mana

High above the steamy jungle of the Amazon basin, rise the flat plateaus known as the Tepui, the House of the Gods. Lost worlds of unknown beauty, a naturalistic wonder, each an ecology onto itself, shunned by the local tribes for centuries. The House of the Gods was not made for men.

But now, the crew and passengers of a small charter plane are about to find what was hidden for sixty million years.

Lost on an island in the clouds 10.000 feet above the jungle, surrounded by dinosaurs, hunted by mysterious mercenaries, the survivors of Sligo Air flight 001 will quickly learn the only rule of life on Earth: Extinction.

Check out other great

Dinosaur Thrillers!

Steve Metcalf

OBJEKT 221

Ruthless multi-national conglomerate Allied Genetics is under siege from a paramilitary force for hire. Allied calls in reinforcements and fortifies their crown-jewel property – an abandoned Soviet military facility in Crimea known during the Cold War as Objekt 221. Fortunately for the future of their research, O221 straddles a stretch of rocky landscape that hides a rift – a portal through time and space. Through this rift, Allied Genetics can travel, at will, to the Cretaceous – 100 million years into Earth's past – and bolster their genetic experiments with dinosaur DNA ... something their competitors want to stop at all costs."Objekt 221" is a story blending numerous science fiction elements such as repurposed military facilities, time travel, rogue corporate armies, dinosaurs and the hint of a super-ancient civilization.

Bestselling collection

PREHISTORIC: A DINOSAUR ANTHOLOGY

PREHISTORIC is an action packed collection of stories featuring terrifying creatures that once ruled the Earth. Lost worlds where T-Rex and Velociraptors still roam and man is now on the menu. Laboratories at the forefront of cloning technology experiment with dinosaurs they do not understand or are able to contain. The deepest parts of the ocean where Megalodon, the largest and most ferocious predator to have ever existed is stalking new prey. Plus many more thrillers filled with extinct prehistoric monsters written by some of the best creature feature authors this side of the Jurassic period.

CHECK OUT OTHER GREAT DINOSAUR BOOKS

PRIMORDIA
by **Greig Beck**

Ben Cartwright, former soldier, home to mourn the loss of his father stumbles upon cryptic letters from the past between the author, Arthur Conan Doyle and his great, great grandfather who vanished while exploring the Amazon jungle in 1908.

Amazingly, these letters lead Ben to believe that his ancestor's expedition was the basis for Doyle's fantastical tale of a lost world inhabited by long extinct creatures. As Ben digs some more he finds clues to the whereabouts of a lost notebook that might contain a map to a place that is home to creatures that would rewrite everything known about history, biology and evolution.

But other parties now know about the notebook, and will do anything to obtain it. For Ben and his friends, it becomes a race against time and against ruthless rivals.

In the remotest corners of Venezuela, along winding river trails known only to lost tribes, and through near impenetrable jungle, Ben and his novice team find a forbidden place more terrifying and dangerous than anything they could ever have imagined.

PANGAEA EXILES
by **Jeff Brackett**

Tried and convicted for his crimes, Sean Barrow is sent into temporal exile—banished to a time so far before recorded history that there is no chance that he, or any other criminal sent back, has any chance of altering history.

Now Sean must find a way to survive more than 200 million years in the past, in a world populated by monstrous creatures that would rend him limb from limb if they got the chance. And that's just his fellow prisoners.

The dinosaurs are almost as bad.